UNENDING
TRAILS

Veronica Mahara

UNENDING TRAILS

ISBN 978-1-7323712-3-1

To my grandmother **Laura**.

Part One

CHAPTER ONE

Rail River Acres—July 1890

THE WARM SUMMER BREEZE LIFTED THE CURTAINS IN THE bedroom where a miracle had just occurred. Jessica Cantrell had just given birth to a healthy son. The midwife swaddled the boy and handed the infant to his father while she attended to the mother.

Jessica watched Caleb closely. He held the tiny infant in his muscular arms, and she hoped he would be strong enough to carry the load of becoming this little one's father. She thought she had prepared herself for the baby not to resemble Caleb in any way, but as she stared at the small replica of Jacob in her husband's arms, she pictured how the real father might look holding his son. She dismissed the thought. This was the price to pay for her decision.

"Does he look like a Henry?" Jessica asked weakly from her bed.

The midwife had left to dispose of the remnants of the birth and to wash up. Caleb returned the baby into her arms. "I suppose, but you don't have to name him after my father. It makes no difference what his name is. He's still not my son."

Jessica cuddled her baby boy. "He will be soon enough," she reminded her husband. "We can draw up the adoption papers now that he's born."

Caleb crossed his arms over his chest. "And how do we explain a healthy child, given that your time was shorter than normal? Besides the fact that he looks nothing like me."

His concerns paled in comparison to what she had just experienced. The infant scrunched his face and let out a wail. Jessica quickly brought him to her breast, and he latched on with vigor. Beyond the pinch of pain, she was relieved her son had a strong will to survive. The pure love she felt for this tiny being was larger than the world. Although his true father must remain a secret, she longed for Jacob to have been present at the birth of his son.

Caleb sat on the bed and leaned into Jessica. He kissed her forehead and caressed the baby's soft cheek with the back of his hand. They both bent to smell the newness of this little being and bumped each other's head. The laugh they shared brought the babe's attention to them. Unlatching from his mother's breast, he looked up at his parents, a milky smile crossing his full, pink lips.

"Henry Thomas Cantrell," Caleb said.

The acceptance in his voice gave great comfort to Jessica as she held tight to little Henry, a tear trickling down her cheek. "Thank you." Their deceased fathers' names—his Henry and hers Thomas—coupled with Caleb's last name made it official. They were a family.

With this battle won, her next challenge was to tell Jacob he had a son and, most heartbreaking, ask him to relinquish his rights to Caleb. Heat rushed through her body, and she felt faint. Taking a deep breath, she knew this was not the time to think about it, yet it hung over their future like a storm cloud.

"My, he looks remarkably big and strong for an early baby." Aunt June cooed and rocked Henry in her arms. Merely weeks old, the infant stared into her eyes. "If I didn't know better, I'd say he looks like Jacob when he was a baby, but then, that would be impossible, now wouldn't it? Jacob does resemble the Stanfords. Isn't that something?"

Aunt June's awareness nearly undid Jessica. Jacob was adopted. It worried her to think she would never know that side of Henry's ancestry. As far as Jessica had gathered over the years, June had little knowledge of her son, Jacob's, origins. Today, she was too curious to let it pass. Nonchalantly, she began her inquiry.

"Do you suppose Jacob's family hailed from Eastern Europe, like the Stanfords? That might explain why he resembles that side of our family." She looked at the baby and smiled.

June pursed her lips. "I definitely remember reading that he had some lineage in Italy. That accounts for the beautiful eyes and dark hair." She kissed Henry's hand and said, "Just like you have, you lucky little one." She brought a finger to her lips. "Oh dear, I can't say a thing like that in front of Caleb. I'm sure he was certain the baby would resemble him, with his blond hair and blue eyes, but he looks more like you, Jessica."

Jessica's mother, Bethany, was quiet as she sipped her tea. She placed the cup and saucer down and gestured for her sister-in-law to hand over the baby.

"Babies look like they're going to look," she said as she re-wrapped the infant. "Your father thought your brother resembled the neighbor's children!" Her mother laughed. "I think he was only teasing me, but William did have the same coloring as the little Chadwick boy."

Ready to get off the subject of who Henry looked like, Jessica fingered the blanket her mother had wrapped tightly around the baby.

"Aunt June, thank you for the knitted blanket. Even in July, his little hands and feet get cool at night."

"He is a big one," Bethany remarked. "You weren't this big at birth, neither was Will. Oh, he is handsome. And look at the grip he has on my finger!"

Watching her mother and aunt fuss over Henry brought joy to Jessica's heart, but it was tinged with grief. Someday, she and Caleb would have a child together.

Hannah came out of the kitchen carrying a tray laden with soup and biscuits.

"Let me take that, Hannah," June said. After placing it on the table next to Jessica, she became more animated, her green eyes brightening. "We must have a party to celebrate our new family member. Will and Jacob have to see him. I'm sure they'll be very proud of little Henry here. Yes, next Sunday!" She clapped her hands, then served up the cold cucumber soup with Hannah standing nearby, shaking her head.

She'd been hungry a moment ago, but now Jessica felt sick to her stomach. Would Jacob be proud if he knew? The thought sent her reaching for a glass of cool water. There would be no time to tell him before Sunday. Would he suspect anyway? The timing was in favor of their lovemaking rather than her reunion with Caleb.

Jessica thought her trials were behind her, but in fact, she had brought more upon herself. The family had thankfully and tearfully welcomed her back into the fold after her kidnapping ordeal. She was just finding her comfort and rhythm again as a wife, daughter, niece, and now a mother. She had explained what she could, and they hadn't pressed her for details. She was glad for that. The experience of being taken from Caleb and her home by a Native man hired by Rex Conrad, the scout who was looking for her husband, had changed her life forever. She'd spent time in the Indian camp, then on the trails.

The reason for her abduction angered her each time she let herself think of it. Jacob, Will, and Caleb had caused her much grief, even though she loved them still. Forgiveness was her only solution. Although she looked and behaved the same to her family, she wasn't the same person who had been plucked from the river on that sunny day in May. Being rescued by her brother, Will, and her cousin, Jacob, would always have her believing in fate, yet finding comfort with Jacob as they made their way home from her months of captivity made her question what other trials fate had in store. Their love had been reignited. Henry was proof enough of that. With Jacob now living just on the other side of the San Francisco Bay, she would have to be careful. It was easier to resist her feelings for him when he was far away on some wilderness trail with her brother.

"Auntie, can we put it off for a couple of weeks while Caleb and I get adjusted? Henry's been fussy at night, and I'm afraid no one is getting much sleep around here. Hannah's been a blessing." Jessica gave the housekeeper a thankful smile. "But we've taken her from you long enough."

"As you wish, my dear, but everyone is anxious to see him. Sophie and Laura keep asking for a proper visit, and Austin can't wait to give him a gift. My dear brother has been holding on to this red wooden train ever since he thought he and Laura were having a son." June looked at Bethany. "They love their Sophie and her family, but you know how men want sons." Bethany returned an understanding nod. Turning to Jessica, June added, "And Laura and Sophie find it too taxing to ride all the way up here, so my house is the natural solution."

As her aunt spoke, Jessica made the decision to accept. Avoiding the celebration might cause suspicion. There would be no getting out of this. "Next Sunday then," she said with a weak smile.

Looking at her dress, Jessica's thoughts went to how she would present herself to Jacob. It had been many months since she last saw him. A silly thought, but she knew if she looked her best, it would give her courage to act as if all was as it should be. Her nerves flared. Would she be able to face Jacob? Would Caleb be able to pretend he was the father around him? Bringing the two men together in the same room was something she'd been hoping to avoid for a very long time, but putting it off would look odd. She would have to muster the courage she had found in her days in the wilderness.

CHAPTER TWO

San Francisco, California

AFTER HOURS OF PORING OVER THE LEDGER IN FRONT OF him, Jacob's eyes blurred. The amounts were right. J&W Imports had broken even last month. It was a slight victory, given that they had started the business only eight months ago. He closed the book, sat back in his leather office chair, and rubbed his eyes. A stab of guilt hit him—he knew the business wouldn't have gone far without the reward money and felt he hadn't earned a penny of it. He stood, took his suit coat off the hook on the wall, and left to join his cousin and business partner. Will Messing was in the modest apartments above their storefront on Market Street.

Will had insisted they hire a housekeeper and cook, and Jeanette Belle was just the woman to help them stay tidy and well-fed. Today, she'd left them with a lunch of stewed tomatoes over a baked potato smothered with molten cheese.

Jacob sat across the table from Will and sniffed the platter of food. "Where the hell does she get these recipes?"

"Who knows. They're damn good, though." Will devoured his share with a piece of crusty bread in one hand and a fork in the other.

Jacob took up his fork and knife and dug in. "We broke even last month," he said before taking a bite of red-stained potato dripping with cheese.

"That's good news. I knew we could do this." Will looked up from his plate. "You don't seem very happy about it."

"Did we do this?"

"Come on, Jake. Get off that train. The money started us off, but we're building something here." Will took a break from his lunch to sip on Jeanette's iced tea. He wiped his sweaty brow with his napkin. The apartment was close and stifling hot.

"As long as you stay away from the gambling tables." Jacob smirked at his cousin. Will had lost a good sum of money the other night.

"It was just one night, Jake. You know I haven't been at the tables for a while. Just letting off some steam. Anyway, who told you?"

"Our maternal housekeeper. She's like having a grandmother around." Jacob mocked her with an old-lady accent. "'Mrs. Leahy has a grandson who saw William at the Rusty Brew and mentioned it to his mother who . . .' You can imagine the rest."

Will puffed out a laugh. "I guess I better behave myself."

Changing the subject, Jacob asked, "Have you seen the invitation from my mother?" The words came out less casual than he'd wanted them to.

"Yeah, June would be put out if we didn't make it over, and I'm looking forward to seeing the little babe—Henry, they named him. My sister's a mother." Will grinned.

Curiosity gripped Jacob, but he couldn't speak aloud the question that kept him awake at night. What if the child was his? His mother had remarked how well and healthy the baby was given his early entrance into the world. He pushed the thought out of his head. "Humph."

"What's the matter?" Will asked.

"Nothing, nothing at all." Jacob threw his napkin on the table and got up. "Back to work." He left the apartment. Stopping in the stairwell, he took a deep breath, his throat tight with emotion.

THAT NIGHT, JACOB SAT IN bed looking over their next orders. Silk scarves from China coming in on the next ship. Tea towels and embroidered cotton napkins arriving from England. He was pleased with more companies willing to stock their goods with J&W Imports. Along with furniture and rugs, they would have enough inventory to sell.

Jacob didn't have the stomach for selling, so Will had taken over the job of greeting the customers and directing them to an eventual sale. "I love the sound of the cash register and the stack of orders!" he'd declared one night after closing the store. Jacob had to laugh. Will was a born salesman. Back in their gunrunning and trading days, he could talk his way out of the stickiest situations. With J&W being the new kid on the block, his skills came in handy. He turned the curious into buyers by convincing them they needed whatever J&W was selling. If a woman picked up a table runner, Will was there to praise her for her fine taste and to encourage her to buy something that would complement the piece. If a man was contemplating an expensive rug, Will would ask him about his home and his family. Somehow, he'd make it sound as if they needed this most precious gift in their lives. Jacob teased him about his ability to bullshit. Will called it "finessing a sale." Whatever it was, it worked. Jacob was content to do the ordering, go over their accounts, and stay out of the way. They'd hired a professional assistant to dress up the store and window displays. The man's flair for detail gave the store a rich, appealing look, something neither Jacob nor his cousin could have pulled off.

Jacob adjusted the pillow at his back to make himself more comfortable, then looked around and marveled at his new life. Though the apartment was small, it had all the necessities and comforts one could ask for. Last year, he'd been in the wilderness, both literally and figuratively.

His thoughts went to Jessica. The time they'd spent together getting her home had taken him back to loving her, wanting her, and finally having to surrender her to Caleb. The loss had almost been too much to bear at first, and he fought with himself to stay away from Clermont City and her home on Rail River Acres. Each day, he was more convinced baby Henry was his child, yet she'd said nothing to him, and according to his mother, everyone had decided the doctor had miscalculated the dates. Of course, they would have to keep their love child a secret, but he wasn't going to hide his knowledge from Jessica. He wondered if Caleb knew. The bitter irony of Caleb—his onetime partner in gunrunning, his partner in murder, the husband of his true love—raising his son hurt Jacob to the core. His heart burned with anger, then defeat. He couldn't avoid seeing them. The invitation to the family gathering would test him in ways being on the trails never had.

CHAPTER THREE

*J*ESSICA STOOD CLUTCHING HENRY, HER HEART POUNDING. Caleb brought the rig around to the stables, and she was alone in front of Aunt June's home. She would put on a happy face. Nothing was going to crack her exterior of confidence and calmness. The August heat was in stark contrast to the day of her return in December of last year. Jessica let the sunny warmth give her comfort. She had come so far. Today reflected her new life, and she welcomed it.

Climbing the porch steps, she entered the house. The drumming in her chest became irregular upon hearing Jacob's voice. The sound of him struck her deep inside with such familiarity, she wanted to sink to the floor and surrender. *Remain strong!* He and Will came out of the kitchen. She held on to Henry, and her feet felt glued in place.

"There's my little nephew," Will said. He lifted Henry from

Jessica's arms and planted a kiss on his head. "Congratulations, Sis." He kissed her cheek, and baby Henry cooed.

Her brother's familiarity settled her nerves. "He seems right at home with you, Will," she said. Jacob came alongside, and she felt his heat. She forced herself to temper her visceral reaction. Stepping away, she introduced Henry to both men. The baby drooled and wrinkled his nose as Will gently bounced him in his arms.

"Here ya go, Jake." Will handed Henry off. "Chubby little one, but he's as light as a feather."

Jessica took in Jacob's hesitation as a signal to her. She brushed the thought aside. Then Henry was in his father's arms. Jacob looked at the baby, and then peered down at her. His jaw was slack, his eyes misty. *He knows.* She bit her wobbling lip. The emotions she desperately needed to hide were surfacing with a mighty force. The tears couldn't be stopped. She reached for her handkerchief as her aunt, uncle, and mother flooded into the room and Caleb entered through the back door. She heaved a ragged breath.

"I don't know what got into me," she said as she wiped her eyes. "Ever since his birth, my feelings are unpredictable."

"It's natural, my dear," her aunt said as she took Henry from Jacob. "You will see in time everything will settle."

"And you'll want another one," Bethany chimed in with a laugh.

The baby was whisked away into the kitchen, and Will and Burt headed for drinks at the sidebar. She heard them discussing the difference in whiskeys, but her attention couldn't wander far with Jacob standing next to her. His stare was penetrating.

"It's good to see you, Jacob."

"Why didn't you tell me?" His whisper was low and hoarse.

Giving a quick look at the others milling around, she felt the heat rise in her chest. How could he broach the subject like this? And here of all places? Her husband was approaching. She shook her head, and Jacob clucked his tongue before turning to Caleb. They acknowledged each other with equal coolness.

"Jacob."

"Caleb."

Jessica rolled her eyes. "I think Henry might be hungry." She turned her attention to her son. *What harm could they do to each other here?*

The two men took little time to distance themselves. Caleb walked over to the table of food, and Jacob went to the side-bar. When Jessica glanced his way, she noticed he was pouring a double.

Once June's brother, Austin, and his brood arrived, the conversation and activity dispelled the tension in the air. Sophie fell in love with Henry and cried how her two boys were growing up much too fast. She stated she would like another one just like baby Henry. Her mother, Laura, reached over and covered her daughter's hand. "That's enough of that kind of talk, Sophie." Her husband, Carl, simply grunted.

By the end of the evening, Jessica was spent. Her emotions had seesawed all day. Avoiding Jacob had been her main goal, and for the most part, she had succeeded, until the last moment when Uncle Burt invited Jacob and Jessica to take a look in the stable at his new mare.

"I think you and Jessica can appreciate her better than the rest," her uncle said. "Why, I remember how you two rode together almost every Sunday in that wide-open field. By the way, Mr. Bishop recently wrote and told me that land is filling with new houses. It's a shame, but that's progress."

Jessica couldn't hear much of what her uncle was saying over the buzzing in her head. She couldn't possibly be alone with Jacob. Before she could suggest Will join them, Caleb stepped in.

"I can see Jessica is getting tired, Burt. Maybe another time," said Caleb. "We should be heading home."

She was saved. They said their goodbyes, and only Jessica seemed to notice that Jacob stayed to the back of the room. She looked his way, and his hooded eyes gave her the feeling she might be in for more of a struggle than she'd thought. The adoption papers had already been drawn up. Time was of the essence for her and Caleb to legally form a family. Henry needed a last name.

ROLLING HER HEAD FROM SIDE to side, Jessica felt the crackle in her neck. The baby was in his cradle, and Caleb was in the kitchen. Alone in the bedroom, she felt vulnerable. Her thoughts couldn't remove the picture of Jacob holding Henry. She must get past her feelings for him. After the adoption was legalized, she would be free to move forward. Jacob would relinquish all rights. Her love for Caleb was strong, and it would surpass her love for Jacob. A shiver seized her body. Though the heat of the day still lingered, she felt cold. Wrapping her shawl around her shoulders, she made herself relax. *Everything will be fine.*

Caleb brought her a cup of tea, and she propped herself up on her pillows to receive the hot brew.

"That was a close call this evening, wasn't it, Jess?" he said as he went to the other side of the bed and joined her. His remark dripped with sarcasm.

"I would have had one of Sophie's boys join us, so you don't have to say it like that." She blew on the rim of the cup, then took a sip.

"Once we finish signing the papers, they will get mailed to Jacob. There will be no need to bring up the subject to him again. You don't need to confront him. He knows Henry is his and surely suspects I will want to adopt him."

Her husband always had a sensible, almost cold approach to such weighted matters. Then he would sulk and want to be alone while things played out. It angered and frustrated her, yet she held tight to his common sense. In this case, her own common sense was unreliable.

"Yes, I think that would be wise." She turned to Caleb. Long blond hair framed his handsome face, and his soulful blue eyes looked back at her as if he wanted to say something but couldn't find the words.

"What?" she asked.

He cleared his throat and turned away. "Nothing."

She placed her hand on his arm. "That means there's something."

"Did you want to go with him into the stables?" He turned to her and examined her face.

"No . . . and yes. I'm sorry, Caleb, but I want to know what he thinks, how he's going to handle the adoption."

"Does it matter? He'll be angry, relieved, saddened. What do you expect? Or should I ask, what is your hope?"

Feeling too tired for a go around with her husband she answered briefly, "I expect nothing."

He chuckled in disbelief, then jerked on his side and fell asleep. He didn't fool her, she was sure neither of them would sleep well until Henry was legally the son of Caleb Cantrell and their secret was buried deep.

CHAPTER FOUR

*T*he wait for Jacob's decision was made easier by the amount of work Jessica had to do. Besides caring for the house and Henry, she had several commissions for her art. Each day, as baby Henry slept, Jessica escaped to the barn, where Caleb had sectioned off an area for her studio.

On this early September morning, the pungent odor of hay and animal dung mixed with the smell of oil paint and mineral spirits. It pricked her nose when she opened the barn door and went into her studio. The large canvases waited, as did the watercolors and her art supplies. It was as orderly as she could make it. There was a small window on the outer wall that let in the morning light, and the ceiling was as tall as the barn. When the beams of sunlight came through the window and pierced the clapboard cracks, she felt as if she were in a cathedral instead of a humble place for cows and horses.

Closing the studio door behind her, Jessica opened the window and looked around. Sketched on the taut surfaces of the canvases were people she had encountered in her time away from home. They stood among the rough backdrop of land she had been a part of. The enormity of her experience overwhelmed her.

Throughout her pregnancy she'd stuck to watercolors—the odor of the oil paint and thinner had made her ill. Now the urge to paint in oils tugged at her. How would she paint what she had observed in the intimacy of the Indian camp and the journey home with her brother and Jacob? Perhaps her feelings for Jacob would never make it to the canvas, or maybe she would one day be brave enough to create the portraits of their time together. She shook her head. Such a foolish thought.

Turning back to her task, Jessica lifted a smaller canvas. Mr. Talbot, the gallery owner she'd once rented a space from and who still sold her paintings from his gallery in town, had suggested an art teacher who was new to Clermont City, an older woman who taught adults from beginners to advanced. Jessica had to admit she was rusty. It would take convincing Caleb and a good going over of their budget, but she might manage a lesson once a month. The thought brought a flush of excitement—she would have help in getting to the next level of her artistic journey.

HER AUNT AND MOTHER WERE more than willing to take Henry for the three-hour sessions with Louise Colter. Caleb had been agreeable, stating, "If this is what it takes, then we will find a way." Jessica was afraid to ask if this was more of his guilty conscience for his part in her kidnapping or simply his business mind speaking. She decided it wasn't worth opening up that can of worms.

Many questions plagued her about her husband and his relationship with the Klamath Reservation. How could he associate with those people after some of them had kidnapped her? Last spring when she was in her full pregnant state, he had left to ride up to the reservation. He'd said he had to find out a few things and wanted to give his friends the good news of his wife returning. To Jessica's chagrin, he didn't mention the coming birth of the baby. Would he tell them? She was afraid and spent the time worrying about his well-being and her safety. He would here none of the pleas for him not to go. It had put another brick on the wall that had been building between them since her return. She realized Caleb had taken on a lot to keep her and the child she carried. He'd agreed to becoming a family, and at times, she had to admit, she took advantage of his words. Thinking he had forgiven her and Jacob was a mistake. He was his own man, and nothing she said or did could change who he was—a man who never forgot and who seldom forgave.

After her chores and taking care of the baby, Jessica practiced her art each day, channeling her emotions onto the canvas. It was exhilarating, and soon the material, stretched over stiff frames, came to life with the spirit of her experiences, her depth of feelings in her work laid out for all to see. The wilderness of Northern California and the ruggedness of Southern Oregon. Streams and valleys, canyons, small towns. She painted the vibrant colors of the clothes worn by the Klamath people in the Indian camp she had been taken to live in, their dome-shaped, stick-and-grass dwellings, the people themselves—Cara, From-Wings, Lea, John Tooth, and especially Blue Heron. She could not and would not forget them. Mallow she would not paint, although his treatment of her drifted to the forefront of her mind from time to time. With it came a whisper of despair and fear as the memory of the beating he had given her when she'd tried to escape crossed her thoughts. He'd hated her and had made her captivity harder. It haunted her dreams. The nightmares had diminished, but she would never forget. At times, it seemed so long ago, and other times, it was only yesterday when she was held for ransom to pay for her husband's past deeds. The whole experience seemed as if it belonged to someone else. If it weren't for her son, she might let it be a crazy dream, dismissed as most dreams are, but Henry was real and a lively reminder of her past.

Her new art teacher, Louise, shared with Jessica her experience with the art community in San Francisco, which she'd been a part of most of her adult life. It harkened Jessica back to the days when she'd been involved in a gallery there. Her other art teacher, Lenny, her friend Jilly, and the flirty French-Canadian artist, Leo Gosselin, came to mind. Louise knew about all of them, but she offered very little in the way of information or even a bit of gossip. Jessica was disappointed. She wondered how Jilly's gallery was and how the eccentric Lenny fared, but each time she sat down to write to them, she couldn't find the right words. So much had changed in her life. Eventually, she abandoned her efforts. At sixty-eight, Louise had more to say about the art community in general. Their talks after each lesson proved to be great lessons in themselves.

Today, they sipped Louise's strongly brewed coffee while Henry took a nap in his carrier. Louise wanted to see the baby, and with a watercolor lesson this month, Jessica had decided to bring him along.

"You're doing quite well, Jessica. It's coming back to you. And from what you've told me, you have plenty to paint," Louise said. Her steel-gray hair was swept up into a loose bun, her dark-brown eyes and brows revealing the color her hair had once been. Though petite, she was sturdy and held an air of authority. Kind and sensible was how Jessica had described her to Caleb.

"Thank you, Louise. I feel a sense of privilege and obligation to continue to be the best artist I can be."

By the time she arrived home, Henry was screeching. He fussed most of the way up the hill, and she had to stop the carriage several times to see what ailed him. He was fed and changed. She soothed him as best she could. "I'm tired, too, my little one. We'll be home soon."

After a warm bath and feeding, Henry lay in his crib, contentedly sucking on his lips as he dozed off. Jessica sat in her paisley chair, exhausted. That would be the last time she attempted to take Henry out alone. The thought of her dear housekeeper came to mind. Hannah was back to living and working at Aunt June's, but perhaps she could borrow her again. The extra hands would surely help. It might mean taking her art lessons every other month to pay for that help. How she felt this afternoon made her think she'd be better off. Besides, her artistic ability was flowing back to her, and she would nurture it between lessons.

Soon, however, her work fell under the scrutinizing gaze of her mother and aunt. "My, this is a bit on the vulgar side, Jessica," her mother pointed out after surveying her studio and paintings.

"I know this isn't the perfect place for painting, but Caleb has tried to make it a proper studio."

"Yes, the space is certainly questionable, but my dear, I'm talking about your new style of painting. I mean, half-naked Indian men and the dress of these women? It seems to me you could pretty up some of these scenes."

"Thank you, Mother, for your critique." Jessica was disappointed but not surprised that her mother would show little support. "They are what they are."

Aunt June was more diplomatic. "Now, these are very interesting, Jessica. Are you sure you want to abandon your nice landscapes? I was hoping to see more of the seaside."

She steered them toward her watercolors to appease them, then suggested they all go back to the house to continue their visit. Nothing more was said concerning her artwork, as if it were a dirty secret. At the next Sunday dinner at Aunt June's, no one asked how she was coming along with her latest work or if she had sold any of them.

Louise laughed when Jessica conveyed her mother's response. "Get yourself a tough skin, Mrs. Cantrell. That's just the beginning."

She finished a canvas that she was particularly proud of. Before wrapping it and taking it over for Louise to inspect and offer her critique, she showed it to Caleb.

"It's almost violently realistic," he said.

Standing it up in the parlor away from her studio gave it a presence Jessica hadn't expected. When she looked at her work, she was moved by what she had expressed—a white woman in an Indian world. The surrounding landscape was raw and beautiful, but it was the faces that made the painting come to life. Sorrow, fear, tiredness, and anger crossed the faces of the Native people. The one face shadowed by a thick braid was Jessica's. Squatting, she stirred a pot held over a firepit while other women carried bundles of wood, skinned animals, and washed clothes by the water.

"I painted what I remember. What I can't forget. The work we women had to do. It was so much more than anything here on our land. We have running water and kerosene, a general store for supplies. They had nothing." She put her hand to her chest and sighed. "It might be too much for the galleries to display."

"No," Caleb said. "This is real, and you've captured it well. Sweetheart, I had no idea. I didn't know this was in you." His expression became somber, and she couldn't help but feel his pain. When he took her hand, she leaned against him.

"I have to show my story."

Their neighbors and friends, Sally and Ben Loggin, had been a great support, and today, Sally happily agreed to take care of Henry. Jessica kissed her baby boy. "Mama will be right back. Thank you, Sally. See you soon."

With Caleb's encouragement and Louise making a fuss about showing her work, she confidently hauled her painting to the Talbot Gallery. Mr. Talbot had always liked Jessica's soft, feminine style since it gave a nice contrast to the other paintings in his gallery done by men. He looked over the painting with his chin in hand, his eyes squinting under his knitted brows.

"I'll get this up to Oakland. The Gates Gallery will be happy to have it. They don't mind a little controversy. Gets people talking." His eyes went to the signature. He pursed his lips. "Oh."

Knowing this was coming, Jessica readied what she was going to say. She had abandoned the male alias he had suggested for her. "I want my art to be recognized as done by me." She didn't want to hurt his feelings, yet she stood her ground.

"I see." He looked again at the painting. "Good for you, Mrs. Cantrell!"

She choked back tears. His support meant so much to her. "Thank you, Mr. Talbot."

Shyly, she asked him something she had wanted to ask ever since she'd begun her more realistic paintings. "Mr. Talbot, would you consider showing this piece here, in your gallery?"

"You certainly do tug at my wild side, but I'm afraid it's too . . . undomesticated for me to take on. Besides, you'll make a better profit with the Gates, and your watercolors do so well here."

"I know, but I'd love to see my oils here, too."

Scratching his graying hair, he looked at the painting, then back to her. His pause was too long. Disappointed, she knew what the answer would be.

"Well." Again, a long pause as he scrubbed his beard. "Why not?"

She bounced into his arms, and he caught her with a laugh. "My dear, control yourself!"

His smile, as she stepped away, gave her a warm feeling. She saw that he, too, was excited about her new art in his gallery. "I'll continue with the watercolors also, Mr. Talbot!"

He gave a sigh of relief. "They are my bread and butter, you know." He carried the painting into his gallery. She followed and helped him bring it to the back room. "I think telling the story behind this painting would greatly enhance its value," he said. "If you have more, we can do a series. A time line of sorts."

A thud hit her chest. The world couldn't see too much of the truth. Hanging this one here for all in Clermont City to see took a great deal of thought on her part. Did she want the townsfolk to see the artist she really was? Hiding her talent was no longer an option for her, but she had to be very careful what she exposed. The newspapers had said she'd been taken by renegade Indians for a short period of time but returned without harm. The group hadn't been found, and the woman wouldn't press charges. "I might be able to do a triptych with the change of seasons." Her heart slowed. The answer made perfect sense.

With a pat on the shoulder, Mr. Talbot accepted the deal. "The missus and I are happy to have you back, Jessica. And now you and the mister with a new little one." He took in a jagged breath and swept at the moisture in the corner of his eye. He swiftly directed her to the door. "That's all for now. Bring in more, and we'll see how this goes."

Touched, and respectful of his pride, she went out the door. "Yes, Mr. Talbot. See you soon. Thank you!"

CHAPTER FIVE

San Francisco—September 1890

In less than a year, with Jacob's father's help, J&W Imports had grown into a respectable business. Burt had warned them not to get too far ahead of themselves. Jacob looked around the cramped apartment and wondered when he'd have a real home. It felt close to him today as he waited for his father's arrival. He was tired and in no mood for another of Burt's lectures on keeping his nose to the grindstone.

His father was out of breath from the flight of stairs up to the second floor. Jacob led him to the open window in the corner of the apartment. The rush of air coming from the busy street seemed to help.

"Come, sit down, Father. Let me get you a glass of water."

Returning with two tall glasses, Jacob made sure his father's breathing had stabilized before questioning him. Finally, Burt was able to converse.

"What's this meeting about?" Jacob asked him. "Oh, and how is Mother?"

"Fine, fine. She and Bethany are good company for each other. The baby keeps them busy, too. Jessica has taken some art lessons and needs their help." Burt took a gulp of water. Coming up for air, he said, "I'll wait until Will gets here to tell you my reason for coming into the city."

Jacob seized the opportunity to inquire about Jessica and the baby—his son, his father's grandson. He brushed a hand over his cheek. "How is the baby? And Jessica?"

"Oh, they're just fine. Caleb purchased a newer rig the other day. It's used but in good working order. Jessica's able to get up and down the hill with a lot more ease. That old flatbed was such a chore for her. It's used mainly for Caleb's supplies now."

This wasn't really what he wanted to know. He longed to ask what Henry was like. Was he a strong boy? Any teeth yet? Or was that too soon for his age? What made him content or unhappy? Yet he couldn't show any real interest, not in this child who looked just like him. No one could know the truth, so he remained silent.

Burt added, "Last time I saw your cousin, she was looking a little peaked. I think she's working too hard."

Jacob tried to visualize Jessica on her land with a baby in tow and her artwork. Did she ever think of him? He was taken out of his thoughts with Will's arrival.

His cousin helped himself to the fresh pot of coffee Jeanette had prepared before leaving for the day. He sipped and then moaned, as if it were the exact remedy he needed. "That was a hell of a night, Jake," he said to his cousin, unaware that his uncle was seated in the corner just behind the coat stand.

Jacob cleared his throat and looked in Burt's direction. Will swung around as Burt rose from his seat.

"I hope you have your wits about you, both of you," Burt said. "As I've told you before, I can help with the legalities of the business, but it's up to the two of you to keep this ship pointed in the right direction. Gallivanting about after hours is *not* the right direction."

Jacob didn't reply. He felt confident in the way he and Will were running their business. The market continued to be prosperous due, in great part, to the railroad companies advertising the virtues of the land surrounding the bay and out into the farming regions. People needed homes, and those homes needed furnishings. It also kept Burt busy at the real estate company he worked for in Clermont City and from getting too involved in J&W Imports.

Will took his coffee and sat down. Burt wasted no time. "It seems Mr. Frederick Moore wishes to take back his reward money," he said.

"Take it back? Can he do that?" Will asked.

"I've been looking into it, and I can't find a precedent for it anywhere," Burt replied. "I suppose it could be recognized as a gift to us and by right belongs to the recipient, but he's claiming that it was money entrusted to us to be allotted to whomever outside of the immediate family found and returned Jessica. We never gave specific instructions about anyone inside the family receiving it. We hardly suspected it would be you." He paced the floor now. "Frederick says it's clearly a case of nepotism and a conflict of interest and that we cheated him out of his thousands."

"For Christ's sake," Jacob blurted out. "I knew we shouldn't have taken his part of the reward. Hell, I don't know if I believe he isn't right."

"Shit," Will said under his breath. "What can we do, Uncle?"

"His letter stated that he expected a reply within forty-eight hours or he would pursue other avenues. What that could mean, I don't know, but he made it clear that he would have no problem taking this to court and putting a lien on J&W. I received the letter while you were off on your trip the other day, so it's already been twenty-four hours. You don't happen to have five thousand dollars somewhere, do you?" Burt asked glibly, looking around their small apartment filled with second-hand furniture.

Jacob gave his father a withering look.

"Well, there is one thing we could offer him," Burt said, "but you may not like it."

"What is it, Father?"

Burt looked at his son, then Will. "You have few options in this matter, so I suggest you weigh my advice carefully. But if we offer him a share of J&W—"

"Hell no!" Jacob and Will shouted in unison before he could finish.

"Damn it, boys, listen to me." Burt spoke over their protests. "Frederick could weaken, if not destroy, everything you've worked for. We must address this in a way that saves the company and satisfies Frederick. The two of you don't understand what he's capable of."

Will ran his fingers through his hair while Jacob stared out the window.

"As you know, our money is mostly tied up," Jacob said. "If Frederick can wait, we can come up with the sum, maybe make payments." Panic rose in his chest. He rubbed his nose and went for his glass.

"I'm afraid that short of raising the five thousand dollars in twenty-four hours, I haven't been able to come up with anything else," Burt said. "I'm afraid Jessica's ex-husband is not a reasonable man, and for reasons I can't imagine, he doesn't care much for you, Jacob." Burt paced, then stopped in front of his son. "Now, I've considered the source, so I say this without any accusations, but Frederick seems to think he has some information about you and your past that might jeopardize your reputation and more. Mostly, I think he's a madman and might find great satisfaction in taking down the business. Sour grapes from the divorce. I heard his own land deals are going badly. He's desperate for money and the power that goes with it."

Jacob wanted to change the subject. His mind went in all directions. *What did Frederick know, and how had he found out?*

Will stepped in. "I know he's been buying parcels for cheap, then reselling them several times over without anyone being the wiser." Burt and Jacob exchanged a concerned look. "The poor suckers who bought that land are out of luck. I'd like to offer him our silence on the matter in exchange for the money and leave it at that."

"I've caught wind of that, too," Burt admitted. "He's been doing business in this county, as well as the ones across the bay. Dunbar suspects that whoever sold the land to Frederick didn't come by it legally, either. We can't get hold of any records to prove it, and nothing comes up to show that multiple sales have been made on the same properties. I'm certain Frederick has found a way to keep his paperwork carefully concealed. The original owners are either dead or out of town with no clue of their land being taken advantage of. Dunbar and I have written to the city council, and they promise to bring up the matter at their next meeting. We couldn't prove our case without documents."

"I'd like to make him an offer all right," Jacob muttered to himself.

"Jacob, you're a businessman now, and you'll settle this in a businesslike manner," Burt reminded him.

"I say we put the threat to him," Will said. "He doesn't know how much we know about his shady business. Besides, Uncle Burt, didn't you find out about his other dirty dealings with the bank some years back? It got his attention. Surely you have the credibility to make him think again. He might just back down."

Burt ran his hand over his full, gray beard. "True, true, it might work. We'd have to have a witness. I don't like approaching these things without enough evidence to back up my claim."

"That's the lawyer in you talking, Father," Jacob said. "Try thinking more like the criminal."

"I'll have to offer him a small part of the company," Burt said. "It will be a fair offer but not enough for him to run wild with. It should set him good, for a while. When he's accumulated the five thousand, his share of it will be dissolved. I'll write up the contract, then set up a meeting with him. If he refuses, I'll try my best to convince him that his claim may bring him more trouble than it's worth."

Jacob and Will looked at each other. Jacob replied, "It's not ideal, but we seem to be between a rock and a hard place." He looked around his office, then out the window. The streets were busy, and he saw commerce in that. Frederick having part of his business was unthinkable. Now he had to accept the fact that this man wasn't going away. "And if he refuses, we look harder into his land affairs, which I barely care to do at this point, but I'll be damned if I let him come near J&W. Make sure that contract limits him in every way possible."

"I'll do my best, Jake, but he will have some clout. I can only hope he'll be too busy with his own affairs to complicate yours. By the way, Will, how did you come by your information?"

Will looked down at his shoes, then up at his uncle. "Frederick seems to have friends and enemies in certain places. I happened on some of them recently."

Burt raised his hand. "I knew better than to ask. Whatever else you learn might help, though." Now Burt was looking somber. "I feel it's my duty to bring this man to justice. He treated your sister badly. June has told me things."

Jacob was burning inside at the thought of Frederick bringing harm to the woman he loved. "Damn him! He should rot in prison!"

Both men looked at Jacob. His father paused, then concluded, "Until we sort this out, keep your eyes on the business, and no more gallivanting off on some adventure. You're grown men now—act like it."

Will stirred in his seat, then got up to refresh his coffee. "Well, there goes our trip to China," he said unwittingly.

A rush of heat flooded Jacob's chest. Why did his cousin have to bring that up?

Burt was incensed. "China? Good God, whatever for?"

"It was just a thought, Father. We could have brought some goods back with us. Save some money."

Burt shook his head. "We've settled on a fine transport company. Let the Union Pacific worry about getting our inventory to us. There's certainly no need for either of you to travel such a distance at this time, of all times! God help me, you boys are going to send me to an early grave!"

With that, Burt left them to consider their circumstances. Will sat heavily in one of the worn leather chairs. "Could you put some whiskey in this?" he asked his cousin as he raised his coffee cup.

Jacob went over to the liquor trolley and fulfilled his cousin's request. "How did you hear about the land deals?"

"I recalled talking with one of the ladies at the Bay Tavern a few days ago. She told me about Mr. Moore suggesting she invest her hard-earned money in real estate. She was tempted until she found out through the grapevine that the properties were dirty and that it was like buying fool's gold. Frederick is as much of a scoundrel as ever." Will then congratulated himself for getting around the city as he did. He raised his liquor-infused coffee. "Gallivanting pays off."

THE NEWS ABOUT FREDERICK HOMING in on his business had Jacob in a foul mood. His dream to one day, present himself to Jessica as a successful man able to take on a family was being dashed. He was impatient. Tonight, he drank too much whiskey as he sat in his study, going over the letter Frederick had sent his father. Although he knew Jessica was content, he thought of Burt's comment about her overworking. He let his mind drift to the house he would buy her and the help he would hire for her. A beautiful studio, her dirt-free nails and rested hands creating her art. His love would embrace her and Henry. He would take them out of the woods and into the city where they would prosper and live happily ever—

He stopped himself. It was a waste of thought. Had she completely forgotten him? Avoiding her since the day he'd met his son had been difficult. He knew his mother and father wondered at his motives to stay away from the family's end-of-summer picnic. He couldn't bring himself to face her and Caleb together, pretending to be a family with his own son. He made his growing business his excuse. Afraid he would never be able to claim Henry as his, he grieved over his loss.

Two days later, his fears were recognized. The certified letter containing the adoption request had left him shaken and empty-hearted. His world was suddenly filled with only a paper cut-out of a finer life from the one he'd lived on the trails. Without Jessica, it all seemed senseless. A campsite fire and a blanket with her wrapped in it and lying next to him was richer than anything money could afford.

As he reread the personal letter, which had come sealed in a separate envelope, his desire to burn the whole thing and pretend he'd never received it grew. Her words offered no solution he wanted to hear.

Dear Jacob,

Please forgive me. I've waited too long to tell you what you already know. Henry is your child. It's been agony to watch him grow, knowing you will not be with him every step of the way. Let Caleb be his father, and you his cousin. Don't disappear from us as you've seen fit to do. I am offering us a chance to be together in a different way.

Caleb will make a good father and has agreed to this most difficult task of raising another man's child—your child. He loves me and he loves Henry, and together, we will love him

in return. It doesn't make my love for you lessen, as much as I wish it would. I feel I will forever think of us and forever be sadden by our circumstances.
I wish you all the best life can offer. Take this piece of it for us and Henry.
Always,
Jessica

He placed the note back into the envelope, then returned it and the rest of the papers to the larger one, refusing to sign away his parental duty. The thought crossed his mind to expose the whole thing to the world and claim his son. With that, he felt ill. Jessica would hate him forever, and his parents and family would be shocked beyond repair. His poor mother, with her innocent look on life, would be shattered. What respect he had cultivated from his father would be forever lost. Yet his hand couldn't put pen to paper. His heart spoke too loudly. But what was the rest of the world's reaction compared to a life with Jessica and his son? Slapping the envelope on his nightstand, he decided it was time to take a bolder course of action.

CHAPTER SIX

Rail River Acres—October 1890

HANNAH REACHED TO RETRIEVE THE WOODEN TOY HENRY had thrown across the room. "Now, little man, no more throwing. You almost hit poor Boones with it." She gave him back his wooden block, and Henry took it with a mischievous smile, bringing it to his drooling mouth. She continued to play with the nearly four-month-old boy as she sat on the floor with him in her lap.

Meanwhile, Jessica was in the kitchen preparing their lunch. At the sound of horse hooves, Hannah looked up as Henry threw his block again directly at the dog. Boones heaved his body from the floor and moved away from danger. Hannah placed Henry on the blanket and shook a finger at him. He whimpered in protest and sucked on his fist, his legs kicking the air. She peered out the window. A man on horseback approached, the brim of his hat shadowing his face. She called to the kitchen, "Jessica, there's a visitor."

Jessica heard the sound of the horse and wondered who it might be. A strange feeling took hold of her. She wiped her hands on a towel and then removed her apron and hung it on the peg by the kitchen entrance. Boones had begun to bark, and she quieted him and looked out the parlor window. Her heart skipped in her chest as she recognized one of Uncle Burt's horses and the rider. Hannah now had Henry in her arms, and Jessica took him from her.

"Should I get Caleb's rifle?" Hannah asked.

"No, no, it's . . . Jacob, my cousin. Stay here."

Placing her fists on her full waist, the English housekeeper commented, "Well, I'll be. Finally coming around, is he?"

Jessica wished she hadn't complained to Hannah about not seeing her cousin, but she was too moved by the sight of him to answer. She wrapped her shawl around herself and Henry before stepping out onto the porch.

Jacob dismounted and slowly approached. He took off his hat, and her heart thumped. Under his coat, he wore a tidy gray shirt tucked into a pair of black pants with a gold-buckled belt. His hair was shorter, and his cleanly shaven face gave him a fresh and youthful appearance. Suddenly, Jessica was taken back to when they were younger, when they stole a moment here and there to touch and gaze longingly into each other's eyes, the horse rides together, and mostly, Mary's pond and their lovemaking. Her feelings for him leapt from their hiding place. She cleared away the past and tried to keep calm. By now, he had received the adoption papers. Was this a visit to concede or refuse? She held Henry close as she walked forward. Standing in front of him, she caught his handsome face staring at their son.

Without looking at her, he said, "Hello, Jess." He took little Henry's hand in his. "You really could have had the decency to tell me before we returned. You must have known." Then he met her eyes. "Sending papers over from your lawyer is a pretty shitty way of dealing with this."

Her breath hitched. "Did you read my letter?"

Letting go of Henry's chubby hand, he said, "Why wasn't I told? You could have written earlier. Keep the rest of the world out of this, but I had the right to know."

"I wanted to, but . . . I couldn't let you interfere. I hoped to hide it from Caleb, but I couldn't do that to him. It was survival and what was best for the child. I needed to have a stable home, and Caleb has already proven to be a good father."

"Interfere? I'm an interference now?" He spat out the words. "I wasn't given a chance to prove anything . . . was I?"

His glare penetrated her. "Hannah, would you come get the baby, please?"

Hannah came from the house and over to where they stood.

"Wait." Jessica stopped Hannah from taking Henry. "Would you like to hold him, Jacob?"

Jacob looked at Hannah, who stepped away. He hesitated, then reached out for his son. Henry gave his father a wet grin and went willingly. Jacob eyed him, as if to examine his every feature. In a whispered breath he said, "He looks like me."

Jessica glanced at Hannah, but she hadn't heard. The sight of Jacob holding his son warmed her heart and confused her mind. It was a natural scene, as if the two of them had known each other from the start. After a while, he reluctantly handed his baby boy over to Hannah, who came forward and took him into the house.

Feeling the heavy silence between them, Jessica shifted her weight and saw Jacob peering at Hannah, who was watching from behind the screened door. His hand was on Jessica's arm, and she willingly let him lead her to the side of the barn. It was private, and she was anxious to hear what he had to say.

His eyes focused on her, his body close enough for her to smell his clean and manly scent, nearly unraveling her.

"Jess, I know I haven't proven anything that would make you want to raise a family with me, but my life is different now. I have a thriving business, and I'm settled . . . in many ways. I want you and

Henry in my life. We can meet in the city. We can be together. I'm sorry I've been such a coward. We can be a family someday. I'll be wealthy. We can make this work."

He bent down to touch her lips with his own. Lifting her head up to meet his mouth, she closed her eyes and accepted his kiss. The flood of love and longing for him threatened to wash her integrity away. It was the declaration she had wanted to hear from him for all these years. Every hurt she had experienced as a result of loving him vanished with his spoken desire to make a life with her, and yet it had come too late.

Jacob gently moved her up against the warm, sun-drenched wood of the house and kissed her again, much deeper this time. Coming apart, his lips went to her neck, and his hot breath sent tingles of desire through her. "Meet me next Monday. You and Henry." His words were hoarse and weighted.

Taking his face in her hands, Jessica raised his head to meet her eyes, which were now swimming with tears. She took one of his hands and slowly brought it to her belly. He pulled away with a jerk. He cursed and kicked the dirt and cursed again, then turned to her with a cold stare. She felt his forceful grip as he held her shoulders.

"Are you trying to make a damn fool out of me?" he shouted into her face.

"Jacob, let me go!" The tingle in her body turned to alarm.

He released her but held his stance, his eyes cutting into her heart.

"And I suppose you'll say that my son is this one's brother, and everyone will be fine with that, too! Is it even Caleb's?"

Jessica's stinging slap across his face shocked both of them. He held his stare as if he hadn't been hit. His breathing was audible, tears welling in his eyes. Her heart broke, and she buried her head in his chest. He brought her away from him, and she saw his anguish. The moment hung in the air until, like the wind blowing clouds across the sun, his expression changed. Was it resignation or defeat? He bit his lip and stood silently. Slowly, he took a few steps backward, his eyes directed at hers. It felt as if he were looking at her for the last time. She heaved a sigh.

"When we meet again, Jessica, it will be as cousins and nothing more. I can't fight with fate any longer. It wins. You win. I have to get on with my life."

Turning, he strode to his horse. She sensed he couldn't get away soon enough. Watching him leave opened an abyss of grief. She cried out, feeling the overwhelming sadness of this and so many departures from him. Her hand went to her mouth as she regained her composure.

Before she knew it, Hannah was by her side.

"Jessica, you must come inside. What has happened? Don't make yourself sick now. You've got to be well for our Henry and that little one inside of you."

Embarrassed by her sudden outburst, Jessica straightened the bodice of her dress. "I'm sorry, Hannah. My cousin told me that someone we loved as children has died," she said. It was a bitter lie, and yet, in a way, it was the truth.

Hannah's usually calm expression failed to hide her confusion. "I see, and he left you like this?"

"Let's go inside. I'll be fine."

Jessica sat on her red paisley chair and looked around, lost in her thoughts. Henry began to cry, and his pathetic wailing snapped her out of her daze. She picked him up and examined her son for the source of his dismay, but as soon as she held him, he looked back at her, his eyes wide and his mouth working as he gurgled out sounds. His happy innocence struck her heart. She cuddled her little boy and found comfort in him. She still had Jacob, if only through their son.

CHAPTER SEVEN

*C*ALEB DROVE THE OLD FLATBED WAGON HOME, SATISFIED WITH his load and the orders he had received from the Higgins Silver Factory. His abilities would be challenged by a few of the pieces, but he had an anxious excitement about the chore. The craft he had fallen in love with was becoming more fulfilling and profitable.

As he got closer to the narrower road that led him home, he saw a horse and rider coming from it and onto the main one. Slowing the wagon to inspect the stranger, he recognized Jacob's straight seat and chiseled features under his drawn-down hat. He sat on a horse as if he were a prince. It had been something Caleb often mused to himself when they rode together as gunrunners on the dirty trails with little to eat and danger around every corner. What was he doing here? He waited. Jacob spied him, and the men stared at each other. Riding casually over to Caleb, Jacob tipped his hat in greeting.

"You had some business up at my house, Jacob?"

"I came to claim Jessica and take her and my son with me, but I see that isn't possible." He paused, and Caleb swallowed the bile rising in his throat. While trying his best not to hurl himself from his seat and drag Jacob to the ground and pummel him mercilessly, he saw the unmistakable sadness in Jacob's eyes. It didn't move him, yet he understood the feeling of loss.

"It's not easy for either one of us," Caleb said. "Sign the damn papers, and let's get on with our lives. It is what it is."

With a curt nod, Jacob turned the horse around and headed down the road.

HEARING THE WAGON BEING BROUGHT into the barn, Jessica composed herself. She asked Hannah to see if Sally needed her help. Between her and their neighbor, Hannah was kept busy, and June was generous to share the housekeeper several days a week. Little Henry was sleeping from his active day of play. Jessica hoped Caleb and Jacob had not passed each other, but they must have. She struggled to settle herself down for the inevitable conversation with her husband.

CALEB SAT IN HIS CHAIR, and Jessica presented him with a glass of wine. He lit a cigarette and waited before talking. He wanted to deal with this calmly, but he didn't remove his boots as he usually did on his arrival home. He was ready to retreat to his workshop, if he needed to, or take his horse out for a good ride to blow off steam.

"What did he want?" Determined to stay in control, he didn't let her speak. "His attorney could have delivered his answer to us. He didn't have to come here and, conveniently, when I was away. And what did you say to him? I suppose it was a cozy meeting." He drained the glass of wine and placed the glass down on the table, hard. "You could have given me something stronger."

"He wants to be a part of Henry's life. I don't think he was speaking in his right mind, Caleb. We can't blame him. Henry is his son, after all. Well, he's more your son by now . . ."

"Enough." Caleb stood and looked at her with defiance. "Don't paint the picture any clearer for me, sweetheart. I can see it just fine. He wanted both of you."

"No, it's over. He made it very clear."

"*He* made it clear?"

"We made it clear to each other." She bit her lip.

Caleb went to Henry's room. The baby was lying peacefully, unaware of the struggles taking place in his honor. Caleb brought the knitted blanket over him and kissed his forehead. He wondered how he could love this child as much as he did. It disturbed him. The thought of Jessica and Henry being taken from him made him ill. He put his hand to his chin and shook his head. He couldn't— and wouldn't—let that happen.

Going back into the room, he sat down and stared into the flames of the potbellied stove. "Is he all right?" Jessica asked.

Quietly, he replied, "He's fine. I swear he's growing before my eyes."

She sat and leaned toward him. "Caleb, remember when you asked me to join your life? You thought it would be too hard for me, or too simple. I'm not sure which one you were most concerned about," she said with a soft laugh. "But it's been neither. I love you, and I love our son and the child inside of me that we created together. I love our life. Jacob has always been a part of my life, and now he's a part of all of our lives. There's nothing that can change that, but I'm here."

He wasn't about to let her off the hook. He was truly hurt and afraid. "But you wanted to be with him, didn't you?"

"Caleb, I've made mistakes, but give me the credit I deserve."

If she wanted to deliver a speech on remorse, he was having none of it. "I wish you had more trusting words for me. This isn't a goddamn confessional."

He stormed out to the porch, holding up a hand to stop her from following. He wanted to slam the door, but he thought of the sleeping child. Remembering his Indian mentor, Soaring Feather, he exercised a meditation. He began to quiet his thoughts and breathe in a more regular rhythm. He closed his eyes, and the wisdom of Soaring Feather spoke to him. "The powers that lift us forward are not always the ones we would have welcomed into our lives." Caleb put his head in his hands, and the truth behind the words made him realize how challenged he had been by his wife and how enriched his life had become since Henry's birth. His need to strive to be a better man was not only for himself.

His fear gave way to peace and then to love. It wasn't easy to let go of all he held as a man, yet he'd recognized long ago that it served no advantage to stay rigid and unforgiving. It was a hard lesson to put into practice, and he admitted to himself he'd failed at it miserably. Perhaps another opportunity would bring him success. Forgiving Jessica would be his greatest challenge. He wanted to shout out to the world how unfairly life had treated him, but he knew he would only hear his own voice echoing back.

After a long while, Jessica was on the porch, standing before him, her arms folded in front of her chest. "So, that's it?" she asked.

He slowly lifted his head. "No. Sit down, Jess." He cleared his throat. "I want to be a good husband to you, better than . . . before, and I think I'm failing at it."

She lowered her arms and sat beside him. "I've handed you more than most men would tolerate."

He nodded in agreement, then lifted himself off the bench and walked to the corner of the porch to gaze out on his land. "Yes, you have," he said, almost to himself.

She rose to stand beside him. The air was still, and into the quiet she whispered, "Too much?"

Facing her now, he looked into her questioning face. "I blame myself every day for your disappearance. I should have gone with you to the river. I should have gotten rid of the scout before he planned your abduction. I don't know why I thought nothing would come of my past if I just carried on with my life. I thought I could hide it or throw it away, never to be seen again. That day, I was only thinking of myself as a man with a wife and a homestead to care for. I'm sorry, Jess. I didn't realize what you really meant to me until . . . you were gone. Knowing you could have made a different choice just minutes ago . . ." His true feelings emerged, pushing aside the man he was trying to be. "But what you did with Jacob was just as selfish, so I suppose, in a way, that makes us even."

"Even?" Her question was tinted with arrogance.

"Yes. Square, if you'd like."

"I'm sorry to know that you've reduced our marriage and this whole situation to a game of tit for tat."

"Jess, don't be like that. You know what I mean."

"Well, then I should confess to you that I broke one of your pipes by accident. Maybe I should give you one of my dresses to burn? I think that would keep us 'square.'"

Caleb took a deep breath. She was right. He brought her to sit down beside him and clasped her hand in his. "All right, but it needn't be one of your good dresses. I know you broke the pipe, but I wasn't very attached to that particular one."

"Caleb!"

He looked down at his pretty wife and smiled. "We'll both do better."

JESSICA LEANED INTO HER HUSBAND with a sense of relief that nearly overwhelmed her, yet Jacob's words rang in her ears. "When we meet again, Jessica, it will be as cousins and nothing more." She looked up at Caleb and felt the freedom to love him with all her heart, even as she tried to dismiss the guilt she felt for having the fleeting thought of meeting with Henry's true father.

CHAPTER EIGHT

February 1891

*J*ESSICA WAS SHOCKED BY WILL'S NEWS. HE'D JUST ARRIVED from the city and now sat in her kitchen, turning a glass of whiskey in slow circles on the table.

"What do you mean Frederick had a hand in my kidnapping? I thought the scout was looking to cash in on whatever my husband and you and Jacob did together." She sat straight in her chair, forbidding herself from thinking too much about Caleb's and Jacob's pasts, not to mention her own brother's dirty dealings.

"Apparently, Rex Conrad put his scouting ears to the ground and found out you were divorced. He sought out Mr. Frederick Moore."

Bracing herself, Jessica knew she wasn't going to like what Will had to say. He paused and stared at her. Nodding for him to continue, she sipped her tea, holding tight to the warm cup.

"I did some snooping of my own and found out the filthy scout paid a visit to Frederick and told him why he was bringing Caleb back to Colorado. Jake and I were on his list, too," Will said.

Jessica placed her cup on the kitchen table and looked out the window. "Frederick knows more about my husband's past than I do." She wanted her brother to stay for supper and pick his brain. The February day was bright, but the sun was still setting early. Will would have to overnight at Aunt June and Uncle Burt's. She knew he wouldn't be missing one of June's suppers.

She looked Will in the eye. Her brother could wheel and deal his way out of most situations, but he had a hard time lying to her. "Tell me what my husband is accused of. And later, tell me what you and Jacob had to do with this."

"Gunrunning, plain and simple."

"Is that all?"

Will's sheepish expression gave her the answer—there was plenty more.

"Jess, I think . . . no, I *know* we are out of trouble. Hell, no marshal is going to send another scout all the way out here when the first one failed."

"Unless the crime is more than selling unlawful weapons."

"I'm not here to tell you things you ought not to know, Sis. What I have to say will be upsetting enough. For now, put the past away."

With a nod, her attention was drawn back to the present. "All right, go on."

"Apparently, Frederick decided to cash in on our family's assets, and he and Rex set up this whole thing with the Indians to take you and hold you for ransom. If it went bad, they could lay blame on the camp of renegades. Then he placed a tidy sum in the bank to show his concern. Through Rex, he would blackmail the family for a whole lot more, keeping his own name out of it. No one would know he orchestrated any of it. The scout got killed, and we brought you back. End of story. Frederick got caught in his own game. I know he isn't sitting on it very well."

Slapping her hands on the table, Jessica rose. "How ridiculous! I went through all of that because of Frederick? Why do all the men in my life have power over me?" Facing her brother, she scowled at him. "I trusted you and Jacob! I thought you left Hartford to join a legitimate business! How naïve I was back then. How naïve I've been all along!" Trying to rein in her anger, she retreated to the parlor, but she found no peace in sitting. She paced the woven rug on the floor.

Will came in from the kitchen. His voice was low. "I'm sorry we took you away from your life. You must know it was no one's intention. How were we to know you and Caleb ... I mean you have to admit this is pretty unusual."

"That doesn't remove anyone's guilt."

"Jess, this was the life Jacob and I chose and the life Caleb chose. It had nothing to do with you."

"Yet it had everything to do with me." Jessica let out a breath. "It's done. Caleb and I want to live a good and peaceful life."

"I'm afraid, Sister, that your actions didn't set up a life of peace."

His words punched her gut. She let out a breath and sat down. "Or your actions."

Will lowered his head. "True." He sat down next to her. "Be careful, Jess. From what I've heard, Frederick's become desperate. His land deals are souring, and he needs money. He wants his part of the reward returned to him."

"Well, then just give it back. And don't worry, I'm not going to do anything rash, though I'd like to see him get what he deserves—time behind bars."

Her brother lowered his head and ran his finger over the rim of his cup, then nervously scratched his chin whiskers. "That would be nice, but in the meantime, I'm afraid he could reveal too much."

"Will? Is there more?"

He tilted his head to look up at her. "You're not going to like this."

"I'm sure I won't, but please tell me everything." She cupped her trembling hands. He hesitated. "Well?" she said impatiently.

Finally, Will spoke. "I know about you and Jake. Have for a long time now. It's not for me to judge, and I've had to come to terms with it on my own."

Jessica brought her chin to her chest, her face flushed with the heat of her shame. If this was what it felt like to have a member of the family aware of her and Jacob's relationship . . . Right then and there, she vowed to take their secret to her grave.

"Jess, I said I've come to terms with it. Look at me."

Slowly, she lifted her head. "It was innocent at first, but we just—"

"And Caleb knows?" he asked.

"Yes. He knows Henry is . . ." Bringing both hands to her cheeks, she mouthed, "Oh God."

"I know everything, but that's not what I want to tell you."

Jessica went to the window, tempering her ragged breath, the acid in her chest churning like a whirl of fire. With her back to her brother, she listened as he unfurled the story.

"The clerk at the attorney's office, where the copies of the adoption papers were ready to be sent out, mistakenly sent a copy to your first husband."

A guttural sound came from deep inside her, and she clenched her stomach.

Will went to her. Jessica turned around, staring past him.

"The clerk was fired, but the damage is done."

As the reality of what Frederick could do sank in, she felt the air leave the room. "This can't be. He knows too much. You have to stop him, Will. He's after revenge. Stop him!"

"Calm down, Jess. We're working on it. You'll have to trust me."

"I should have warned you not to take his share in the first place." She walked past Will. "Oh, I want to strangle that clerk! Of all the incompetence!" Pacing and wringing her hands, Jessica asked, "Where are those papers now?"

"Frederick has been asked to return them immediately. The office will notify you when they have them back. They had Jacob's signature and consent."

Bringing her hand to her chest, she closed her eyes and took in a deep breath. *Jacob signed his son away.* A mix of relief and failure played with her emotions. Opening her eyes, she saw Will run his hands through his hair. Was there more? She waited.

"As for the money, we can't return it," he said. "The business has absorbed every bit of cash we had. Jake and I are barely able to pay ourselves. We shouldn't have taken it, but it was too tempting. You saw how we were living. Uncle Burt says we can give Frederick a share of J&W, just until he makes back the five grand. That might take a while. Now, as far as his knowledge of the adoption, we have an ace up our sleeves. His land deals are pretty dirty. If we can get proof that he's selling the same parcels multiple times, we can hold that knowledge over his head. He'll be tried and I'm sure found guilty—if we have the evidence."

"So, we're trading scandal and greed for pure greed?" Jessica's words were filled with anger. "Has he signed anything concerning J&W?"

Will shook his head. "Not yet. Burt is meeting with him in a few days."

A flare of nerves skidded across her chest. What if Frederick told Uncle Burt what he knew? What if he exposed all their secrets? The memory of her miscarriage after their separation and Frederick unable to have children flooded into her mind. The room clouded, and she felt Will catch her as she dropped to the floor.

THE ROOM WAS WARM, AND the light had changed. An amber glow engulfed her as the sizzle and pops coming from the tiny bedroom stove brought Jessica back from her faint. The last thing she remembered was Will bringing her to bed and telling her he would fetch Hannah. She must have needed the sleep—or an escape from life. Feeling stronger, she got up and went into the parlor, where Caleb rocked a contented Henry. The fire had been lit, and the aroma of roasting chicken and biscuits, along with the wood fire smoke, filled the air. It warmed her heart.

Caleb immediately rose with Henry. "Are you well, Jessica? Will said you just needed a bit of a rest. He left before I arrived home."

"I'm fine." She took Henry and brought the now awake and grumpy boy into her lap as she sat down. "Was Hannah here?"

"You smell the chicken." Caleb smiled, then became serious. "What happened, Jessica? Hannah said Will came to visit, and you fainted."

"Caleb, Frederick knows about everything—our past, the baby, the adoption." Her voice cracked, and he leaned forward in his chair, hands clasped on his knees.

"How?" he asked.

As Jessica related the story to him, his face turned ashen, and his blue eyes intensified. "Will didn't tell me why the scout was looking for the three of you, only that you were gunrunners. I'm not sure I want to know the rest. Is there more, Caleb?"

Henry squirmed in her lap, and she laid him in the cradle, handing him a toy. Caleb watched his young son grab a wooden duck and put it to his mouth. He gurgled, and Caleb gave him a smile, then sat back in his leather chair.

"You might as well hear the story," Caleb said. "If it all comes out in the open, I don't want you to be the last to know."

In the low evening light, with the sounds of Henry's nonsensical gurgling and the steady slap of Boones's tail as he lay splayed in front of the baby's cradle, Jessica held her arms close to her body. Her breathing became shallow as she stared at her husband.

Caleb cleared his throat. "It was in Colorado. Me, Will, Jacob, and Levi—he's one of my friends in town."

She nodded. She hadn't met his friends but wasn't surprised they were involved in this.

"We rode out for most of the morning, carrying the guns and ammo, until we came to a cabin. Three men were inside with the money. It was supposed to be a straight deal, cash for guns. We soon found out they were working for the government. The money was too fresh—new bills. I gave Jacob the signal to warn the others. He went outside and ..."

Jessica crossed her legs, and her breath hitched. Her curiosity wanted him to continue, but her heart wanted to hear no more.

"Suddenly, bullets were flying everywhere. I might have killed a man. I'm not sure whose bullet reached him."

"Oh God!"

"Jess, please, let me continue. I know this is hard to hear."

The sound of the wooden duck hitting the floor took their attention. Jessica got up and wiped the toy before handing it back to her son. Her legs were shaking as she lowered herself back into her chair. She nodded for Caleb to continue.

"It all happened within seconds. Before I knew it, one of the men was on top of me, his gun stuck under my chin."

She brought her hand to her chest with a gasp. Caleb stopped. "Sorry. Go on," she said.

"I thought it was the end until Jacob ..."

As her eyes widened, her head shook from side to side. "No." Her bottom lip trembled. "No."

"He shot the man in the back and saved my life."

The tears came, and her sobs brought Caleb to her side, his hand on her arm. Feeling his closeness, she lifted her head to meet his watery blue eyes.

"I want to say it was in self-defense, but we were riding a dangerous path. Anything could happen and for any reason."

Through her tears she asked, "Then what?"

"The three men were dead. We took the money and left. Rode as long and fast as we could in the opposite direction of the camp, which was burned by the men hired by the government. One out of our gang survived, and for his clemency, he gave our names and likenesses to the marshal."

Caleb stood above her, his arms crossed in front, his chin elevated. "So that's it. The scout was sent to bring us all back to hang. Instead, he decided to make a quick deal. I gave him two hundred dollars to leave us be." She watched Caleb withdraw into his own thoughts for a long moment. When he came back to her, his expression had softened. "I had no idea Rex had communicated with Frederick."

Slowly, Jessica rose, her eyes glued to his. "Thank you for telling me."

He embraced her, and she sank into him. She held on tight to his strong, vital body, his heartbeat loud against her ear. His soft yet stubborn heart would have been gone before her ever knowing him. Her life with him, the child she carried—their child—the homestead they'd built together, all would have been nothing if Jacob hadn't killed another man.

"What are you thinking, Jess?" he asked, his breath warm on the side of her face.

Pulling away from him, Jessica stood as tall as her five-foot-four-inch frame could manage. "I can't judge you or Jacob or my brother for what you did in the past. It's hard to take it in, but it's done. You're here and alive. For now, we must stop Frederick from revealing any of this to my family. Will knows about Henry's origins, and now Frederick has physical proof of something that would break the hearts and minds of my family. I feel it all unraveling before me!" She slumped her shoulders and looked away.

Caleb stepped back. "Will knows? How would that have happened? On the trails? Geez, I don't even want to think of what you and Jacob did together and how long."

"Don't then."

He jerked back. "Jesus."

"Caleb, let's not get into this again. We have to put a stop to Frederick. He wants the reward money back, and Uncle Burt is about to give him part ownership in J&W until he makes back the five thousand."

"I have nothing to do with that business. Will and Jacob are on their own with that."

"What about the adoption, Caleb? What are we to do?"

"What do you want, Jess? I can't do a damn thing."

"Will says they will blackmail him. His land deals are apparently unlawful."

Caleb chuckled. "Imagine that. Well, I say let them deal with this. I want nothing more than to resume my life. Our lives." With that, Caleb sat down and lit his pipe. "Dinner smells ready."

Jessica went to the kitchen. Before entering, she looked back at Caleb. The smoke from his pipe swirled around his head. He seemed unburdened now. She wondered if what he had just revealed to her was one incident among many. The man she knew was nothing like the picture he had painted. She imagined him lying on the dirty floor, a gun to his chin. His beauty, his strength, his reasoning had been in another man's hands. Jacob's hands. She knew he carried burdens beyond her imagination. Another part of her was in shock. How was he able to reconcile the spiritual man with the outlaw? The chambers in her husband had many compartments, and she had only come to know a few.

As she stirred the gravy, Jessica thought of Jacob, her love for him growing instead of falling back. He was now her hero. *Oh dear.*

Chapter Nine

San Francisco—March 1891

$\mathcal{B}$URT WAITED AT A TABLE IN THE HOTEL FAIRMONT DINING room and tried to remain calm. The time was nearing for Frederick to arrive. He fiddled with a glass of brandy and went over the plan in his head. Soon enough, Frederick was there. Burt rose to greet the Englishman. Last time they had spoken was in '89 when Frederick asked to donate to the reward money in a show of solidarity for Jessica's safe return. Burt quickly noticed that the younger man had become gray around the temples and his eyes were dull and tired, though he still remained a strong, proper gentleman. Putting aside his disdain for Frederick, Burt offered him a seat.

"You look well," Frederick said as he signaled to the waiter.

Burt nodded. "Thank you, Frederick. Shall we get down to business, or shall we wait for your drink?"

"Do I need one, Burt? I recall another meeting in my study that certainly required one. But indeed, let's get down to business. Do you have my money?"

His directness was so unlike the man Burt had come to know as Jessica's husband. "No, I do not." Burt took the papers from his old leather briefcase. It was the one he'd used back East when he was the head prosecutor in Hartford. "We have an offer for you."

"There was no conveyance in my letter concerning any offers. I simply want my money returned, plus whatever interest it has accrued," Frederick replied without missing a beat.

"I'm placing an offer on the table. Look it over, and we'll go from there." He laid the paperwork in front of Frederick.

"What is all this?" Frederick asked as he leafed through the pages. He slid it back to Burt's side of the table. "I have no use for this," he said with a dismissive wave. "Now, how will you be getting my money to me? Cash? A bank note?"

"I won't mince words with you, Frederick. The funds are tied up in J&W. Either you take the offer, or we give you nothing more than our promise that . . ." Burt swallowed. What was he getting himself into? He had dipped his toe into the murky waters of blackmail. Never before had he done such a thing.

Frederick leaned in. "Yes? Promise of what?"

"The promise that we will expose the land deals you've been making. We know they are illegal. It could have a very costly outcome for you, more than the five thousand." Burt held Frederick's stare, then broke it by sliding the papers back. His heart beat unevenly. Was it his conscience or his age catching up to him?

Frederick, now with a drink in hand, smiled broadly. He took a long sip and placed the glass on the white linen tablecloth. "Is this blackmail? I expected more from you, Burt. This must be the foolish doing of your son and nephew."

"It's your own doing, Frederick."

"You're neither jury nor judge, may I remind you," Frederick said. "Do not forget I was once an attorney myself. I hope you don't expect me to feebly accept your offer or let you ruin me with your false accusations."

"No one has formally accused anyone of anything. I'm sure your attorney skills are not that rusty, unless perhaps you feel you have something to worry about."

"I have nothing to hide, Burt, and I resent your remarks concerning my business affairs. However, I certainly don't need to have another blow to my reputation, as you so skillfully planned before."

"Frederick, you know damn well I was the one who got you out of your troubles with the bank." Burt stopped himself from going further. He wasn't going to become embroiled in a battle of right and wrong with this man. He took a breath and stayed on track. "Very well then. I hope you are dealing in clean properties. I'm sure my friend at the attorney general's office would be very pleased about that. He's told me that several schemes to sell land multiple times have come to his attention, and being a thorough agent of the state of California, he'll find out what's what in no time." The lie was coming too freely, but he had to play this to the end.

"You're bloody good, Burt. You came well prepared, but I still want my money back. Please give my regards to your son and nephew. You've betrayed your good sense in allowing them to take any of the reward and, in doing so, have stolen from me." He drained his glass. "By the way, I have some disturbing news. It's come to my attention that your niece's son is illegitimate." He gave the older attorney a hard look.

The comment slammed into Burt. He steadied himself. "Don't start, Frederick. I know your schemes and lies."

Frederick chuckled. "Don't think you know everything, my dear old man. My information would ruin your family beyond belief."

A sharp chill ran up Burt's spine. He was speechless. Finally, he found his voice. "What could you possibly do to us? Your vengeance toward my niece is insane."

"Your niece and your son. They plotted against me. Jacob ruined my marriage!" Frederick slammed his glass onto the table.

The other diners turned to stare. Burt needed to defuse the situation.

"I'm sorry if my son was concerned for his cousin, but I'm sure he couldn't have given her any advice that would make her leave you. That was clearly her choice."

Frederick stood and gave a rueful laugh. "As you wish to see it, but mark me, I will ruin them if you go after me in any way."

The Englishman wove his way through the lush golden dining hall, its large pots of leafy palms soon camouflaging him. Burt took a drink from his water glass to soothe his dry mouth and then a swig of liquor to calm his shaken nerves. He was getting too old for this sort of business.

CHAPTER TEN

*W*AITING ANXIOUSLY FOR HIS FATHER'S ARRIVAL FROM THE meeting with Frederick, Jacob paced in front of J&W's storefront window. He cursed as he considered the secrets Frederick could expose. How could this man wield such power over his life? Their plan to blackmail him had to work. The future of his business and family depended on it. The former outlaw in him pondered darker things—the "accidents" that could occur in the blackness of night. He brushed those sinister thoughts away and continued to wait.

The street was teeming with industry. Carriages, horses, carts, people, and the occasional new horseless buggy sped by him in a flurry of activity. In it lay his success if he could keep certain secrets under a heavy veil of silence.

By the time the carriage stopped in front and his father descended, Jacob had drummed up so many scenarios, he felt his mind spinning out of control. Was the truth about to spill over the tightly sealed vessel he and Jessica and Caleb had put it in?

"Jacob."

"Father."

They entered the building, and Jacob led him straight to the back, where his crowded office waited. "You must be tired from the trip. There is a room ready for you at the Fremont. I'll have our driver take you there shortly."

Burt dusted off his coat. "A driver? How worldly."

Jacob clucked his tongue. "Our deliveryman, Father." He offered his father a seat and hung his coat on a hook.

"Yes, of course. Don't mind my foul mood. Frederick was as supercilious as ever." Burt rubbed his back as he sat, grimacing in discomfort.

Jacob took a chair opposite, his nerves tight. "What did he say exactly?"

"That he doesn't want anything to do with J&W Imports and wants his money. I told him we knew of his land deals, and he laughed in my face, then threatened me."

"Threatened you? Father, what could he threaten you with?"

"He said you ruined his marriage. He claims Jessica's son is illegitimate. I don't know where he gets such crazy ideas."

Jacob took a breath and let it out.

"Unless, Son, you know what he might be talking about? Henry didn't look premature."

The look his father gave him was one of a lawyer trying to extract the truth from a client. With his heart beating like a bass drum, Jacob stared back, blank-faced. "No, I don't."

A heavy silence engulfed the dimly lit office. The tension was broken by the clink-clank of the door's bell as someone entered the store. Jacob went into the hall to see who it was. Will gave a nod. "In here," Jacob said. "My father's back from his meeting with Frederick."

Will entered the office. "Hello, Uncle Burt. What's the news?"

Burt stood up and faced Will. "Not much. I may hear from him later, but he says he wants no part of the business. We'll have to find another plan."

Will grinned. Jacob and his father exchanged a wry look.

"I'll find another plan. Give me some time," Will said with a wink.

"We'll get to the root of his dealings," Jacob replied.

Burt sniffed. "Well, I see you both feel you can manage this without me."

"You want me to behave like a grown man, yet you treat me as an adolescent. Which is it, Father?"

Will stepped aside. To his surprise, Jacob saw his father soften. "I'm sorry, Jake, I just don't—"

"Don't trust me?" His heart lurched. It hurt him to even ask the question.

"I do trust you, Jacob, but this has to be handled with some expertise. You and Will should let me take care of it."

"We want to take care of it ourselves," Jacob replied.

His father's eyes held the sadness of a man being told he was too old for the job. A pang of empathy ran through Jacob. Burt's stern voice brought him back. "Sometimes you can fight fire with fire, Jake, but be careful. You and Will are no match for this scheming bastard."

Aged or not, the man still had fight in him. "Was that all he said about me?" Jacob asked.

"What do you mean is that all? It's quite an accusation. He seems to believe now as he did back in the days of his divorce from Jessica that you had a hand in their marriage and its demise. He's also alluded to knowing something else about you." Turning to his nephew, he brought Will back into the conversation. "And you as well. Something about working outside the law. What's this all about?"

Jacob was determined to keep his autonomy. "My past is my business."

"And these claims that you ruined his marriage?"

"When we visited in September of '86, I saw how miserable Jessica was," Jacob replied. "She needed to get away from him. I gave her a shoulder to lean on." He avoided his cousin's raised eyebrows and the smirk covering his face.

His father looked away. "Yes, we saw it, too. Why do you think I helped her get a divorce? He blackmailed her with accusations I do not care to go into. And, well, I heard from Hannah that he laid a hand on her—and more than once."

"And I'm the villain in his eyes?" Jacob barked.

"Now, Son, that's all in the past."

Jacob composed himself.

"Let's stick to the problem at hand," Burt said. "Besides, I don't hear of you visiting Jessica and her family. It seems you've distanced yourself from them over these many months. That isn't very family-like, Jacob. I thought you two were close."

Jacob nodded to his father, a sharp pain etching his heart. Loving Jessica was a never-ending story, and now he held that same love for his son. "Yes, well, time and circumstances change people." He cupped the back of his neck.

Burt scratched his chin. "Whatever it is you two have in mind to take care of Frederick better be above-board. If it isn't, just be damn sure you don't get caught. The Stanford and Messing names cannot be involved in any wrongdoing. If this got back to the board, I could have my license revoked. Thomas's good name back East would be tarnished, God rest his soul. And I don't have to tell you how this could affect your mothers, not to mention Jessica's artistic ambitions and Caleb's business." He puffed out a breath as if weary from the possible consequences.

"Don't worry, Father. It will be as above-board as it needs to be." In the back of his mind, he was praying Will wasn't about to gamble away their futures. A whisper of his own gunrunning, gambling, and whoring days ran through Jacob, sending a shiver up his spine. If the truth were to come out, it could be the end of their import business. He was desperate to put his past behind him.

CHAPTER ELEVEN

WILL WAS CONSIDERING HIS LOUSY HAND OF CARDS AND pondering his next move when a tap on his shoulder took his attention. Turning his head, he found a long, thin finger attached to an equally long, thin man in a plain brown tweed suit.

"Excuse me, sir," the stranger began. "My sources tell me you have business with a Mr. Frederick Moore. I was wondering if it might be possible to discuss some matters with you."

Will looked at him with amusement. "You aren't familiar with card playing, are you?" he asked the gentleman who had just broken his concentration.

The man flustered. "No, I'm sorry."

Will tossed his cards on the table and threw in a few coins from his small pile, then pocketed the rest. He rose to face his savior. "I was losing anyway. Who are you, and what's this about?"

The man gestured toward a more discreet table. Will followed his lead, and soon there was a drink in front of him. A whiff of it revealed it was his favorite whiskey.

"My name is Kendall Southerly. You are William Messing, are you not?"

"How do you know of me when I've only just met you, Mr. Southerly?" Will took a sip of his whiskey and showed his teeth as he swallowed. "Aw, that's good."

Kendall Southerly tilted his narrow head. "My sources know you, Mr. Messing. You seem to bring them as much pleasure as they bring to you, if you get my meaning."

"I get your meaning." Will quickly replayed what he had said to his latest whore. "Talk straight, man. What do you want?"

"I heard you were interested in Frederick Moore's land company, if you can call it that. It seems more of a fool's folly."

"I take it you invested your hard-earned money and are dissatisfied?" Southerly's tipped chin gave him the answer. "What's that got to do with me?"

Kendall Southerly brought his glass to his lips, sniffed, then took a swig, followed by a short cough. "My sources tell me you may want some help in getting out of a sticky situation with him. Money owed? I'd be happy to be of service and would charge a sensible amount for the satisfaction of seeing Frederick Moore run out of town, or better yet, thrown in jail for an extended period of time."

"I see," Will said with a chuckle. "And you think we can be of service to each other?"

"Yes, since my sources tell me—"

"Your sources are decent women trying to make a living," Will remarked.

Southerly squirmed in his chair, looking guilty for having indulged in the houses of ill repute. "I can see you lack discretion, Mr. Messing. I feel meeting with you may have been a mistake."

"I'm as much a gentleman as any," Will replied, defending his rougher manners against this haughty stranger's contempt. "Please tell me what's on your mind, *Mr.* Southerly."

"Please call me Kendall. You see, my job as an accountant for a funeral home had become routine and depressing. When I learned of Mr. Moore's land investments from, well, a certain *lady* . . ." Southerly paused and took a gulp of his drink, coughed again, and continued. "I became excited by the prospect of a different way of life for myself and my bride-to-be, Maude. One day, I received an invitation to a dinner party at Mr. Moore's home. Maude's name was also on the invitation. We were greatly flattered, as you might expect."

He told the story of how Frederick had not only been able to take his money with ease but had also lured away his fiancée.

Will listened to the sad tale and felt pity for the man, remembering that, at one time, he, too, would have invested with Frederick. The word "blackmail" entered his mind again. Will's determination to be clear of entanglement with Jessica's ex-husband gave Kendall Southerly an audience.

"Although I'm beginning to recover financially, my dignity as a man has been stripped from me," Southerly concluded. "If he had only played me for a fool, and not my Maude as well, it might have been different. It seems he turned her head his way. She thinks he loves her and she told me she might be in love with him."

"Yes, a promise of marriage is a solemn agreement. I'm sorry to hear he was able to take her from you. He has a wife, a mistress, and now another mistress. A very busy man," Will said.

"I heard that your dear sister was married to him at one time. Rumor has it he cheated on her as well."

"My sister's name will be kept out of this or our conversation is over."

"Yes, yes. Indeed, she has paid her dues," Southerly responded quickly. "I have seen her paintings in the gallery not far from here. They are . . . provocative." He went for the small napkin by his drink and wiped the beads of sweat collecting on his forehead.

Will was slightly sickened by this man. "Let me get back to you, Southerly. I think we may be able to help each other. Now, if you'll excuse me."

Kendall Southerly ignored him. "I think Maude feels Mr. Moore can provide her with a life beyond anything she can imagine. I suppose his charm had something to do with it." He looked down at his drink, his protruding cheekbones and sullen eyes defining his hardship.

Standing, Will again expressed his sympathy and thanked Southerly for the drink.

The unfortunate man continued more loudly, clearly desperate. "I met his current wife, Mrs. Annabelle Moore, at their dinner party. I provided her a sympathetic ear as she revealed to me how unhappy she is with her circumstances. I feel she might be willing to help us."

"Not *us*. You," Will insisted.

"Oh, yes, of course." Southerly ordered Will another drink as Will reluctantly reclaimed his seat.

"I'm not as worldly as most men." Southerly stared into his empty glass. "I know unhappiness and despair when I see it. Annabelle, Mrs. Moore, seems to be quite depressed." He looked up at Will. "Maybe she would trust me to offer her a way out."

Will thought for a moment. If anyone looked like an empathic creature, it was this man, but he was hardly the gent to lure a woman from her husband. "Are you saying that Frederick's wife would hand over information about her husband's land deals to you?"

"She may if I approach her with my story. She claims he uses her as his secretary at all hours of the night. Her first-hand knowledge of his records could be invaluable. Besides, why wouldn't she want revenge for her husband's infidelity?"

"Women are funny animals, and some breeds are damn unpredictable. Good luck, my man. Now, I really must leave." Will swallowed his drink and rose.

Southerly jumped up and grabbed his arm. "Wait!" he hissed. "Please help me. I need money to get Maude back. Annabelle is penniless without Frederick and helpless to move on with her life. I need to pay for her help. In turn, we will get the information we need to bring charges. I know your uncle is a lawyer. He must know how."

The man's eyes protruded from their bony exterior. Will shook off his hand. "How the hell do you know all this?"

Kendall Southerly straightened his back. "Women talk."

Will ran his hand through his hair. "Jesus."

"Losing a business such as J&W is almost as heartbreaking as losing a wife-to-be. I wouldn't want anyone to feel such pain."

Will wasn't sure what to make of this tall, elegant, but sorry soul, yet his story was intriguing. "One hundred, not a penny more," he said in a lowered voice. "Meet me here next Tuesday. If what you have is worth my time and money, I'll pay you. Mind you, I need clear documentation."

Southerly extended his hand without pause. "That's more than generous of you, Mr. Messing."

Will left the saloon, wiping his hand on his trousers. Where this would lead, he didn't know, but his gut told him it wasn't good.

CHAPTER TWELVE

FTER HER CHORES WERE DONE AND HENRY WAS SETTLED,
Jessica sat at the kitchen table with paper and pencil. She began
her letter to Jacob, then scratched out her words and ripped it up.
Balancing their intimacy with practicality proved difficult. She
plodded through with another piece of her precious stationery.

> *My brother has told me everything I'm sure you already know.*
> *Jacob, I'm afraid. Frederick could hold this over our heads*
> *forever. We would be his puppets. Please let me know what*
> *you and Will are doing to prevent the complete unraveling*
> *of our lives.*
> *Burn this letter, for I must convey to you that you are still in*
> *my heart and mind. Henry grows healthy and well and looks*
> *more like you every day.*
> *Yours always,*
> *Jessica*

She placed the letter into the envelope. In spite of her growing belly that demanded she slow down, she would take the carriage into town today to post the letter herself.

As Jessica approached the barn with Henry in her arms, Caleb came up the road on horseback. She never took Henry into her studio. He would know she was going somewhere. Dismounting, he walked to them.

"Where do you think you're going?" he asked with a droll smile.

"I have a letter I want to post today. It's important. I've written to Jacob to let him know how concerned we are about this situation with Frederick. I've asked him to inform me of their plans." She stood more defiantly than she intended.

Caleb shifted his weight and grimaced. "Jessica, the doctor warned you about taking the carriage down the hill by yourself." Henry reached out for Caleb, and he took him. "Hello, little fella. Have you been a good boy today?" Henry spoke in his own language, explaining his entire morning. Jessica and Caleb laughed at their sweet son.

Turning back to her, Caleb was more serious. "I don't want you writing to him. Besides, I heard from the lawyer. He has the adoption papers back. Unless Frederick had them copied, I think it's safe to say we are in the clear with that situation. The other situation has nothing to do with you. Is this just an excuse to write to him?"

Avoiding his question, Jessica relaxed. "I'm glad they were returned, but you know as well as I do, he had a copy made."

"Come inside."

Jessica followed Caleb back to the house. Once they were inside and Henry was placed in his cradle, Caleb sat down and asked her to sit as well.

"I've had a letter from Will."

Her eyes widened. "You have?"

"What they plan is something you should stay clear of. Not knowing ensures you don't have to lie."

"I see. I already know they plan to blackmail him."

"Will met a man who says he has information from Frederick's wife."

"Annabelle? I thought she worshiped the ground he walked on."

"I think she worshiped the actual ground he walked on." Caleb chuckled.

Smirking, Jessica nodded. "Yes, she was taken from a lowly position as his receptionist at the bank to the mistress of a fine house with servants, jewelry, and a wardrobe of the current fashions."

"I suppose it would turn a feeble mind. Anyway, from now on, I don't want you having any contact with your brother or Jacob. The less you are involved, the better." He reached into his shirt pocket and took out the letter, then opened the door on the potbellied stove. Together, they watched Will's letter burn. Extending his hand to her, Caleb waited. She handed over her letter to Jacob. It, too, burned to ashes.

"He'll never know that you sent your fondest wishes."

Her husband's sarcasm hurt, but his intuition made her mad. He knew her too well.

Closing the door to the stove, they sat, silently watching the flames. Jessica's thoughts crisscrossed in her mind. Everything would be fine and life would return to a sense of normality, or Frederick would feel trapped and tell her uncle exactly what he knew with proof to back it up.

She looked over at Caleb, and he returned her stare. His beautiful blue eyes were reassuring and knowing, yet she felt the tinge of guilt so familiar to her now. If they got to the other side of this without harm to anyone, it would be a miracle.

Chapter Thirteen

San Francisco

*A*nnabelle Moore nervously awaited Kendall Southerly's arrival. Spring blossoms sat in large vases around the parlor, scenting the room. Normally, the profusion of flowers would renew her spirit. Today, however, they were merely decoration in a house she no longer wished to live in.

She had arranged this meeting for afternoon tea after receiving a note from Mr. Southerly asking to see her privately. He wasn't much of a man. His slight build and thinly drawn face did not move her, but during their first meeting, her heart had been tugged by his understanding and compassion, and this had sparked her interest. With her family intentionally unaware of her plight, she would find a way to get back to them with dignity. British Columbia was a world away. She had written home of her marriage to a banker in San Francisco and the fine life they led while leaving out the lies and deception, the unlawful dealings, and her role in keeping the ledgers of the actual figures secret while doctoring others.

Frederick held this rich lifestyle over her head and threatened to throw her into the streets if she dared speak of any of it. Somehow, she'd found the courage to take this step. Would Kendall Southerly be her savior?

With no personal assistant or any house employee she could trust, Annabelle was alone in her decision to extend Mr. Southerly the invitation. She was keenly aware of the rift between him and her husband, though she knew none of the particulars. She assumed it had to do with another land deal. This meeting had been arranged carefully. Frederick was away for a few days on business.

Having dismissed the housekeeper and the kitchen help, Annabelle asked the cook, Betty, to bring the tea service into the parlor. She pretended not to see the cook's dagger looks at being forced to stoop beneath her station. This was the housekeeper's duty. Betty's contempt wasn't unusual, however. Annabelle knew the staff preferred the first Mrs. Moore to her. The vile whispering around every corner made for a lonely life, but as long as they kept her husband happy, she could endure their coldness. Even those she herself had hired had been turned against her by the older staff.

But if things went well today, she'd have to endure her unhappy life only a little while longer. She shuddered to think how freely she had given herself to Frederick. The lure of being married to a handsome, wealthy man had made her giddy with the hope of a grand future. She would have done anything to live in the luxury that she craved, but the truth haunted her—she had let herself become a secretary to a criminal, and now she felt betrayed and dirty.

"Thank you, Betty. You can arrange it over here," she instructed, pointing to a small table between two chairs. Annabelle swept a hand over her neatly arranged blonde hair, then adjusted the lace on the blue-gray bodice of her dress. She fidgeted with the figurines on the mantel and moved the large vase of flowers to the other side of the mirror that hung above the white, marbled fireplace. Its ornately carved surroundings had been her design. The whole house had been too plain when she'd arrived. His first wife must have been a dolt not to outfit this home with the very best. She considered bringing luxury to every room one of her greatest feats. The house was a showpiece, and all their guests admired her good taste.

Betty did as she was told, but Annabelle was acutely aware of the cook tracking her every move. Was she Frederick's spy? Were they all tracking her for him? Taking a sharp breath, she steadied her thoughts.

"Must be a special guest this afternoon, Mrs. Moore. Will simple biscuits suffice?"

"That's none of your business." She reached into her skirt pocket and brought out a piece of paper. "I've arranged for Sam to take you into town to pick up the items I will need for our next dinner party. Here is the list. He's ready to take you now."

Betty studied the piece of paper. "Right now, ma'am?"

"Yes."

"Mrs. Moore, I'll have to stop at several shops for these things. I have a lamb stew cooking. You gave the other girls the morning off. Who will tend to it?"

"Take it off the heat until you return. It will be fine."

"But, ma'am—"

"I said it will be fine. Now go!"

Betty immediately left the room, murmuring under her breath as she removed her apron.

Annabelle looked at herself in the ornate mirror. She pinched her cheeks and lifted her small chin, then adjusted the feathered pin nestled in her bun. She tried to overlook the dark circles under her eyes and her lackluster complexion. After all, she reasoned, it had been an unusually cool, wet winter.

Listening carefully for the sound of horses taking Betty and Sam away, she stood still. She figured their chores would keep them out of the house for several hours. As the clip-clop of the horses' hooves left the cobblestone drive, her anticipation grew. The minutes ticked by, and she was afraid he might be late or not come at all, and she began to question her decision. Perhaps Kendall Southerly's purpose was to make amends with Frederick through her. *Or maybe he wants to see me just for me.* She pondered a few scenarios, including one in which he would sweep her off her feet and away from her tragic life. Together they would travel to Canada and forge a new life. She quickly came out of her delusion. *Don't be a fool, Annabelle. You're twenty-eight years old and a married woman. Who would want you now?* She wiped a tear from her cheek and sighed, concluding Kendall Southerly wanted something from her husband and needed her help. He might pay well for her information. Acquiring money was her only hope of escape. If only she knew how to get to Frederick's store of cash. She had yet to discover the code to his safe.

There was a soft knock on the front door, and she had to listen to make sure she was hearing correctly. Then it came again. Annabelle took a deep breath and let it out before opening the door.

"Mr. Southerly, what a pleasure it is to see you again." In truth, the meek, thin man repulsed her. Her dream of a brave, handsome knight coming to take her away dissolved in disappointment.

"The pleasure is mine, my dear lady. Please forgive the vagueness in my note."

She offered her hand, and he took it with his spiny fingers. She was surprised at their warmth. "Come in." She gestured toward the parlor.

Kendall walked into the ornate room and stopped abruptly. She nearly collided with him.

"What is it?" she asked.

"The impressive fireplace, the flowers, the delicate figurines. Everything is the same as that night—the night I lost my Maude and my future to Frederick."

Annabelle looked around the room, then back at Kendall. He sent pins and needles up her spine.

As if he stood alone, his words poured out of him. "She told me she had fallen in love with Frederick. He offered her a better life. And . . . and she became a woman with him. He told her to be strong and act like the woman she had become. She told me all this and more. My dear, sweet Maude. She invested her money in his land, the money for our wedding. Her dowry."

Annabelle listened, wide-eyed, mouth agape. Another mistress? "Do you need to take some tea, Mr. Southerly? Or perhaps something stronger? I know I need the latter."

"Yes, thank you," he replied, coming out of his trance.

She went to the liquor cabinet, drew out two glasses, and poured them each a drink.

Kendall accepted his and sat down. He took a small sip of the brandy. "That's better," he said. He placed the glass on the table and looked directly at her. "Madam, it has come to my attention that your husband is dealing in bad properties and that your future prospects may be in jeopardy. As someone who cares about your welfare, let me help you." He wiped his sweaty hands on one of her delicate napkins, then placed it on his knee.

The brandy tasted good, and she took another sip. Flattered, she proceeded cautiously. Her involvement in Frederick's land deals could prove disastrous for her. "I don't know what to say, Mr. Southerly. Thank you for your concern, but I'm sure you are mistaken."

"Annabelle. May I call you by your first name?"

"Yes, I suppose." She touched her lips.

"Annabelle, is it not upsetting to you that your husband has taken up with my fiancée?"

She sat still as her mind instantly went to the past several weeks. Frederick had told her he would have to be away more on business.

"I'm not sure what you're talking about, Mr. Southerly. It's very inappropriate of you to blame my husband for your woes." Taking a gulp of her drink, she felt her head filling with cotton.

"I know where they meet," he continued. "He put her up at

the Hotel Regale. She bragged to me as if I was nobody. It's all so below her. He's possessed her."

Annabelle was still not convinced. "Please calm yourself. What proof can you give me?"

"My proof is my word. She broke off our engagement to be with him!"

"Mr. Southerly, you're talking about my husband." Her statement was weak at best. She knew Frederick. This man's assertions fit her husband to a tee. Annabelle fingered her napkin. She stood up and faced the mirror.

"They could very well be meeting there now," Mr. Southerly said, his voice rising to an excited pitch.

Annabelle felt light-headed as she turned back to him. "I thought perhaps you were here for other reasons. Maybe I can help restore your investment with my husband?"

Continuing his line of thought, Mr. Southerly was now pacing the floor. "We'll go there and expose this devilish thing!" he cried, as if going to war.

His excitement chilled her. "We must be prudent. This is a very delicate matter, and we're not even sure of it. Now, tell me, is there something else you want? Concerning business?"

"Let's go there now and be sure!"

"This is madness! My husband is on a business trip and will return in a few days. I will wait and confront him with it then. I will not go off on some wild goose chase simply on hearsay!"

"Madam, they could be in each other's arms many times before he returns to you. Will you be able to wait, knowing you could have shortened their involvement?"

She looked around the room for answers, then she thought of Molly Ambers, his longtime mistress. "His other woman has a room in a home not far from here," she revealed unexpectedly. "He has brought that whore into our own neighborhood. He says he will send her back to England as soon as he finds the money for the ticket! But that was months ago!" The stinging tears flowed freely now.

"How awful for you, my dear woman. What have you got to lose?"

"What about his land deals? I know where the key is to his files. We can ruin him that way." She wrung her hands. "I would need money in exchange for my help to you. I will leave him as soon as he is arrested. I have family in—" She brought a hand to her mouth, deciding she didn't want a future with Mr. Southerly.

The air around her was tingling with energy. Annabelle felt she was on the brink of changing her life forever. There might be plenty to lose, but she suddenly didn't care. A taste of revenge slithered in her mouth.

"Yes, I have money. Tuesday. I can get it then. I will need documents," Kendall Southerly said as an afterthought. "But what about today? What about catching them in the act? We must leave now."

Although it felt perverse, Annabelle had an overpowering need to find Frederick with one of his mistresses. She got her wrap, and soon they were on their way to the Hotel Regale.

CHAPTER FOURTEEN

THIS IS MADNESS, ANNABELLE THOUGHT. SHE WANTED IT TO BE a folly, nothing more than this man's crazed mind. They'd go back to her home, and she'd find the documents he needed. Waiting for Tuesday would be difficult, but three days wouldn't matter if she was to get money for her freedom for a train ticket up north. If anything, catching Frederick in the act before she left him would bring truth to the shadows of lies surrounding their marriage.

No, today was her time to seize this sudden opportunity.

When they arrived at the Hotel Regale and its less-than-opulent lodgings, Mr. Southerly helped Annabelle out of the carriage. She stood on the sidewalk and looked up at the modest building. It gave her a chill, and she drew her shawl closer. As she contemplated whether or not she would have the courage to go inside and ask for her husband, she glanced at Mr. Southerly, who was reaching into the cab of the carriage. To her horror, he placed a pistol in the inner pocket of his coat.

"Where did you get that?" she whispered.

"Never mind where. I purchased it. In case."

"I want to go home," she demanded.

"What? What do you mean? We are too close to our freedom, your freedom, madam."

Southerly told the driver to wait. Grabbing Annabelle's hand, he led her toward the entrance.

Annabelle's heart raced, and her mind snapped. Frederick in bed with yet another woman. When would it stop? He had to be stopped! She got to the front desk, and with all the confidence she could muster, she proceeded with the plan.

"Hello, I believe you have my friend, Maude Jennings, staying with you?"

The man studied his book and placed a finger to a line, then looked up at Annabelle. "Yes, we do. However, it says here she's gone out for the day and won't be dining with us. Was she expecting you? If you'll give me your name, I will leave a note telling her you were here."

Annabelle's heart was in her throat. She had to think quickly. "Oh dear. Where did she say she was going?"

"Let me see if she left a note for you."

Annabelle waited on wobbly legs while the desk clerk searched for the correspondence. She leaned into the counter. He continued his search to the waste bin and retrieved a crumbled piece of paper.

"Here is something. Are you M? This has her room number on it. It must have been tossed by mistake. I'm sorry."

"Yes, yes." Annabelle took the note with clammy hands.

My sweet M, it read. *Meet me at 124 Roosevelt Drive.* She placed the note on the counter and turned to leave.

"Madam, don't you want to save this for the address?" the clerk asked.

She kept walking until she was outside.

Southerly quickly went to her. "What is it?"

"Are they in there? Are they?"

"They're at the cottage he once rented for Molly," she said in a daze. "Why would he still rent it?" Her thoughts went to the time when she was Frederick's go-between for him and Molly when he was married to Jessica. The irony was not lost on her, and it made her entire body fill with anger, pinning her to the ground.

"Come, time is wasting." He grabbed her arm. She recited the address to the driver.

They arrived at a small house perched atop a steep hill. The fog had rolled in, and wisps of the gray clouds surrounded the upper floor of the house. Annabelle peered out the carriage window at the eerie sight. Southerly came around and helped her out, and she saw the handle of his pistol peeking out from his open coat. Her stomach reeled.

"I don't want you to do something foolish, Mr. Southerly. Now, if you will please leave the pistol behind." She shook at the very words coming from her mouth.

"I said it's just in case. I may have to defend my honor. I feel braver with it. I can assure you, it's just for show." He hurried her up the wood-encased stone stairs as she fought to keep her balance on the slippery surfaces. Once at the top, she stopped to catch her breath at the door.

Turning the knob on the door, she found it was unlocked. *He's so sure he's safe, he didn't even bother to lock the door.* Annabelle looked at Southerly. Even in the cool air, sweat moistened his nose and upper lip.

"I don't want to do this," she said in a panic and began to step back down, her footing unsteady.

"Go back to the carriage then!" he shouted, taking the pistol from his pocket.

Annabelle rushed down the stairs, nearly slipping on the stones. Once on the ground, she immediately went to the driver, who was enjoying a bit of rest in the cab. She called out, and he jumped from the cab, explaining that he was just cleaning the seats for their return.

"Something awful is about to happen!" she shouted. "You must get the police!"

"The police, madam?"

Annabelle looked up at the door. Kendall Southerly was no longer there. "Mr. Southerly has a gun, and I'm afraid he's going to use it!" She could barely get the words out. "Please do something!"

"Madam, I think you should get into the carriage and calm yourself. I'm sure it will be fine. I didn't see that he had a gun." The driver took her arm to guide her to the cab, but she pulled away and raced back to the house. Climbing the slippery steps, she got to the top and leaned against the door, taking in gulps of air before carefully entering the house.

Her thoughts whirled in hope. *Maybe this could be resolved peacefully. Frederick would quit Maude and ask for my forgiveness. Molly would return to England. I would manage our home better. Frederick could make amends for all his philandering.* Leaving him to go back home to a poor, outback town in British Columbia? What was she thinking?

No one was on the first floor. She gingerly climbed a narrow, two-level staircase. As she got to the first landing, she heard muffled voices. At the top was a door, slightly ajar, voices coming from the inside. Annabelle pushed the door open to see Frederick, his crisp white shirt untucked from his pants, his hair tousled. Standing beside him was a beautiful young woman dressed in a mint-colored skirt and matching blouse, the top buttons of the lace collar undone, her light-brown hair in loose tendrils. Annabelle took it all in as if time had slowed down. Southerly's back was to her.

"Annabelle!" Frederick's shout jerked her out of her trance.

Southerly whipped around, pointing his pistol at her, then he immediately turned back to Frederick, his hand shaking. "Get out of here, Mrs. Moore!" he yelled.

"Thank God you're here, Annabelle!" Frederick said. "Now tell Mr. Southerly he's making a big mistake."

She looked at Maude, now cowering behind Frederick. "Why are you here with her?"

"Not now, Annabelle!" Frederick shouted. "Southerly, put down the gun and let's talk about this."

"Kendall, please. Listen to him," Maude begged through her sobs. "I love you." She moved forward. "Take me home, Kendall. Please!"

The sweat on Southerly's forehead trickled down his temples. He steadied the gun with both hands. "No," he said flatly. "No, this was no mistake. You both planned to ruin me."

"Kendall," Annabelle pleaded, using his Christian name for the first time. "You're too good to do this. Let's leave them to their filthy sins and go back to the house. We'll figure it all out there. Come on now, let's go. Remember what we talked about."

When Southerly turned back to look at Annabelle, Frederick lunged, grasping at the hand that held the gun. The two men struggled for the weapon, both landing on the floor. Frederick was stronger, yet Southerly held tight to the pistol. But he was no match for Frederick's heft. Annabelle watched in horror as Frederick twisted the gun into Southerly's chest, her husband's steely focus revealing his intent.

There was a sudden, echoing pop. Annabelle and Maude screamed as Southerly went limp.

Frederick stumbled to his feet, and the gun clunked to the floor. He bent over and swayed, staring at the still form. Maude fell beside the lifeless body. "Kendall!" she screamed.

Frederick gripped Annabelle's arm and pulled her down the stairs. "Go home!" he commanded.

"Aren't you coming? We need to call a doctor, the police!"

His hands were on her shoulders, his fingers digging into her flesh. "Go home and keep your mouth shut! Do you understand?"

Through hitched sobs, she nodded. Her hand shook as she turned the knob. Annabelle looked over her shoulder and saw him running to the back of the cottage. She waited and listened.

A door slammed. He was escaping. She would, too. She moved down the front stairs, her legs trembling, her arms flailing as she tried to steady herself. When she got to the carriage, she saw the driver's concerned expression and commanded her body into composure.

"Are you all right, madam? Shall I wait for your companion?"

Annabelle felt her head shake and her spine tingle. "No, he and his fiancée had a terrible fight. I think something awful is about to happen. I told you he had a gun. Did you hear anything?"

He shuffled his feet. "I took a short stroll. Always with an eye to the carriage, madam, I can assure you. It was just a short stroll."

She breathed a sigh of relief. "Take me home."

"Yes, of course. Should I alert the police?"

"First, take me home!"

She let the driver help her into the cab, and once the carriage began to move, she bent and cried into her gloved hands.

Burt stood over Jacob's desk, the open newspaper between them. Tapping the article with anger and impatience, Burt asked, "Is this your idea of a plan?"

Jacob had read the article that morning.

"What the hell happened here? This is more than a lover's quarrel," Burt said.

Jacob looked up at his father. "You read the same story I did. What more do you want? Will isn't an accomplice. You know that. He's already testified he knew nothing about Southerly. The man came to him looking for an accountant job with us. Simple. Done." Jacob slapped the newspaper closed.

"His name is tainted! Your business is tainted!" his father shouted. "And now it's come out that Frederick filed papers to sue J&W Imports for money we owe him. Witnesses at the saloon said they saw Will talking to Southerly just before the incident." Burt's cheeks were flushed red.

"He was asking for an accountant job. That's the story. Nothing more," Jacob replied.

"Is that where you conduct interviews with job applicants now?"

Jacob chafed at his father's anger and controlling tone. "We're not children. We see the scope and the repercussions of this."

Burt turned to retrieve his coat and hat. "Well, make sure you do. My God, if it got out that this lunatic approached Will for help with Frederick, blackmail could be on the table tied to murder. I don't have to tell you what this could do to us." Burt shook his head. "I should have known not to meet Frederick in a public place. My instincts are failing me. I won't get the peace and quiet I've longed for until this bad business is settled." He placed his hat on his head. "Frederick charged with murder. To think my niece was once married to such a beast."

After his father left for his hotel room, Jacob returned to the paper and thanked God Jessica was safe from Frederick. He reread a part of the article.

Mr. and Mrs. Frederick B. Moore are being questioned in the murder of Mr. Kendall Southerly. Mr. Moore is a financier in the area and highly respected in many social circles. In a statement to the police, he and his wife regret the accident and intend to fully cooperate with the investigators. In her own statement, Maude Jennings, the deceased's fiancée, told police Mr. Moore shot Mr. Kendall. In a side note, Mr. William Messing was seen only days before the incident and has testified that he was approached by Mr. Southerly for a job opportunity in his newly established import company—J&W Imports on Market Street.

Jacob swallowed hard. He threw the paper into the fireplace and watched it burn. He was certain Will had spun the lie perfectly to the authorities and signed the affidavit with utter confidence. He'd been released without further questioning. Just this morning, Will had told him, "Don't worry, Jake, I got it all taken care of." Yet Jacob was tense, and the acid churning in his stomach told him to be careful.

He sat down hard behind his desk. He rubbed his chin and thought back to the time he himself had pulled a trigger and taken a life. It had happened in a flash. He suspected that might have been the case here. Or maybe he just didn't want to believe Jessica's ex-husband was capable of murder. He rested his elbows on his desk, bringing his clasped hands to his mouth. *Our lives are still very much intertwined, Jess, and still so vulnerable.*

CHAPTER FIFTEEN

Rail River Acres—July 1891

*J*ESSICA RODE SIDESADDLE ON HER GENTLE MARE, CARLIE, along the Rail River heading in the direction of Ben and Sally's home. Boones traveled alongside, zigzagging as he explored the ground. The waters were calm, and a slight breeze ran through the grasses along the bank. Her waistcoat was unbuttoned now, and her belly was big with child. She knew she shouldn't be on a horse at this stage of her pregnancy, but the day was hot and she was restless, needing solitude with the sway of a horse beneath her. Henry was safe at home with Hannah. There would be little chance to contemplate life once another child joined the household. A sudden movement from the baby inside startled her. Catching herself, she held on tighter to the reins and moved the horse gently forward.

Today, she needed to settle her feelings. The shocking news of Frederick being accused of murder had left her in a state of confusion. She grieved for him. It was a strange feeling. Had he not been a brute? Had she not fled from his rages and abuse? But murder hardly seemed a fitting accusation for the Englishman who had seemed above it all. After they'd heard the news, Caleb's response had upset her. "He probably did it. I hope he gets what he deserves." She'd retreated to the bedroom, sad and angry. When Caleb came to her, she had no explanation for her actions. He left with a huff and a shake of his head.

Jessica could think more clearly today. Frederick had been her husband, and there had been times she had felt love for him, yet she'd never loved him the way she loved Caleb. Just as she could never love Caleb the way she loved Jacob. She wondered if love was this complicated for everyone.

Taking in a breath of the heated summer air, mixed with the far-off scent of the bay, she rode past the Loggins' home. The aroma soothed her as much as it gave her an excitement for the new life to come. Her family would be complete with this new baby. She trotted along the path that would take her far afield if she let it, and oh, how she wanted to. Although she was about to have another child to care for, today she felt freer than she had in quite some time. After riding for a while longer, she felt a heaviness between her legs. She was tempting fate, and Caleb would certainly be angry with her if he found out, but she continued on. The singing birds and Boones's wagging tail delighted her. The day was for healing, and the world around her seemed in harmony with her thoughts. She inhaled a deep breath, and on letting it out, a cramp seized her womb. She stopped the horse and waited. A wave of tightness and a thorny pain wrapped around her back and abdomen. The baby wasn't due for a few weeks. As she took in steady breaths, it began to relent. After a few more minutes, another pain came on. She knew the waves of child birth. Turning the horse around, she headed home.

By the time she got back to the Loggins' homestead, she knew it was time. The pressure between her legs was becoming painful. She clumsily dismounted by the Loggins' mounting block and tied the mare to a post nearby. Holding her belly, she made her way to their front door. The pounding of her fist on the hard wood as she breathed through another contracting pain brought Sally to her in short order.

"Jessica!" Sally ushered her in and toward the stairs to the bedrooms.

"No, I want to deliver in my own home. Walk me over there, Sally."

The pain slowly disappeared. Another wave would soon follow. She had to get to her bed. Noticing her friend's shocked expression, she said, "You can scold me later. For now, help me make it home."

WRAPPED IN A COTTON BLANKET, the infant sighed. Caleb smiled down at his son. "You're here, little man. Safe and sound."

Jessica was relieved all had gone well, considering the midwife had arrived just in time to catch the infant. "He's perfect, isn't he?" The mesmerized look on Caleb's face gave her the answer. She knew this boy, Johnathan Many-Miles, would be the apple of his father's eye. One-year-old Henry stirred next to her. There would be little rest with him demanding her attention.

"Momma, up! I wan teddy! I wan teddy!"

His little tongue, working to pronounce every word, almost broke her heart. When had he gotten so big? Choking back tears, she suddenly missed baby Henry. He was a big brother now, even if he was just learning to walk.

"Jess, he looks like me and my brother, John," Caleb said without taking his eyes off of Johnathan. The baby squeaked, then fussed, and Jessica knew what he needed. "You will travel many miles to find your destiny," Caleb said as he handed him over to his mother.

Henry couldn't keep still, and Jessica traded one child for another as Caleb picked up his other son.

"What do you mean he has to travel many miles to find his destiny?" Jessica asked as the baby clamped on to her nipple. She took in a breath. Letting Caleb pick the baby's name was fine with her, but now she was having second thoughts about his middle moniker.

"He will be like his father . . . seeking, wandering, and maybe, like me, finding some happiness and peace."

"Some?"

Henry squirmed out of this father's arms. "Down!" the little boy proclaimed.

Caleb put Henry on the floor, and he crawled out of the room like a scurrying crab. Caleb shook his head and leaned over to give her a kiss.

She brought her lips to his.

"It's more than I could hope for," he said. "And today is one of the happiest days of my life. I have a son of my own flesh and blood."

Jessica contemplated his words. "You have two sons and a very tired wife, so please, no deep reflections right now. Hannah has to get back to Aunt June, and Henry needs attention. I'm sure he's confused about what's going on."

Caleb straightened. "Yes, ma'am." Before leaving, he said, "Thank you, sweetheart, for delivering us a healthy son."

At that moment, she wanted him to crawl into bed with her and together cuddle their new baby. Then Henry screamed for milk, and Caleb rushed out of the room. She chuckled and examined the sleeping infant. His perfect little face was that of her husband's. He had the same fair skin and hair. She was sure his eyes would be as blue as his father's. She was glad for that, but something stirred in her, something foreboding. She didn't know why, but she worried for Henry. Would Caleb take favorites?

MONTHS PASSED, AND JESSICA NOTICED how different her two boys were. Johnathan was a much calmer baby than Henry had ever been. He was easily soothed and smiled often. Henry was warming to his new brother, although he would refer to him as "that boy." She hoped he would grow out of such behavior and that the two of them would become good friends.

The worries she had over Caleb and Henry's relationship, for the most part, were unfounded, yet every so often she could see Caleb's love for Johnathan was different than his love for Henry. What she saw was adoration, something he didn't show for Henry. Yesterday, Caleb had scolded the toddler for calling his brother a dog, then held the baby as if he had been wounded by it. Johnathan, unaware of the slight, gurgled and smiled. It seemed a trifle, yet it disturbed her.

This morning, she would mention her concerns to Caleb. She needed to make him aware of his unconscious behavior before the boys grew old enough to feel it themselves.

Taking his cup of coffee off the counter, Caleb sat down at the kitchen table to eat his breakfast. The morning was warm and sunny, and Jessica hesitated to bring up the subject, but she couldn't hold back.

"Caleb, the boys need to be treated equally. You seem to favor Johnathan."

Swallowing his first bite, he raised his brows at her. "Of course I'll be more attached to a child from my own flesh and blood."

"How can you not see how this could be bad for Henry?"

"You worry too much."

After he was nearly done with his meal, she continued to mine his thoughts. "They are different. Can you treat them fairly?"

He scraped his fork across the remains of egg, then dabbed the rest with a piece of bread. "Henry is my adopted son, but I've come to love him."

"I don't want them knowing there's any difference between them."

He gave her a look of impatience, as if waiting to be dismissed from a reprimand. It was a response that sent her blood boiling.

"Caleb, this is a serious matter, and I need you to be aware of the consequences if you favor one son over the other."

He relaxed his stiff stance. "I think it's all in your imagination. I treat the boys equally. Johnathan is a baby, and it's natural to favor the baby of the family. My parents did it with my brother, and I endured it."

"They're only a year apart," she reminded him. Henry was still her baby, too. From the kitchen, she peered into the parlor, where Henry played with his blocks while Johnathan slept in his cradle. "You know this is different."

"Yes, it is, and I would ask you to let me be the father I am, not the one you wish me to be. I will not be Jacob to Henry."

The sting of his words caught her off guard. "I . . . you know I don't want that." Since Johnathan's birth, she'd struggled to rein her emotions in. Tears flowed unchecked.

Caleb reached for her hand. "I'm sorry. I shouldn't have said that. I'll keep those thoughts to myself next time."

That made it worse. "Keep them to yourself?"

He nodded and rose from the table with a kiss to the top of her head. "I'll be in my shop, then off to town for supplies."

Puzzled and disheartened, she had failed again to find the words to make it right. It was clear he would always hold her accountable for her actions with Jacob. She prayed Henry wouldn't have to pay the price for her weakness.

CHAPTER SIXTEEN

Clermont City—March 1892

$\mathcal{W}$HEN JESSICA LEARNED OF THE DATE OF FREDERICK'S TRIAL, she knew she would have to be there. In two weeks, Will would be called to testify. He'd come to Clermont City to see his uncle Burt to prepare for his time in court, then stopped in to visit her.

Scooping Henry up in his arms, Will gave Jessica a peck on the cheek. "How's this little man doing?" He raised the toddler up and pretended Henry was a bird flying high in the sky. The guttural laughter coming from the jubilant boy gave Will his own fit of laughter, and he put Henry back down on his blanket, kissing his cheeks. Henry raised his arms and cried, "Moh, moh!"

"He'll never take his nap now," Jessica said.

"Oh, Uncle Will is in trouble again," Will said to Henry, and the boy giggled and rubbed his eyes. Then Will went over to the cradle holding Johnathan. "He's his father's child, all right. Caleb must be over the moon."

"He is. And they are *both* his children."

"Of course," Will said, looking at her.

"I'm sorry. It's been on my mind that he favors John."

"He may, but I have a feeling Henry isn't having any of it."

Jessica laughed. "Coffee is in the kitchen. Let me try and get him down."

With a few squeaks and whines, Henry finally slept, and Johnathan was now in the smaller cradle in the kitchen. As she rocked the cradle with one foot, Jessica got right to the point. "Why are you testifying for the defense? What have you and Jacob got to hide?"

Will put his cup down. His dark blue eyes held the look she was so used to seeing when he did something he shouldn't have done. Growing up, she knew when he lied, when he deceived their parents. Many times, he would impatiently tell her to be quiet, even if she hadn't spoken a word.

"There's nothing to hide, really. Jacob and I thought we could use this guy to help us get out of debt with Frederick. Blackmail is ugly, but it was what we could do to get Freddie off our backs. It was harmless. A little exchange of knowledge, that's all. We had no idea what this Kendall fella had in mind. Burt told me I'm to say nothing more than he was a stranger inquiring about an accounting position with J&W." He took a sip of coffee. "If you're there, it will look good. I would like your support."

"Do you think Frederick is innocent?"

"Hell no. From what the wife and lover revealed to the press, Frederick is at least guilty of manslaughter."

Jessica brought her hand to her chest. "This is dirty business, and I don't need to hear more. The less I know, the less I have to lie for you and Jacob. All I can say is, you shouldn't have taken Frederick's money in the first place. Now look at the both of you, scheming and hiding from the truth, dealing in unlawful practices." Her anger was on the edge. Will's usual offhanded explanation wasn't enough. She lashed out. "There's more at stake here than just the two of you!"

"Yes, I know. It will all work out, and none of us will be harmed. Frederick is the one who shot the guy. Why are you so concerned? Jake and I had nothing to do with it."

Looking at her brother with annoyance, she said, "I feel that you and Jacob and Caleb had plenty to do with all of it. It's like a house of cards!"

Will raised both eyebrows. "I have a feeling you know more than you let on. Can you forgive the past, Jess?"

He was so sincere. It took her aback. The sarcastic and devil-may-care attitude was gone. He was asking for forgiveness.

"I will try. I have tried." She looked down at Johnathan, then back to her brother. "I will be there for you. We will get past this."

He took her hand. "Thanks, Sis." His wink gave her the feeling his sincerity was short lived and he had returned to his true self.

"By all means, Will, don't change," she said with a smirk.

He laughed, and she smiled in spite of herself.

Her brother had left her house with Jessica at odds with her feelings, and now she would have to watch him lie under oath on the witness stand while she showed her support.

Leaving Johnathan and Henry behind as she took the journey into San Francisco was difficult. She grieved with each mile she traveled and every minute that passed. Her mother would stay at the house for the few days she was gone, which doubled her worry. Bethany and Caleb were not on easy terms. She had to remind herself she was doing this not only for Will but for the whole family. Being present in the courtroom would bring validation to his innocence. Caleb gave his disapproval, but could hardly keep her from supporting her own kin. With Uncle Burt and Hannah, she made her way into the city. She would need the housekeeper to help with her corsets, dresses, and hair if she was to look appropriate for the courtroom. Besides, she needed Hannah as her own moral support—Frederick would be there.

CHAPTER SEVENTEEN

San Francisco

$\mathcal{S}$ITTING IN THE THIRD ROW OF THE COURTROOM WITH Hannah on her left, Burt to her right, and Jacob beside him, Jessica waited along with everyone else for the judge to return to the bench. Will was about to take the stand, and the minutes seemed to tick by like hours. They had heard from the first two witnesses for the defense. The carriage driver, who was told by Annabelle that the fiancée and Kendall were having an argument and something bad might happen and a neighbor who said she had heard a couple quarrelling and then a gunshot. Neither one seemed very convincing to Burt, who whispered his comments to Jacob. "They'll have to do better than this." Jessica overheard and wanted Will's testimony to be done. Her sweaty palms under her gloves and perspiring armpits beneath her tight bodice strained Jessica's patience. A woman offered her a glass of water from a table at the back of the room, and she gladly accepted.

The air held the scent of sweaty bodies and varnished wood

as the tension filled the high-ceilinged courtroom. The hanging lights added to the warmth, even with the blades of the rotating fan laboring above them. Soft murmurs floated around the room but stopped suddenly when a loud voice asked all to rise as the judge entered, his black robes floating behind him as he seated himself above the court.

"You may be seated," he said. Once he related a few rules to the attorneys, he struck the wooden plate with his gavel. Jessica's heart leapt to her throat. A uniformed man stood in front of the stand, and in a loud, echoing voice announced that court had come to order. The judge spoke to the defense attorney, a short fit man in his mid-thirties. The man turned to Will and asked for him to be presented as a witness. Jessica thought she might be ill. What would Will say? How deeply was he involved? She was regretting being here. She found herself agitated with the whole affair. She exhaled in a huff, and a few in the gallery turned to her. Did everyone know she was his sister? She averted her eyes and caught Jacob leaning forward. He looked at her and whispered, "It will be fine." She gave a quick nod and turned her attention back to her brother.

Will looked confident in a deep-blue suit and matching vest over a crisp high-collared white shirt. The knot of his blue paisley tie was perfectly centered. She had to chuckle at his slicked-back hair and tidy beard and mustache. Quite a respectable gentleman. If anyone could look and sound convincing, it was Will.

He took the stand after being sworn in and giving his full name. Frederick's attorney began his questioning.

"Mr. Messing, have you met the deceased, Mr. Kendall Southerly?" A sob went out in the courtroom, and everyone turned to a woman dressed head to toe in black. Jessica assumed it was the fiancée. Loud whispers ricocheted around the room. The judge struck the gavel and called for order.

"Yes," Will replied clearly.

"Where did you meet Mr. Southerly?"

"He approached me in a saloon."

Jessica met her uncle's look. He'd said he instructed Will not to give any information that wasn't asked of him. She grimaced and thought, *This will take all day.*

The attorney asked about the saloon, time of day, and other details. Finally, he asked why a man would come to him in the middle of the day in a saloon to ask for a job.

"Did you arrange this meeting?"

"No."

"Why would he meet you there?"

A pause. Jessica swallowed the bile rising in her throat.

"You would have to ask Mr. Kendall that."

"And as we know, he is deceased, Mr. Messing. Can you give us your best guess?"

"It's a well-known fact that I have a weakness for the tables. I suppose if someone wanted to find me and I wasn't in my office, they would search the saloons and gambling halls."

A few women gave a cluck of their tongues. He was apparently a guilty party in their opinions.

"How did he appear to you, his manners, his approach?"

"He was . . . fidgeting. He said he was desperate to find a new job in his field of accounting."

"And you replied?"

"I don't need an accountant at this time."

"Why was he desperate?"

Will shook his head. "I don't know."

"Was that all?"

"He bought me a drink, and we parted ways."

"Did he mention Mr. Frederick Moore to you?"

"No."

Jessica sat stoically. She knew her brother was lying under oath and cringed inside, but she dared not move a muscle in her face or body.

Thankfully, she could not get a good view of Frederick. He was flanked on either side by clerks. She let her eyes roam to the jury box. The men looked serious and thoughtful. She reminded herself Will was not on trial.

"Do you see Frederick Moore in this courtroom, and if so, would you point to him?"

"Yes," Will said, pointing in Frederick's direction.

"How long have you known the defendant?"

"I believe it's been . . . about nineteen years."

"Yes, you know him quite well. He was your brother-in-law, wasn't he?"

"Yes."

A hushed murmur went through the room.

"He is divorced from your sister, Miss Jessica Messing, now Mrs. Caleb Cantrell, is he not?"

Jessica wanted to disappear.

"He is."

"Have you had any recent dealings with Mr. Moore?"

"My cousin and I borrowed money from him last year, and we are in negotiations to pay it back."

"I see. And Mr. Southerly had nothing to do with these negotiations?"

"No."

"Why do you think Mr. Southerly went to the cottage that day?"

Will shook his head. "I have no idea."

The questioning went on for another fifteen minutes without Will giving anything away. Finally, it was the prosecutor's turn. Burt moved uneasy, and Jacob took in a deep breath.

A stout man with a large belly walked back and forth in front of the stand, then stopped and looked up at Will.

"Mr. Messing, you're a respectable businessman, albeit a bit of a gambler. But we all have our weaknesses." He turned to the jury and smiled. A few of the men nodded.

Jessica rolled her eyes.

"After knowing the defendant, Mr. Frederick Moore, for nearly twenty years, would you say he is capable of committing murder in cold blood?"

Jessica's heart skipped a beat. Sweat ran down her back.

Will hesitated, then gave a resounding, "No."

Again, the murmurs in the gallery rose. She sat back in her seat, suddenly aware she had all but been on the edge of it.

"But Mr. Moore was quite cruel to your sister when she was his wife, was he not?"

"I … I don't know. That is not my …"

"Just answer yes or no, Mr. Messing," the attorney said.

"No."

"In your sister's divorce records she, Jessica Moore at the time, claims infidelity on his part. And there is proof of his mistreatment of her. If a man can beat his wife and cheat on her, what else can he be capable of?"

"Objection!" cried Frederick's attorney.

"No further questions, your honor."

Before anyone could speak, the attorneys were standing in front of the judge arguing, then quietly returned to their seats.

"The last testimony will be stricken from the books, and the jurors are instructed to ignore it.

Jessica caught a glimpse of Frederick. His smug grin shook her. It was as if she was the one testifying, and his behavior toward her in their marriage was to be ignored and stricken from the record. This was not her case, yet she wanted to sit on the witness stand and say yes, he did mistreat her, and he did cheat on her. He was capable of cruelty. It beckoned the question, was he capable of murder?

Will was released and told to not leave the city, for he may be needed for further questioning.

Jessica let out a sigh of relief.

They all stood, and Burt addressed her.

"He did well, but I'm sorry you had to go through that. I didn't know the prosecutor would take that line of questioning."

"I'll be fine," she replied.

"I will join you at the hotel," her uncle said.

She gathered her waistcoat and purse and hurried to the waiting carriage with Hannah at her heels. She heard Jacob's voice behind her.

"Jessica, wait."

She turned, and he caught up with them. Newspapermen gathered, and the questions were hurled at her. They got to the door, and she was ready to escape. It opened, letting the sharp light of day into the wood-and-marble hall. More newspapermen, photographers, and curious spectators swarmed her as she fought her way to the carriage. Jacob tried to fend them off. Before joining them in the cab, he gave the driver instructions to take them to the hotel. As the carriage sped away, Jessica leaned back, flustered and teary-eyed.

Hannah placed a hand on Jessica's shoulder. "Your brother did good, in my opinion."

"What will this do to my reputation? To my husband's? I didn't want my name associated with Frederick Moore ever again and never in this way." What she didn't say was the deep sadness she felt at her uncle's obvious involvement in Will's lies. She looked at Jacob, seated across from them.

"Your father, Jacob . . . he . . ."

Jacob held on to the hanging leather strap as the carriage jostled them about. He glanced at Hannah. "We can talk later, Jess."

WILL AND BURT JOINED JACOB and Jessica for dinner while Hannah took her meal in the room adjacent to Jessica's in the Hotel Fairmont. In the dining room, the large fireplace was blazing, staving off the cold, early spring evening. The braised lamb and scalloped potatoes, along with several tempting side dishes, including marinated artichokes and roasted vegetables, did not charm Jessica's appetite. She picked at the food on her plate.

"I'd say we can put this behind us in short order," her uncle said.

"I think I gave a convincing performance," Will said in a low voice for only their ears.

"Don't get a big head, Will," Jacob said as he cut his lamb and devoured a piece.

"Lying is lying," Jessica said softly, "and now I'm part of the whole awful drama."

She raised her hand to indicate to the men at the table she wanted no apologies. She finished what she could eat of her supper and excused herself.

"Let me escort you to your room, Jess," Jacob offered.

She didn't reply either way, and he followed her up to her room. Once there, she stopped at the door. "Thank you. I can manage now."

"Why are you mad at me? I had very little to do with any of this."

"Oh, is that so? So, the right hand didn't know what the left hand was doing? Please." She took the room key out of her reticule and unlocked the door.

"May I come in?"

"No, Jacob. It will only lead to disappointment. You made it very clear the last time we spoke that you wanted nothing to do with me."

"What? I made it clear? You made it very clear to me."

"Yes, well, despite who made it clear, it doesn't change a thing. I'm too upset to think about it. Uncle Burt was in on a lie, and Will was under oath."

Jacob gave a chuckle. "My father does what a lawyer needs to do. You think he's a saint?" Jacob gave a short laugh. "We needed to save our asses. Excuse my language."

It occurred to her that she was still naïve. "Of course. I understand now. All men lie. That's it, isn't it? To save their skins. Does that wash away their sins?"

"Hey, where do you get off talking to me as if you've never done a wrong thing in your life? Is your memory so short?"

She turned to let herself in. "Good night, Jacob."

He caught her hand. "Wait. Don't be angry."

Turning to face him again, she reined in her emotions. "Where does this leave your business with Frederick?"

"We'll see if he's found guilty or not."

"What do you think?"

Nudging the door open, Jacob gestured for her to go inside. He followed. She looked back at him.

"I'll be good," he said. "I think the jury will find him guilty, but for a lesser charge. My father says manslaughter."

She nodded. "I can't believe this. His poor wife and mistresses! Mr. Southerly!" She let out a puff of air. "It was the right thing to leave him when I did."

"You were brave. Now, let's be friends. I forgive you."

Bringing her chin in, her brows ruffled, and she let out a laugh. He could still tease her and make her feel light again. But the subject wasn't light-hearted, and she knew she shouldn't have let him in to her room.

"I couldn't think of my life without you in it," he said. "How is my son?"

The question took her by surprise. She had nearly forgotten that part of their legacy. "He's beautiful. Walking quite well now. He says lots of words, mostly Mama and Dada."

An awkward silence flashed between them.

"I'm sorry," she said, looking down at her feet.

"No, it's good. Thank you for telling me." Jacob cleared his throat. "I have to go now. Rest well, and safe travels home. And, Jess, try to put this whole trial and Will's testimony behind you."

She nodded. "I'll try."

"Good night, Jess." He kissed her cheek.

"Good night, Jacob."

She closed the door, and his presence lingered with her.

CHAPTER EIGHTEEN

ONCE HOME AND SETTLED, JESSICA GAVE HER RENDITION OF the trial to Caleb. He and the children had come through her absence with no apparent harm, even with Caleb relegating Bethany to day visits only. "I couldn't stand her being here at night as well. She gave me plenty of instructions. The boys and I did all right." She was very proud of Caleb's efforts and was glad she hadn't known about him being alone with the baby all night. He smirked when she told him of Will's demeanor and his pointed answers, his obvious lies, and her disappointment in her uncle's involvement. She left out anything to do with Jacob.

"God, some people never change," Caleb said about her brother. "Out in the wilds, we faced a band of Lakota, and by all that is fair, that should have been our last day on Earth, but Will charmed them into letting us be on our way. He knew a few words in their language, and he smiled and bowed and gave the leader of the group his rifle. His damn rifle!"

Jessica laughed, but it gave her no comfort. Another peek into the life her husband and Will and Jacob had lived added to the story she didn't need to know. Now this. When would it end? Would her brother always be in harm's way? It reflected on her now, and she didn't like it.

"Seriously, Caleb. We were under scrutiny too. My name, *your* name, will be in the papers in association with a murder."

Caleb became serious. "You know how I feel about the whole damn thing. I want to ring Will's neck. He and Jacob are no better now than they were when we were on the trails. If this doesn't clear up soon, it will affect my business."

They sat in silence. Jessica would talk to her uncle and get his perspective. For now, she could only hope the trial wouldn't lead to Will's involvement and Frederick would be judged to be innocent. Her heart wouldn't let her believe her ex-husband could kill a man. Her mind told her different.

AT THE END OF THE weeks-long trial, there was sufficient evidence for the jury to find Frederick guilty of manslaughter in self-defense. He was given ten years. To everyone's surprise, his wife, Annabelle, was the key witness in favor of the prosecution. According to the newspaper, Frederick had spat at her when they took him away in handcuffs. The papers also wrote of his association with a Miss Molly Ambers of Liverpool, England, who was without documents and would be deported back to her country as soon as possible. Jessica read the article and didn't see her name or any of her family's names. She gave a sigh of relief. For all the hurt he had caused her, she felt no revenge. She took no satisfaction in his long jail sentence. The men she loved were all guilty in one way or another.

CHAPTER NINETEEN

Clermont City—May 1892

 $\mathscr{A}$ LTHOUGH THE WHOLE OF SAN FRANCISCO TOOK INTEREST in Frederick's trial and the tantalizing details of the lovers' rendezvous turning to murder, it soon became old news, replaced by other crimes and other trials.

Clermont City was different. The small town lapped up every detail, and the gossip ran rampent The ex-wife of a convicted murderer lived among them! Her own brother had testified in favor of the murderer! Jessica couldn't walk into town without stares and whispers. To her surprise, her art at the Talbot Gallery was in high demand, and other venues asked if she would show with them. This was not how she wanted to create a buzz about her work, and she declined the new offers. Caleb's more highbrow customers weren't as impressed, and several orders had suddenly been canceled. It put him in a foul mood.

Tonight, as she and Caleb sat in the parlor after dinner, Jessica asked, "What are we going to do?" It was nearly a whisper. She looked down at Johnathan in her lap and Henry playing on the floor. The one- and two-year-old brothers were oblivious to the situation.

"It'll blow over. It shouldn't be too long before people get bored with it."

"I hope you're right." She kissed the top of the baby's head. A sudden bark from Boones, followed by a loud knock on the door, brought her arms tighter around him, and Caleb got to his feet. He had barely brought back the curtains when a flash of light filled the house with a loud pop.

Caleb cursed as Jessica quickly gathered Henry up and brought the boys to their bedroom while her husband strode to the closet where he kept his rifle. Boones growled and barked.

"Caleb, tell us about your wife's kidnapping!" a muffled voice shouted from behind the door. The questions spun in rapid-fire succession. "Was your wife's brother paid off to call the murderer innocent? What's your connection with the murderer and Rex Conrad? Are your sons legitimate?"

Jessica peeked out from the bedroom and watched from behind her husband as he swung the door open and cocked his gun, aiming at the reporter and photographer.

They stepped backward from the porch. "Calm down now," the reporter said.

"Stay away from my home and my family!" Caleb shouted. He let off a shot near their feet, and they ran away like two scared boys caught stealing eggs from the chicken coop.

Jessica rushed back to her boys and held them, her heart pounding. "Shh, everything's all right." She soothed the scared, wide-eyed children. She heard Caleb shut the front door and secure the bolt, then place his rifle back in the closet.

He stood in the boys' doorway, flushed with anger.

"My God, Caleb. What does this mean?"

"I don't know," he said, breathing hard. He reached for Henry, and the boy went willingly into his father's arms. Johnathan was sniffling, and Jessica rocked him. They went into the parlor and took a moment to regain composure.

"I'll see the sheriff tomorrow. Trespassing is against the law," Caleb said, peering out the window.

Jessica tried to relax, but the reporter's questions made it difficult.

"I want you to stay away from town. Be on your guard, and don't go to the Loggins'. They don't need to get involved. I'll tell Ben what happened." He cursed under his breath.

The following day, Burt brought up the newspaper. On the front page of the *Clermont City News* was a picture of Caleb, standing in the doorway of their home, rifle in hand. The headline read, MORE TO THE STORY THAN MEETS THE EYE. Jessica took the paper from her uncle's hand. The article was vague with hypotheticals.

"How desperate of them to run such a silly piece of gossip!" she said. Some of the article was true. She was taken captive by Indians hired by a scout to get ransom money from her husband, who was involved in illegal activities in Colorado. How could they know? She felt in danger again.

Caleb was looking over her shoulder. "Damn them. I'll show them what meets the eye."

Burt looked at him. "If you need to take them to court—"

"Hell no! I won't waste my time and money."

"Maybe a letter from me will suffice. Sometimes the threat of legal action is all it takes."

Jessica folded the paper. "The damage is done. Right on the front page."

"We can get them to make a retraction," her uncle said.

"Thank you, Uncle. I don't know what this family would do without you," Jessica said.

Burt ran his hand through his thick silver hair. "I'd like to retire soon, just so you all know." He gave a slight grin.

Jessica wrapped her arms around him. "And it will be well deserved. I'm sorry we've caused you so much worry and grief."

Once Burt had left, Jessica faced her husband. "Are we in danger? How do these newspaper men know about Colorado?"

Caleb settled into his leather chair and lit his pipe. "Hell if I know. I doubt anything will come of it. Just newsmen stirring up trouble to sell papers."

Jessica was not so sure and waited impatiently in the coming days for the next issue of the *Clermont City News*.

Jessica laid low, hoping her uncle's attempts would pay off. Over the next few days, Caleb had his hands full with curious townspeople wanting to get a look at him and Jessica. Again, his rifle came out of the closet, and with a few shots in the air, they scurried away.

Focused on her family and her art, today she would finish a watercolor of the sea, a view from the courthouse the day of Will's testimony. With her sketchbook and pencil always tucked into her coat or skirt pocket, she sketched a drawing, making notes of the colors. Mr. Talbot had asked for more of the ocean, and this would be the starting point. It was a lovely scene, and she had wanted to hide in it, if just for a few hours. Her mind wandered, and she thought of Jacob. They had made a truce, and it felt good. No matter what came up in her daily life, he was in her heart and mind.

The paper was finally out, and to their great relief, the publication had retracted the story and publicly apologized to the Cantrells. Jessica decided she'd had enough of her isolation. The pink cherry blossoms were cheery, the air was warm, and everything indicated that spring was finally here. She drove the carriage into town with her sons tucked in the back. Avoiding Main Street, she wove through the narrow dirt streets until she came to her aunt's home. She knew her mother would be there, too, even though she now had her own home just across the street and a few houses down.

June met her at the door with Bethany close behind.

"Jessica, my dear!" Her aunt wrapped her in a tight embrace. "What an ordeal!"

"How are you?" her mother asked, giving her another hug.

Hannah brought in the children and helped them out of their coats. Sitting on the floor, she supervised as they took toys out of a small wooden crate.

"The retraction has helped," Jessica said, removing her coat, "but it might take a while for Caleb to regain his usual commissions."

"Your uncle told us how Will helped a great deal in the case and how your support was very much appreciated," her aunt said. "Why would they smear you like this?" She shook her head in disbelief.

Jessica nodded and smiled. "I was happy to help." Their conversation turned to the growing children and the summer ahead in the garden.

After the visit, Jessica headed home with a clear heart. Her mother and aunt were safe in their own world. She wished she was as innocent as they were of the unsavory parts of life, *her* life. If only she had done this or that differently. *If only . . .*

Johnathan squealed and Henry shouted. There was no time to dwell in the past. These two needed to get home and take a nap.

After the boys were down, she peeked into her studio and saw what needed to be done on her latest commissions. Jilly Gaines of the Billingston Gallery had recently contacted her to ask if she would become a regular contributor to her and her husband's San Francisco gallery. Jessica was thrilled and surprised.

She had met Jilly while still married to Frederick. In those days, Jilly had been full of excitement about the new gallery she and her husband were a part of. Jessica had been happy to meet another artist, since her life had become quite sheltered, and Frederick watched her every move. After the divorce, she was glad to know that her friend found no offense in it. The other women in her social circle at the time were not so forgiving. Having purchased the Billingston Gallery, Jilly was asking her to become a part of something she could only have dreamt of back then.

Jessica leaned against the doorframe of her art studio and wondered at Jilly's motives. Was she joining the bandwagon, looking to profit off of scandal? Her heart said no. She would respond with an enthusiastic yes. Joy raced through her. This was a highly regarded venue. Had she finally made it? The past troubling weeks slid away as she returned to her easel, paints, and brushes.

CHAPTER TWENTY

Rail River Acres—October 1897

*F*ive years passed, and as the scandal of the trial faded into the distance, Jessica found success in the Billingston Gallery. Her dream of showing her art in a large venue had come true. She had mustered the courage to present to Jilly the works that told of her experience in the Indian camp—a time that would never be lost to her. Mr. Talbot had forced her hand when he told her he was getting on in years and it was time he retired.

"I'm getting too old to discuss the fine points of realism versus impressionism versus post-impressionism, or . . . or why a woman paints such scenes. Even those who are aware of your captivity, my dear, say that you should keep it to yourself," he had said as he waved to her two canvases. Out of the three he'd consented to show, only one had sold, and that was to an out-of-towner.

"My son will be taking over the gallery, and I will paint in my little studio away from all of their opinions. I wish you the very best, and please come to see me sometime. We can talk about the weather."

Sadly, he was good on his word, and Jessica soon found his son taking down her art and handing it back to her. Only her little watercolor renditions of the town and its surroundings remained for travelers passing through. It was an ending to her relationship with the senior Talbot and the beginning of finding a new home for her provocative oil paintings. To her great relief, Jilly had welcomed them, and they now had a prominent place in the gallery.

Henry tossed the ball to his brother. Johnathan sprang forward and missed, falling onto the dusty ground. Standing, he brushed himself off and tossed his light-blond hair around to get the dirt out. "You did that on purpose, Henry! Why can't you ever play fair?"

Henry retrieved the ball. "Don't be such a baby. You could have gotten that if you tried." Johnathan stormed off, wiping his eyes.

Watching from the kitchen window, Jessica observed Henry bullying his brother again. It had gotten worse lately with the passing of their faithful dog, Boones. It was grievous to all of them, but Henry seemed to take it the hardest. Now he was showing his grief with anger. His competitive nature would always get the best of him, and she tried to come up with another way of making him see his error. She didn't want to squash the seven-year-old's spirit, yet she worried he would outshine Johnathan and leave the younger boy feeling bad about himself. Johnathan was his father's son—thoughtful, kind, and quiet. At six, he showed no signs of wanting to compete, and he often avoided Henry's constant assertions.

It hurt her to see this gap between her sons. Caleb seemed hurt by it, too, but in a different way. He blamed Henry for most of Johnathan's mishaps, even when Henry was clearly not at fault. Jessica was the sounding board for the brothers, their referee, and a soft place of understanding. She had let Caleb do all the disciplining. At times, his heavy-handedness with Henry concerned her, and she thought of how Jacob would have handled the situation. Taking on the task herself might be a good solution, but today was no time to dwell on the matter. The yellow telegram that still sat on the kitchen table was more important. Aunt June was ill. Her fever had become worse.

Caleb was at work, and Jessica loaded her boys into the carriage. "Be mindful of the pot of soup, Henry. Stop bouncing in the back, John."

She glanced at her sons before taking the reins. Henry had brought the warm pot onto his lap, and Johnathan had settled in. "Thank you, Henry." A warm glow of pride touched his face. Her motherly emotions pulled at her to stop what she was doing and give him a hug. She instead smiled, and his brown eyes met hers with understanding. It swelled her heart. Henry looked so much like Jacob, and his eyes sought out her approval in the same way Jacob's did. These brief moments kept her wondering how she could make Jacob a part of Henry's life. It never went well whenever she suggested to Caleb that Jacob needed to see Henry. Her husband saw this as black and white—either he was the father and no one else, or Jacob was the father and let the chips fall where they may. He knew he had her trapped. Jacob would have to wait.

She started down the hill toward town with the heavy load of concern for Henry and Aunt June. One was finding his way, and the other may be traveling away from her. Her throat tightened, and she swallowed hard. She must be strong. Everyone had come to expect that of her.

THE BRIGHT AUTUMN SUN SHONE into June's bedroom, and she winced from its intense light. She motioned for Jessica to draw the curtains. The movement of her aunt's hand commenced her deep, rattling cough.

"Here, Auntie, take some broth." Jessica went to the nightstand and brought the cup to June's lips.

"No, no, dear. I can't stand it." She pushed her niece's hand away.

Bethany tried to get her to take some warm honey water, but that failed to stop the violent fits of coughing.

"I'll have Hannah get Dr. Grant again," Bethany said as she fussed with June's bedding.

"Mother, I'll do that. You look tired." Jessica took her mother's place by the bed. Their vigil had made both women weary, but Jessica less so.

June had thankfully fallen asleep, clearly exhausted from the coughing spells. The doctor said the pneumonia had invaded only one of her lungs. He was cautiously optimistic. Before leaving yesterday, he'd given them more medication and instructions. "Call me if she worsens."

Her uncle slipped into the room. "She's as strong as they come, never a cold or headache. She'll be fine."

"You're right, Uncle. I feel this will actually make her even stronger once she's recovered," Jessica replied.

"She saw her brother and Laura yesterday," Burt said. "Sophie, Carl, and the boys are staying away." In a whisper he said, "They feel she might be contagious."

Henry and Johnathan entered next. "May we say hello, Mother?" Henry asked.

Before Jessica could usher them downstairs, June stirred. Johnathan went to her.

"Hello, Auntie. You'll get better soon. I know you will. I placed rocks in a circle outside my bedroom window with leaves and feathers in the middle. The leaves and feathers are you, and the rocks will protect you from all bad things."

Henry was more practical as he came around the other side of her bed. "Uncle says the pneumonia is not as bad as it could be. That means you have a good chance of getting well. Do what Mother says. She always makes me and John feel better."

Tears streamed down both sides of June's face. She touched their hands with hers. "My dear, thank you for that, Henry. I will keep that in mind. And Johnny, I'll take any talisman I can get." She coughed and covered her mouth.

"Come now, boys, let Auntie rest."

Jessica brought the boys downstairs and into the kitchen, where her mother had a bowl of soup and warmed biscuits waiting.

"I don't know what else to do but pray this will pass soon," her mother said. "Come sit and eat, boys."

"She will recover, Mother. She has to." Jessica sat down and nibbled on a biscuit.

"I meant to tell you that Jacob is on his way," her mother said. "He should be here soon."

Jessica nearly choked on her bite. "Jacob is coming?"

"Why, of course he is. His mother may be taking her last breath at any moment." Bethany brought her fist to her mouth. "I'm sorry."

"We'll all be brave, and Aunt June will get well," Jessica said. She was about to serve herself soup when she heard her uncle come down the stairs, then a knock on the front door. Burt welcomed his son. Jacob's voice was clear and low. It rattled her, and she dropped the ladle, sending the liquid splattering onto the table. She scolded herself for her clumsiness as she wiped up the mess.

"She's upstairs in the flower-ceiling room," her uncle said. "The doctor was here yesterday and said it was best we keep separated."

"My goodness, Jessica! Be careful. It's hot," her mother scolded.

"Yes, Mother."

Jacob went straight upstairs without stopping to greet them. Jessica waited a moment before joining him.

Each step gave her time to compose herself. It had been almost a year since they'd seen each other, briefly, at Christmas. He and Will had business with her uncle. They had returned to the city the day after the holiday dinner. He had a few sporadic visits to his parents' home, coming and going nearly in secret. Jessica heard

114

about these after he was gone. Her aunt would sigh happily over his visit. An empty feeling would embrace her each time she heard he had been in town.

Jessica stood for a moment outside the slightly open bedroom door. Listening, she heard Jacob say, "I told you I would come. Now, promise me you will get better. I have a new home, and you need to see it. It's grand, Mother, but not auspicious. I think you'll love it. The view seems as if you're standing on top of the world."

Jacob's voice was low and clear. It sent a shiver up her spine. He could still arouse her. Uncle Burt widened the door, and she stepped back. "I didn't want to intrude," she said in a low voice. "Would she like some soup?"

Jacob looked up from the chair he was sitting in, holding his mother's hand. He met her eyes. His were sad, and hers were misty.

"Hello, Jessica."

"Hello, Jacob. I'm sorry you're visiting under these circumstances, but"—Jessica looked at her aunt—"our lady here is going to make a full recovery." She smiled before meeting his eyes again. There was no smile on his face.

"I'll get her that soup, Jessica," her uncle said, then left.

"Thank you, Uncle."

"I don't want any more liquids," June said. She began coughing, and Jessica rushed to her side to plump the pillows and smooth the quilt. When the coughing stopped, she said in a raspy voice, "Go visit now, you two. Burt will take over. Jacob, your young cousins would love to hear about business. I bet Henry most of all and—" The coughing took the words from her, and they waited for her to settle. She waved them away. "Go. I'll be fine."

Reluctantly, they did as they were told. Jacob slowly closed the door behind them. "She's a fighter. I'm glad for that."

The awkwardness between them reminded Jessica of their last meeting. She passed a palm down the front of her day dress. Since the last time they'd stood together in this hallway over a decade ago, her hands had become worn and her eyes less bright. She was thirty-two but felt much older. Still, in his presence, her youth bubbled up inside her.

"How have you been, Jacob?"

"Fine. And you?"

Why they weren't moving to the stairs, she didn't know, but she was not taking the first step. "I've been well, thank you."

"The boys have grown since I saw them last. Especially Henry."

"Yes, like a weed. I can't seem to keep up with his pants and shoes."

A smile crossed Jacob's face. Jessica took it as an invitation. "He'd like to get to know you. I mean, both the boys would."

Jacob nodded. "You've kept my son to yourself."

Taken aback by his words, she answered in a loud whisper, "Kept him to myself? There were plenty of opportunities for you to visit with him."

"The invitation never came." He stepped closer. "I'm not sure I would have responded to it anyway."

"Well, then, we are both to blame."

Furrowing his brows, Jacob shook his head. "Do you think I'm made of steel? You think that because I've gone on with my life, I don't think about him, about us? Look at us. We're standing outside the room we once made love in."

The very thought of their bodies entangled on that September night sent a tingle up her spine. "We weren't thinking. It was careless."

"As careless as you and I ever were." Before she could answer, his stance became less rigid. "When Henry comes of age, say fifteen, I will have him stay with me in the city. I want him to know who I am, what I do, and how I view the world. Caleb has taught him his own truth and what he's learned from the Indians, but he will learn other ways from me." He stepped back. She opened her mouth to speak, and he shook his head. "You owe me this, Jessica."

Moving past her, he went downstairs. Stunned, she stood with her back to the stairwell, listening to him pad down every step. Jessica looked at the closed door of the flower-ceiling room. The room now held her sick aunt, but it had once been the place where Jacob had made love to her, where she had stayed after her divorce from Frederick, and where she'd lost Jacob's baby. Those sacred memories would have to sit alongside this new one.

She moved downstairs and entered the parlor.

"Thank you for coming to be with her, Jessica," Burt said. "She loves seeing you and the boys. I think it cheered her up."

"It was no hardship, Uncle Burt. I do hope we hear good news soon."

Her mother came out of the kitchen. "You've been a great help." She sat down with her nephew and grandsons. "I have to say, she does wear Hannah and me out, going up and down those stairs twenty times a day."

"Hannah should be doing most of that, Mother."

"I know, but I have to check on her myself." Bethany unfolded her handkerchief and wiped her nose.

Jessica stood by the window. The cool air coming off the panes helped to hide the heat that rose in her. Jacob sat silently with one leg crossed over the other. Would she ever be calm around him?

Looking at his son, Jacob noticed the boy return his stare. They exchanged a smile. It was as if he were seeing himself at this age. "So, how do you fare in school, young man?" he asked, feeling more like his father than himself. He cringed inside. No boy wanted to be asked about school. He never did.

Henry shrugged his shoulders. "Fine."

It was the natural response, and Jacob had to grin. "Yeah, I was bored in school, too."

"I want to be a lawyer like Uncle Burt and my grandpa was."

Jacob considered his past disdain for his father and uncle's profession. Their offices, their clients, the well-defined edges of their lives, their status. None of it had ever appealed to him, yet he now had his own life, and the business he ran defined his boundaries. He gave a short laugh. His life had become much the same. "Well, that's something to consider. Life is full of opportunities. You might change your mind as you discover what else is out there."

Henry shrugged again. "I like the law. Uncle Burt has been teaching me. He tells the best stories. I want to help people get out of trouble. Then, when I earn enough money, I want to travel to all kinds of different places."

Burt smiled. "We have fun with it. I hope he does take up the profession, though. Henry, you will be the first to carry on the tradition."

Knowing the hidden meaning in his father's statement, Jacob drew his attention back to his son. Thankful for the child's curious nature, Jacob yearned to educate him in a world outside of Clermont City.

Johnathan piped up. "I want to be just like Mama and Papa. I want to be an artist. I can already paint, and Papa says I will learn to weld pieces together soon. I made this, Cousin Jacob." He brought the neck piece away from his chest and close to Jacob's face. "See?"

Jacob raised his chin and took a look at the crudely hammered piece of silver hanging from the thin strand of rawhide. "Yes, indeed. That is a fine job you did. You can be very proud." He felt an unexpected twinge of love for both boys. Was it because they came from Jessica? Johnathan resembled his father, yet he also held a look about him that was distinctly hers—a softness around the lips, a gentleness in his eyes. For a moment, Jacob was lost in the charming innocence of Henry and Johnathan. He glanced up to see Jessica across the room, and tears welled in his eyes. Reality crashed down on him, and his heart ached. Rubbing his chest, he stood and excused himself. Going out to the porch, he leaned on the rail.

"Mother, it's time we were leaving," Jessica announced. "Can you and Uncle Burt manage all right?"

"Yes, my brother and I will be fine, my dear. I'll send a message to you if you're needed. She may just sleep now."

"Boys, collect your things and say your goodbyes."

"Come give your grandma a hug. I'll see you again soon." Bethany grabbed her grandsons and squished them to her bosom, after which the boys scampered to the carriage, a giggle or two escaping from them.

Jessica stepped outside. "Let me walk you out," Jacob said.

Taking her around the back of the carriage and out of view of the house, Jacob brought his lips to her cheek. It was a gentle kiss, and they lingered too long out of sight. "I will see you at Christmas," he said.

"That will be nice."

"I want him to get to know me. When the time comes, I'll be making my request."

He walked away, leaving her heart pounding in her chest and her moist cheek tingling in the late-autumn breeze.

CHAPTER TWENTY-ONE

Christmas Day—1897

$\mathcal{T}$HE DECEMBER AFTERNOON LIGHT CAST ITS SHADOWS OVER June's vacant garden, and the roses that had danced during the summer on the white picket fence now stood dormant with only their thorny stems as a promise of their return.

As their carriage approached, Jessica peered in the window and caught a glimpse of her aunt walking toward the foyer, a festive apron tied around her much-slimmer waist. She felt a twinge of sadness then joy at having almost lost this person so precious to her. The Christmas celebration would bring together the ones June loved the most. Jessica braced herself for another family gathering where she and Jacob and Caleb would continue their lie. June had hinted at a special guest. She was curious who it might be, and surprised her aunt had kept the secret so long. She was relieved to know that Austin and his brood would celebrate the day at his home. Caleb always found them taxing, and they put him in a foul mood. Who was this special guest? Could her brother have a sweetheart? Could Jacob? The latter riled her. Mostly because she really shouldn't care, but she did.

Contented with her life revolving around caring for her children and husband and trying to meet deadlines with her art, she didn't need this pull on her emotions. She and Caleb were immersed in their work and had developed a rhythm to their lives.

Caleb escorted her and the children into the house, which was decorated with all the Christmas frippery a child could imagine. Soon, she would find out who this person was.

"Merry Christmas!" June sang out. "Come in! Come in!"

The children entered the warm home with eyes wide and mouths agape. The smell of oranges and cloves filled the air, mingling with the heavy scent of baking turkey and ham, followed by a trail of pipe tobacco floating from the parlor. After he greeted June, Caleb took a seat near Burt, who sat comfortably, smoking his pipe filled with his favorite tobacco. Caleb removed his own pipe from his shirt pocket, and Burt offered him some. Before Caleb could fill his pipe, Johnathan planted himself on his father's lap, nibbling on a decorated cookie he'd snatched from the table on his way in.

Jessica gave her blond-headed son a stern look. He smiled his sweetest smile, and she forgave his rudeness. Her mother was coming from the kitchen, followed by her brother and Jacob. Hannah was right behind them with a platter of food. Jessica met Jacob's eyes, and for a brief moment, the connection sparked a rush of nerves. Both he and Will looked dapper in their tailored suits. Jacob's hair was short and slicked back, and his trimmed mustache showed off his etched cheekbones and strong chin. Her eyes drifted down his long neck, and stopping at his collar, she looked away. His success was evident, and she was glad for it. Feeling beautiful in her deep-maroon dress with the latest style of leg-of-mutton sleeves and lace trim, she exuded her own prosperity. Settling her nerves, she reminded herself she was a married woman with two children.

She was proud of Caleb and the success he earned with his silverwork of jewelry, household wares, and adornments. He and their children were dressed in new clothes, and she thought Caleb looked especially handsome today. His long blond hair was tied back in a neat ponytail, and his face was clean-shaven around his goatee. He was a beautiful man. She looked beyond Hannah toward the kitchen. No one else followed.

"Greetings and good tidings to all," Will sang out as he placed the turkey on the table.

Jacob let his mother take the plate of ham. She arranged it, along with the other plates and bowls of food. Will and Jessica exchanged a smile of mutual understanding—June was in her element.

"Thank you for your help," Bethany said to Will and Jacob. "Now you both sit and visit, and we'll call you all to the table soon. Let me look at my fine young grandsons." Bethany gave her approval of their clothes, and her generous tone included Caleb, although with a tinge of irony. "You look very much the gentleman today, Caleb."

Jessica winced. To her relief, Caleb gave no mind to his mother-in-law's slight. She looked beyond Hannah, and the kitchen door swung open to reveal the surprise guest. Reverend Tandy came out with a broad smile and a bowl of steaming vegetables.

"Greetings and blessings on this holy day," he recited.

Jessica greeted him warmly as her mother whispered in her ear, "It was our turn to invite him for Christmas."

"What a nice surprise, Reverend," Jessica said, squeezing her mother's hand.

Soon, Henry circled the Christmas tree. The brightly adorned gifts below caught his eye. With his hands behind his back, he looked as if he were a detective deciphering a case.

"Henry, come away from there," Caleb said. "Sit down and wait."

"But, Pa!" Henry whined.

Noticing Jacob watching the exchange between Caleb and Henry, Jessica wondered how Jacob would have done as Henry's father. Would he have taught him to respect nature and the world around him as Caleb was doing, or would he have encouraged him to ignore the rules while he cut a path of his own as Jacob had done? To her surprise, he weighed in.

"Henry," Jacob said. "I think your Uncle Burt has the new picture books I brought for you and John in his den. I'm sure he wouldn't mind you getting them." He looked at his father. Burt nodded and waved the boy toward his study.

Caleb turned to Jacob, his expression less than approving.

"Yes, that sounds like a wonderful idea, Henry," Jessica said.

"Really, can I?" Henry bolted to the study.

Caleb's blue eyes steeled as he addressed Jacob. "My son doesn't need to be encouraged. Waiting for self-gratification is a skill every man needs to have."

Jessica winced at her misstep in agreeing with Jacob.

"It was merely a suggestion," Jacob responded as the door to Burt's study was thrown open.

"Oh, come now, Caleb," Will interjected. "He's only a boy. What youngster wants to be around us old folks?" He laughed and went for the bar. "Another drink, anyone?"

Caleb met Jessica with hooded eyes. She tilted her head with a smile and received, in return, his raised eyebrow and curled lip. He looked at his son. Johnathan sat on the floor, eating another cookie and simply admiring the wrapped presents. Jessica bit her lip.

For all her husband's endearing traits, his lack of understanding in the fundamental differences between their sons made her want to shout at him to be reasonable. Today, she said softly, "Everyone learns things differently at different stages of their lives." When their eyes met, Caleb stared into hers as he did when he felt betrayed. It was an old wound, and she had just given it a scratch.

"But you're right." She looked at the others. "Henry can be very impulsive at times." Knowing Caleb wouldn't be easily appeased, she stood and excused herself, then went into the kitchen.

The day unfolded more easily as the meal was enjoyed and the presents to the children were unwrapped. Jacob and Will had bought a train with all the trimmings for Henry and Johnathan. The boys' delight at such a gift gave everyone joy, except for Caleb. His own gifts to his boys were modest, as was his intention.

"This is too much," Jessica said to her brother and cousin. "You shouldn't spoil them like this."

"We get them at a great price," Will said out the side of his mouth. "Let them be spoiled. It's only once a year."

Helpless to argue, Jessica took cheer in her boys' happiness and told herself she would deal with her husband's disapproval later. "It's a fine train set. Thank you. Both of you."

Jacob's sincere smile told her he was proud to present such a gift. She felt her throat tighten. Pressing her lips together, she gave him a nod.

THE DAY'S LIGHT HAD BEEN extinguished, and Caleb lit a lantern for Henry to hold onto for the carriage ride home, the light revealing his still-chubby hand. The festivities had worn Johnathan out, and he laid his head in his mother's lap. Their newer carriage was a hooded four-seater, which shielded them from the droplets of rain forming along its edges.

Sitting in the back, stroking her son's head, Jessica looked at the backs of Henry and Caleb, Henry with his hand outstretched with the light while Caleb held the reins. Their quiet banter caught in the breeze. Father and son. It gave her a sense of well-being. Until their next encounter with Jacob, her family was whole. Her heart would remain true to Caleb, and she would set aside her feelings for Jacob. It must be this way. She would carry on without his love.

Once home and the children in bed, Caleb let his thoughts be known. "I have no doubt Jacob was proving to you he can make a living. So, he has. Good for him. That's the end of the visits, however."

"I don't know if that will be possible. Aunt June will be upset if we don't show for family occasions."

"Then I will not be seeing him again, nor will Henry. Your brother and Jacob are not the kind of influence I want on my sons. They deal in profit on the backs of poorly treated workers. Just look at the vulgar way they dress. They forget who and what they once were."

"They're allowed to forget those times, but I'm sure they haven't. We are living in the present, are we not?"

He turned away to stoke the fire. "Your eyes don't lie, sweetheart. You were quite taken with his appearance."

"I'm very happy for them both. Would you prefer they fail?"

The stirring of the embers brought the flames shooting up. Caleb leaned back and replaced the iron poker to its holder. "I want you to rid yourself of him." He turned to her and stared into her eyes.

The paisley chair had warmed under her, and she felt the heat rise to her chest. "He doesn't take up my time. I have you and the boys. If you think it's better that we have no more to do with him, then we won't." Putting aside Jacob's request to be with his son when Henry was older, she would keep her promise to Caleb. Her heart was another matter. Her feelings belonged to her and no one else. Loving two men confronted her again. She'd come to realize it would never get easier.

CHAPTER TWENTY-TWO

June 1899

*J*ESSICA CAME OUT OF THE WARM KITCHEN AFTER MAKING A savory pie for supper and a cherry cobbler for dessert. She wiped her hands on her apron and hung it on the peg by the pantry. Wondering how she could persuade Caleb to attend her aunt and uncle's anniversary celebration had occupied her thoughts most of the day. Jessica knew how important it was to her aunt. Her family, as well as friends from town, would be there. She went over her speech. *We can't hold on to the past. It's been a year and a half since the boys saw their cousin Jacob. We can't hide from him forever. Aunt June will be crushed if you're not there.*

After dinner, Henry and John went to their room to do their homework, but not without some horseplay and a reprimand from their father. She and Caleb sat alone in the quiet parlor. Deciding to throw out her well-rehearsed speech, she simply handed him the flower-decorated, hand-printed invitation.

He cocked an eyebrow and gave a crooked smile.

"*Everyone* will be there," she said.

He placed the invitation on the table by his chair and scratched his chin whiskers. "We can't miss their anniversary. June would never forgive me, and I dare say what your mother would do to me."

Her breath hitched. "Thank you, Caleb. It means so much to them to have everyone together. They're not getting any younger."

"No, none of us are." He cleared his throat and sat back in his chair, staring at the floor.

Seeing his sorrowful expression, she asked, "What is it?"

Without looking at her, he replied, "My grandmother died. She was just seventy-eight. I always thought of her as being so old, but that doesn't seem so old to me now."

"Oh, Caleb, I'm so sorry." Jessica leaned forward to take his hand. He squeezed it briefly and let go.

"I wasn't very close to her, although she raised me for a short while before I set off on my own. I know she wanted more for me. She'd dress me in fine clothes, and we'd go to fancy restaurants. I was meant to be seen." He chuckled. "Many a debutante had their eye on me."

Jessica listened as Caleb talked and thought how she would be taken with him as much as those debutantes. If only she had met him then. He rarely spoke of his childhood, and when he did, she felt as if she were an intruder into his thoughts, his secret memories. Hanging on every word, she was hungry for those memories of him as a youth.

"I can't say I even loved her," Caleb continued. "I've kept in touch with her very little over the years, just enough to let her know I'm still alive. The last time I wrote was after John was born." Caleb was silent for a moment. "She was there for me after the accident. When I lost my family, I felt I should have died, too. Why should I be alive and not them? My grandmother got me through that. She was quite a woman, actually. I feel sick when I think of how little I thought of the fact that she had lost a son, daughter-in-law, and grandson. I was all she had left."

He looked at her, and Jessica gave a slight smile. "You were young," she said. "It's lucky you had her, but why didn't you stay closer?"

Caleb shrugged. "I don't know. After graduation, she had great plans for me. College, the right fraternity, the right people. I wanted to run far away. Her plans didn't appeal to me." He raised his brows and laughed. "Who knows what I would have become. My choices have made me who I am today, if that's saying anything." He puffed out a breath. "Well, maybe I'd take a few things back."

Jessica nodded. "Your life choices brought us together, and I'm very grateful for that. We all have regrets."

A silence filled the parlor until John came out of his room, pencil and paper in hand.

"Pa, I don't get this. Can you help me?"

Henry followed. "John, I told you *I* can help you."

"I want Pa to help me. You're too mean!"

Caleb sat John on his lap. "Let's see what you've got here."

"You're such a baby," Henry said under his breath as he walked out of the parlor.

"Henry, we heard that," Jessica said.

Henry turned. "Sorry, but he is. Why do you both baby him? Especially you, Pa."

Caleb looked over at his son, and Jessica held her breath. She didn't want them to argue about this again. Before Jessica could intervene, Caleb was defending himself. "I don't treat either of you differently. When you need help, don't I give it to you?"

"I guess. Sorry, Pa," Henry said and sulked back to his room.

As always, Caleb and Henry came to a truce, yet Jessica wondered how it would be when Henry was older and Johnathan still held his father in the palm of his hand.

Looking over at Caleb and John working through the math problem, she saw a father who had lost his family and now was engaged with his own, perhaps filling a gap he needed to fill. How he must have missed the love and the everyday ups and downs that make up a family. Her emotions rose. She wanted to go to Caleb and comfort him, but she knew he was past their conversation. His childhood was tucked back into himself and no longer reachable.

In bed that night, she wrapped her body around his. "I love you. I'm sorry."

"I love you, too," he whispered above her head. "Don't be sorry. Let's stop being sorry. Life is too short." He paused and kissed the top of her head. "By the way, my grandmother left me some money."

Jessica looked up at Caleb, his profile etched in the moonlight. "Oh?"

"It's a good sum. We can do a lot around here with it. We'll build a proper art studio for you. Mostly, it will sit in the bank for a rainy day, so to speak."

She smiled broadly at the idea of getting out of the barn and its permeating odors.

"Don't tell the boys. They don't need to know they have a cushion under them. I've seen what money can do to a person. And don't tell your family, either. I won't gain your mother's approval just because I have money, nor will I buy a bigger house because I can afford one."

Jessica pressed her body to his and said, "It will be our secret, and I love our home."

He turned and moved his hands to her bottom, bringing her into the front of him. With a feral growl, he brought his hands up her back and into her hair, and his lips came down to meet hers. It sparked her lust for him, and she returned his passion with her own.

Caleb could melt her fears and anxiousness away with his love-making. Tomorrow, he would return to his usual state of business with a peck on her cheek before he hurried off to his workshop, or some errand, or a meeting with friends in town. Possibly more than a peck, maybe a longer hug. She would resume her chores and art and worry about the anniversary party and the boys. But tonight, he was all hers, and her heart only belonged to him. Nothing else mattered.

His mouth slowly moved to her neck, taking pleasure there until he cupped her breasts and teased her hard nipples with his tongue. She moaned and was swept away to their private realm.

CHAPTER TWENTY-THREE

July 1899

*J*UNE HELD UP THE INTRICATELY PAINTED, BLUE-AND-WHITE vase so that everyone could see the anniversary gift her son had given his parents. The red-and-black velvet box it came in was a gift in itself. The room was filled with at least twenty people and buzzing with voices. June's other niece, Sophie, was the loudest, instructing her sons to stand straight, show some interest, and stop eating all the canapés. The pipe and tobacco smoke swirled around the room in a haze, and the liquor cart was nearly depleted.

The cheers and applause at the exotic gift rang in Jessica's ears. Standing back from the crowd, she felt dizzy and sick. She shouldn't have had that last glass of wine. Caleb was talking with Will, and her boys were running around outside with the neighbor's children. She took in a breath and let it out. She knew it wasn't the wine or the food or the smoke. Looking over at Jacob, standing next to his mother with a wide smile on his gleaming face, was the reason. He was happy, and not because of the joy the gift brought to his mother.

"Jessica! Jessica, come here and look at this close-up," her aunt said.

She moved to the front and smiled at the beautiful vase. "It's lovely, Auntie." Turning to meet Jacob, she said, "What a thoughtful gift."

"Mother, it's from both of us," Jacob said and brought the Mexican woman closer to him. She was tall and beautiful, standing out among the others.

"My Aldonza and I both picked it out."

"Well, then it's twice as special," June said.

"Jacob, please, it's Donza," the woman said with an accent. She turned to June and added, "He loves my full name, but I am not used to such a formal way of being addressed."

Jessica slipped away. *His Aldonza?* She went into the kitchen, where Hannah was refilling the canapé tray. The door swung shut, and the receding noise was a welcome relief.

"My, that lot is hungry," Hannah said as she arranged the crab-filled puffs.

Jessica leaned against the counter. "Can I help?"

"No. Why are you in here?" Hannah asked with a squint of an eye.

"It's too crowded out there."

Hannah tilted her head. "One too many, ah?"

Jessica examined the tray. "I don't know what you're talking about."

"Come now, *Mrs. Cantrell.* We have too many years between us."

"They met at a convention on Chinese affairs, of all things," Jessica said.

Hannah wiped her hands on the towel hanging from her apron and waited for more.

"It's really none of my business," she continued, placing another puff on the tray.

Hannah clucked her tongue. "You know it has upset you."

Jessica placed a hand to her chest. "I'm not upset. It's just very sudden."

"It's about time your brother and cousin settle down."

"She went to college at the University of California. Jacob was planning on going to China someday. China, of all places!"

Hannah lifted her brows.

"She was studying their trade policies. She's very young, don't you think? Just out of college only four years. What could Jacob be thinking?"

The English housekeeper patted Jessica's arm. "There's no use in fussing about it. People do what they want to do. And she's not that young, just younger than him."

"By ten years is what I heard!"

Bethany entered the kitchen. "Hannah, what's keeping you? Fill a tray of cheeses, please."

"I'll do the cheese platter, Mother," Jessica said.

Her mother gave her a side glance and left.

"I'd love to chat, but duty calls," Hannah said. She lifted the tray, then pushed the swinging door open and scooted around it.

Jessica unwrapped the cheese and found a knife, then began to cut slices off the block of cheddar. At a sudden breeze from the door, she addressed her mother without turning. "It won't take me long."

"Jess."

His voice penetrated her body, and she closed her eyes and squared her shoulders. Resting the knife, she slowly turned to Jacob. "I thought you were Mother," she said.

"I didn't know how to tell you. I thought it would be best if I just introduced her to everyone at the same time." He looked at the door. "I think she's overwhelmed, but she's being brave."

"Your parents like her, especially your mother."

"They met her last night. I knew they would like her. She's a fine person, and I—"

Jessica raised her hand. "Say no more. It's written all over your face."

"It's hard being alone with no one by your side. I'm getting close to being forty. I don't want to be alone for the rest of my life."

"Jacob, you don't have to explain. I'm happy for you."

He smirked and let out a laugh. "Yeah, it's written all over your face."

She went back to slicing the cheese. He reached for the flatbread, and they both arranged the platter without a word. His hand touched hers, and their fingers entwined. She withdrew suddenly. "I can manage from here. Please go back in."

He touched her shoulder and returned to the parlor, the door swinging in his wake. Jessica brushed his touch away. Tears welled in her eyes, and she swiped at them. It was no use spilling a drop from her eyes. She would have to come to terms with the fact he was now lost to her forever.

Part Two

CHAPTER TWENTY-FOUR

San Francisco—February 1904

$\mathcal{J}$ACOB STUDIED THE SMALL PAINTING IN FRONT OF HIM. HE unbuttoned his finely tailored waistcoat, stuck a hand in each pocket of the matching trousers, and leaned forward to look at the detailed picture that captured a piece of his own past as well as a piece of his heart. It hung by itself on a narrow wall dwarfed by Jessica's other paintings throughout the expansive Billingston Gallery, yet it created no less of an impact, especially for him.

The large canvases surrounding it held the richly textured, vibrant scenes of days gone by. The detailed facial expressions, as if carefully carved from leather, revealed the hardships and rewards of the Indians' lives. Simple, makeshift, wood-and-thatch dwellings in the forest conveyed the efforts of a lost camp of renegades. His mind swirled with the memory of he and Will finding her there. How extraordinary it was. It confirmed to him that he and Jessica would always be a part of each other. He didn't think about the trails. His own journey to her. Only that he had found her among the Indians and rescued her to return her to a husband, his campmate in the gunrunning trade and a man whose life he'd saved. It seemed long ago and yet still so near to his heart. What if it had been different? What if he had let Caleb die in that unholy cabin in Colorado?

He peered at another canvas. This one a surreal image of a strong warrior with only a wrap of deerskin around his waist. He had risen out of the blue-green waters and stood with water dripping from his muscular body. A war raged behind him, threatening to destroy his world, while a peaceful meadow of soft grass stretched out before him, vulnerable and optimistic. The title, *Blue Heron, Blue Horizons*, sent a shiver up Jacob's spine. The Indian who claimed to have married Jessica and held her in the Indian camp. The small battle that proceeded, then the long hours of negotiations with the elders and Blue Heron before they could finally take her with them. The days that followed filled his empty heart as she rode in back of him. So close were their bodies in rhythm with the horse's stride. The heartbreak of losing her again to another man was still a tender wound. He rubbed his chest and continued to peruse her works. Depictions of Native people in elaborate ceremonial wear with the backdrop of a breath-taking, untamed wilderness came from a perspective different than his own. He was impressed by the way she brought the past to life. His own past would look different if he had a way with a brush and paints. Her renditions were almost optimistic.

Turning back to the small frame, he wondered what she had felt while painting this scene. "Excuse me," Jacob said to a young woman walking by with a name tag pinned to the lapel of her crisply pressed, navy-blue jacket.

"Yes, may I help you, sir?"

"I'd like to purchase this painting, but I don't see a price. Is it for sale?"

"No, I'm afraid none of the paintings in this particular part of the gallery are for sale." She bent down to retrieve a small plaque from the floor. It had fallen from its position on the wall beside the artwork. She pressed it back into place. Jacob read, *Heart's Journey—Artist's Personal Collection.* "I'm sorry for any confusion, sir. The rest of Jessica Cantrell's canvases and watercolors are in the next room to your right. Those are for sale."

"Thank you." Turning his attention back to the small piece of framed history, he heard voices coming from the far side of the hall.

Recognizing the one voice that had brought him here, he stood still and let it penetrate his being. When he turned to look at her, he saw a confident woman in a tailored outfit. She was even more beautiful than when he'd last seen her nearly two years ago. A few silver strands wove through her simple updo, and her figure held its curves. He chuckled to himself, as if he took inventory. She spied him, and her smile lit up his world. Clearing his throat, he acknowledged her with a nod.

A FEW PATRONS ENGAGED HER in conversation about the origins of her ideas and the choice of her mediums. Once she saw Jacob, Jessica politely answered, then let them talk among themselves. She observed the well-groomed, neatly attired figure looking intently at her. He stood in front of the one piece of art she had hesitated to share with the world. She'd hung it herself for one person to see, and he had found it.

Age had been kind to Jacob in spite of the life he had led before his present one of comfort and advantage. But for a few gray hairs around his temples, he was still the handsome, vital man she knew. Jessica walked toward him and extended her hand. He took it and then embraced her. The warmth and strength of him overcame her, and she stepped away.

"Jessica, this is an incredible body of work."

She could tell he was as nervous as she was. "Thank you, Jacob. I'm so happy you came to see it."

"I just tried to buy this one, but I found it isn't for sale." He hesitated, then smiled. "I'm glad."

She smiled back and was satisfied her intention had found its home.

They stood together, looking at the portrait of a horse with two riders. One was a tall dark-haired male riding with the reins, looking strong and steady, his hat pulled forward, the other a female rider with long wavy dark hair, one hand tucked around the waist of the man. They rode away from the viewer—no faces, only the two intimate figures.

"I can almost feel the rocking of ol' Otis and your warm body shifting behind me," he said in a whisper. His hand was in hers. "Thank you."

The memories of so many lifetimes with this man welled up inside her. It was unfair that her feelings for him had never abated. She lightly squeezed his hand, silently telling him what he needed to know—she had not forgotten.

It was difficult to express in words what she had experienced at that time. Her brushes and paints were her tools, and art gave her the outlet she needed while keeping a safe distance between her viewers and reality. This one painting, however, was to be held as a kind of photograph of a memory, and she had bravely shown it to the world, including Caleb.

While it still sat on her easel, her husband had commented, "It's quite good, Jess, but excuse me if I don't ask you to hang this one up in the house as I have with some of the others."

She could only say, "I understand, Caleb."

"Do you?" he had replied. "You do realize that the past is truly over with, don't you? He's married now. Painting your experiences over the years has been a great help to you, I'm sure, but this is too much for *your* husband and *his* wife."

It had taken her many years to come to terms with what she and Jacob had done, what Caleb's actions had cost her. In spite of

Caleb's urgings to keep the small rendition of her time with Jacob hidden, she had exposed it to everyone, caring less of what secrets others might glean from it, including Jacob's new wife, if she ever saw it. Jessica was surprised Jacob had even bothered to come to one of her exhibits.

"It was a long time ago, yet it feels so near to me," Jacob said.

"Yes, so much has happened since then. It seems life never settles down. There's always something." She sighed, then asked, "How are Donza and Jocelyn?"

He looked as if he had just come out of a dream. "My wife and daughter are fine. They're with her family in Sacramento. I stayed behind to get some work done."

Over the past few years, Jessica had collected more information from her aunt about Jacob's wife and their courtship—an all-too-brief affair, in Jessica's opinion. They'd been married by a judge in a no-nonsense courtyard ceremony in San Francisco. Donza Cortez and her parents, along with June, Burt, and Will completed the family attendance. Jessica was relieved to have been spared witnessing Jacob say his vows to another. She decided he had done it that way to protect her.

Soon afterward, their daughter was born. All the while, Jessica kept her distance, focusing on her own family and career. It surprised her that Jacob could still tilt her steady, matured heart.

"So, how are you, Jess? Besides being a great success as an artist. This is a fine gallery."

"I've been fortunate. They like me here. I sell paintings."

"I'm sure you do. And how is your family?"

"Caleb and the boys are well. Johnathan is following in his father's footsteps and is becoming quite a young artisan, and Henry is still very interested in the law."

"Ah, yes, my father told me. Well, your father is looking down and smiling. He will get his wish after all—one of his heirs will be a lawyer," Jacob said, shaking his head in disbelief. "It's hard to believe that my son, raised by a man like Caleb, would want to aspire to the law profession. And what is your influence, my lady?" His raised eyebrow goaded her on.

Jessica gave him a smirk and a tilt of her head, and for a brief moment, she was drawn back to their youth when she would tease him and make him declare with arms outstretched that he surrendered to her. The thought caused a rush of blood to her head. She changed the direction of her thoughts.

"Will tells me your daughter is a beautiful little girl."

"She keeps us busy. You know how curious a two-and-a-half-year-old can be."

She laughed. "I remember those days. Henry was never still." There was so much she wanted to tell him about his son. A tap on her shoulder took her attention. It was the young woman who had previously helped Jacob.

"Yes, Claire?"

"I'm sorry to interrupt, Mrs. Cantrell, but you're needed in the other room for the presentation."

"I'll be right there, thank you." Jessica turned back to Jacob, regretting having to cut their visit short. "I have to go."

"Presentation?" he asked.

"Yes, my friend and owner of the gallery, Jilly Gaines, is thanking me for my contribution to their gallery. I really should be thanking *her*. This venue has come a long way, and she had asked me to join her gallery after my . . . ordeal." She looked down at her shoes, then up again. Was her kidnapping and rescue now only referred to as the "ordeal"?

Jacob seemed to catch her meaning. Wanting to see him later, she ventured an invitation.

"I was wondering . . . would you like to have dinner with me?"

He stepped forward. "Yes, I'd like that."

His eyes lit up, and she felt a warmth blanket her body. "Good. Let me finish up here, and I'll meet you at the restaurant of my hotel. I'm staying at the Fairmont. Around six?"

"Sounds perfect. Until then." He made a slight bow, and with a chuckle, he was gone.

She took a deep breath and let it out. *It's only an innocent dinner.*

CHAPTER TWENTY-FIVE

*T*HE MAGICAL AMBIENCE OF THE HOTEL FAIRMONT BROUGHT Jessica into another world far from her home in Clermont City.

The maître d' escorted Jacob through the intimate hotel dining room to Jessica's table. Heads turned to see where the tall handsome man would be seated, and a low whisper filled the room as he leaned down and took Jessica's hand to kiss it. She pursed her lips and bowed her head shyly. He gave her a wink and sat down.

"I must be late?" he asked.

"No, I'm a bit early," she replied, her cheeks flushing.

"You look beautiful, Jess."

She was happy she had brought the emerald, velvet, lace-trimmed gown, selected at the last minute in case of an unexpected evening event. It fit her womanly figure very well, and with her hair turned up high on her head, she felt as beautiful as Jacob said she looked.

"And you're looking very dapper this evening."

He raised an eyebrow. "I liked being the dirty cowboy better."

"I liked it, too." Her words were barely audible, but he heard them. They exchanged knowing looks. She smiled and cleared her throat. "Let's not go back in time, Jacob. It doesn't serve us well."

"Yes, ma'am. I'm sorry." He twisted his lips.

She gave a short laugh, and the evening began with cocktails and small talk. As they shared their lives with each other, the energy between them was as if a light had been turned on in a dark room and they wanted to see everything. After several glasses of wine and a satisfying meal, the conversation turned more personal.

"Do you know how many times I've thought of us and what could have been?" he asked.

"Yes, I do."

He pressed his lips into a grin. "I suppose you do. You're the other half of this whole."

"Of course, we would wonder what else might have been possible with the years we've already spent," she said, "but we shouldn't dwell on it."

Rubbing his forehead with the back of his thumb, he looked at her sheepishly. "Geez, I think I'm getting more romantic in my old age."

Pursing her lips, she knew it wasn't his age. Her marriage was good, and she had no right to complain about the life she had created thus far. "It's not just you, Jacob," she said. "I feel the same, but we have both found happy lives in our sacrifice of each other."

A short silence followed. Then Jacob leaned slightly forward, as if he needed her complete attention. She anticipated his next remark with caution.

"Jess, Donza and I," he began. "It's never been true love. She's a warm and intelligent woman, and I'm very grateful to her. She gave me an incredible daughter." He cupped his hands and brought them to his chin. "Truth be told, I've never found in her what I lost with you."

Jessica sipped on her wine and cocked one eyebrow at him. If she allowed herself to engage in this romance, she could be swept away. "Our timing seems to lack perfection," she replied with a playful smirk. "Why did you marry her then?"

He lifted a shoulder. "I thought it was time to settle down. And . . . well, we didn't exactly plan for her to become . . ." He pursed his lips.

"Oh. No honeymoon baby then?"

"Not quite."

She gave him a crooked grin.

"And as far as our timing, you and me, well, someday it will be perfect. I can't live without that hope."

"Let's talk of our children," Jessica said, trying to get them back on track.

"Yes, let's talk about my son. When will you tell him?"

"Jacob, don't turn this into a melodrama. Too many years have passed for that. I don't think he needs to know. Why confuse him when he's just beginning his own life?"

"Christ, he's turning fifteen this year. He's old enough to know where he comes from."

"Jacob, please." She gathered her white cotton napkin and looked around for the waiter.

"I will let you have your way on that, Jess, but I want him to visit me for the month of April. My schedule is lighter then, and I will make sure it stays that way. The city will be good for him. Let him get to know me."

Jessica weighed what it would mean for Henry to get a taste of the city against the risk of leaving Jacob alone with his son. "I don't know. Caleb will never agree to it."

Jacob fingered the porcelain bowls of salt and pepper in front of him as he continued to make his case. "Not seeing Henry has been more difficult for me than you know." He paused and looked at her with curiosity. "How have you not seen that? Why haven't you offered something yourself? Why has it taken you so long? I shouldn't have to beg."

Jessica flushed. She had no answers for him. In protecting herself and her family, she had built a wall against Jacob's desires. She hadn't expected to be enlightened like this, and especially not by Jacob in a public space. Sensing the other diners' looks, she clasped her cold fingers. Jacob quietly suggested they continue their visit in her room.

She took a breath and gave him a barely perceptible nod. This wasn't prudent, but they had to talk, privately. She straightened her back and said loudly, "My dear cousin, it's been such a pleasure to dine with you."

Jacob rose and offered her his arm. "Yes, indeed it has, Cousin. Shall we go?"

They left the dining hall, but instead of saying good night in the lobby, she allowed him to escort her up the grand marble staircase. She didn't look around and stepped as nonchalantly as possible, her hand tucked into his extended elbow. Once at her room, the door closed quietly behind them. The small sitting area off the bedroom would be a safe place for them to talk.

"I can ring for some coffee or tea to be brought up," she said.

"I'll take a bourbon," he replied.

Jessica smiled. "Well, aren't we all grown up?"

"You know me too well." Jacob laughed. "I can't pretend with you, even if I wanted to. Yes, we've grown up, my dear. It's time for me to know my son."

What was she getting herself into? This conversation was overdue, but she'd hardly expected it today. She will sip her tea, indulging in the peaceful respite from her life and in the company of a man she had longed to be alone with. For a moment, she imagined they had been together all along and were about to discuss their son's future. Jacob cleared his throat.

"Would you like some water?" she asked and poured herself

a glass from the decanter on the side board against the wall. She looked briefly at the tacky painting of still life hanging above it.

"No. Thank you."

"Will has his hands full with Miss Hillsboro," she said, easing into another topic.

"He does. Julia is a wild thing. She thinks she can save the world. Will agrees with her. All that campaigning for the Chinese and shopworkers."

"I think it's admirable."

Jacob snickered. "It takes Will's mind away from business too often. I tried to steer him away from her, but it was no use."

"Jacob! You, of all people, should know what the heart wants cannot be reasoned with." Wishing she could take back those words, she looked down into her glass.

"I said I had no luck with it," he snapped. "Now, let's get back to Henry."

His coolness brought her back to the matter at hand. She found herself riding the ups and downs of their relationship, and it angered her.

"You can be as cold as a fish when you want to be, Jacob Stanford. I see you have a one-track mind, and it's to get hold of your son. I'm not sure you'll get your way." Having vented some of her anger, she settled down. He stared at her with lifted eyebrows.

"I'm sorry. Was there something else you expected from me?"

She dropped her chin. "Of course not."

"Tell me about my son."

Now that was an easy subject. She could talk about her sons for days. She told him about Henry's first steps at only eleven months, the first tooth he'd lost at six while playing ball with his brother, and his broken arm at ten when he fell from a branch by the river and landed on solid ground instead of his intended target—the water. "Thank goodness it wasn't a bad break." She bragged of his accomplishments in school and how he picked Burt's brain about the law, capping it off with examples of his stubborn and wild personality. "It's good he has a mind of his own, yet I feel he needs a lot of guidance."

She saw how intently Jacob listened, smiling from ear to ear. How she ached to have had him involved in it all, and how futile it was to imagine a world where that would have been possible. She continued.

"One day, I think Henry was only about seven, Burt was telling us about some of his cases—just the amusing ones—and talking about my father as well. Henry's ears perked right up. He's been on the subject of law ever since. Henry's proud of the grandfather he never knew, even if his Uncle Will isn't. My brother has tried to discourage him from becoming a lawyer at every turn. He tells him to go out and explore the world before settling into a career. I don't like the ideas he puts into both of my sons' heads. They don't need to mimic the two of you. Besides, Caleb has his own hopes for them."

"Mimic us?" Jacob said with a laugh. "Christ, what makes you think that? I agree, I don't think they need to go to such extremes to experience the world. I'm offering to show Henry the city for a few weeks and give him a taste of life outside of a small town."

"What does your wife think about having a boy around to feed and watch?" His hesitation gave her the feeling Donza might not be excited by the prospect of caring for Jacob's "second cousin."

"Donza won't mind. She has her own work as a college professor's assistant. It keeps her very busy."

Concerned about the hint of discord in his words, she said, "Maybe he can stay with Will. He and Julia have a nice apartment in the city." She didn't want her son to be an unwelcome guest in anyone's household.

"Jessica, Henry will stay with me. Let me know before the end of March, and I will make the arrangements. Donza and Jocelyn will welcome him with open arms. You've kept him from me long enough."

Their eyes locked in mutual battle for the right to have their way.

"Let it be your idea, Jess, or we'll never get anywhere."

Jessica straightened her back. "Don't tell me how to convince my husband into getting my way. I can do that just fine without your help." Flustered, she shook her head. "I mean to say, we discuss our affairs together, equally. Stop grinning! You know very well what I meant."

Jacob laughed out loud. "Oh dear, the cat's out of the bag!"

She was half-embarrassed and half-amused. "As for keeping Henry from you, you know he had to grow up with stability. I was afraid your lifestyle would steer him in the wrong direction."

"Was that really it? I've made amends for my youth."

The mood in the room shifted. Jessica looked at the unlit fireplace, then the floor. "I was afraid of what I would feel if I saw you hold him and love him, so I kept him from getting close to you." There, she had said it—the raw truth. It was freeing, and she continued. "Whenever he asks about Cousin Jacob, I tell him you have a busy life." She felt the words tumble out of their hiding place. She caught his eyes. "I have also told him that you and I grew close as young people, and if I wasn't a girl, we would have traveled together and had all kinds of adventures." Jessica smiled at the thought.

"Thank you for at least talking to him about me. I know it couldn't have been easy."

A chuckle escaped him. "But as for you not being a girl, well, my life would have been a whole lot easier!"

"As would mine." The state of their affair unearthed her sadness. Her eyes misted over.

"So was our fate, and here we are. And to be honest, I'm damn grateful I didn't have to deal with another Messing brother!"

"I would have been a great partner," she said smugly.

"In life or in business?" he asked, enjoying their tête-a-tête.

She lifted her chin. "Both!"

He grinned. "Well, we shall never know, Jess. The past can't be changed, but the future holds great promise. Let's make it good for our son. I promise you it will be nothing more than an adventure and a learning experience. Now, as much as I would love to stay, I must go."

"It's been a good visit, Jacob. I hope we can do this again sometime."

"Most definitely," he replied with gusto.

They rose together, and she walked him to the door. He kissed her on the cheek and prepared to make his exit until their eyes locked. It was that look that made her weak for him. He hesitantly bent down and kissed her lips. A thrill ran through her body, and she kissed him back. It would be easy to give in again even after so many years. No one would know. Their secret would be added to the many between them. He tugged at her collar, and his warm breath caressed her flesh as his full lips found the sweet spot on her neck.

Jessica closed her eyes, letting the familiar wave of lust crest over her body. His scent lived in her, and one whiff was all it took to bring him completely back to the forefront of her heart. As she was about to fall off the edge, she pulled away, and he quickly followed suit.

"I'm sorry," he said. "I shouldn't have taken advantage."

"No, it was me as well. I seem to always forget who I am when I'm near you. There's nothing to forgive, Jacob."

She knew in her heart there was plenty to be forgiven.

"You always did forgive me, Jess. I don't deserve it. I should have fought for us. I love you more now than I ever have. I thought I could make it go away, but it just keeps getting stronger."

She listened without finding excuses for him.

"I suppose I'm paying the price for my youthful pride and foolishness," he continued. "Jess, Henry's all I have of us. Can't you see why I need to be with my son?"

Jessica saw the truth in his eyes. "I understand, Jacob, but he's not me. You can't use him as a way to get to me." He pulled away, and the void between them filled with the cool air of the room. She shivered and brought her loose shawl up around her shoulders.

"I'll tell the front desk to come light your hearth," he said.

They stared into each other's eyes.

"I'm not trying to get at you through him. I just want to know my son."

Taking a breath and letting it out, she gave a slight nod. "You had this all planned? Coming to the gallery and all?"

"Yes, I wanted to see you *and* your paintings, but of course my main reason for seeing you was to ask you to let me spend time with Henry. I didn't expect for it to lead to this." He touched his lips.

"It's your damn stubbornness that just won't let you accept what is."

"*My* stubbornness?" he said with half a laugh. "I'd say you've been the more stubborn of the two of us. And I suppose you've accepted us being apart?"

She was startled at the nerve he showed with such a comment. "Did I have a choice, my friend?" she asked, boldly staring into his eyes.

Jacob walked to the chair he had been sitting in, and she to the one she had occupied. Jessica felt childish as she inwardly sought justice in a most unfair situation.

"Our fathers would call this an impasse and stay up all night trying to find a resolution," he commented.

"And would they find a resolution?"

"I suppose we'll never know, but I do know we're not our fathers. Their lives were designed by them to have crisp, clean edges, ones they could clearly see and stay within." He paused.

"I sometimes envy the simplicity of having defined boundaries. Even with my wife and child, J&W, and all the rules and regulations that surround my life, I still haven't figured out where my boundaries truly are."

"I never figured you or my brother would seek boundaries or clean edges. This is quite a revelation."

"You mock me."

"No, not at all. I'm happy to see you have finally realized that there are boundaries in life and that we all need them. They don't have to be shared by our fathers or mothers."

"Do you like the edges you've built around your life?"

She had to think. Was her life as boundless as she'd once thought it was, or were there still too many locked gates?

"I really don't know. You certainly have given me something to think about. Caleb has traveled more in recent years. Maybe I understand now why he goes up into Oregon to be with his Indian friends, or family, as he refers to them. He doesn't want to close himself in."

"Jessica."

"Yes, Jacob?" she replied, coming out of her thoughts.

"I'm still in love with you."

Jessica reached over and took his hand. He squeezed hers. They stayed holding each other's hands without a word for several minutes until it was time to say goodbye.

This time, he simply rubbed the side of her shoulder and left.

That night, she went over their visit, recounting every word he'd said and each one she hadn't. How could she let him into her life like that? Henry was a bridge to him whether she wanted it or not.

CHAPTER TWENTY-SIX

*T*HE MARCH LIGHT WARMED JESSICA FROM HEAD TO TOE AS she sat on her front porch. To the left, the meadow flowers and grasses swayed, their fragrance giving comfort while the singing birds delighted her. After being away in the city, it was good to return to the simplicity of Rail River Acres.

Their home had grown in size and comfort, thanks to Caleb's inheritance and their thriving careers, but it was still their "homestead." They had built an upper floor and expanded the first floor, taking it from a cabin to a real farmhouse. The kitchen had been updated with the latest in modern conveniences of the new century. The large wooden kitchen table had been refinished into a finer piece of furniture, though it still held its original form along with all its secrets.

The land around the house had been somewhat tamed to complement the new style. Shrubs and flowers purchased from the nursery in town wound their way along garden paths, while the field remained open, and the forest beyond, still wild. Jessica's sunlit art studio on the southeast side of the house overlooked the field that led to the river, and on days like today, she wanted to run through the low-growing grass and chain together tiny daisies. She was in love with her surroundings. Leaving it always reminded her how much she appreciated home.

Leaning her back against the house, the shade of the porch roof providing just enough cool air, her mind wandered to her visit with Jacob a few weeks ago. What he'd asked was not unreasonable—he wanted to see his son. When would she find it in herself to broach the subject with Caleb? Jacob waited for her answer. Although Henry would finish his exams by the end of the month, April seemed too soon.

She let herself indulge a few minutes more in the bliss of the sunny afternoon. The boys would be home from school shortly.

THE DOOR TO CALEB'S WORKSHOP was open. He was inside, sizing up a piece of metal. The descending sun fell from the tall windows like a beacon from heaven, casting golden light across the tidy shop. This was not only her husband's workspace—it had become his sanctuary. She hesitated and then said, "Hello."

"Hello, sweetheart. What brings you out here?" His voice was like music to her ears' especially when he called her "sweetheart." She knew his tone would change once she told him what she had planned for Henry.

"I have something to talk with you about."

He put the metal down and wiped his hands on his heavy cotton apron. Jessica looked at the man she still loved. His long blond hair, threaded with white, was tied back. Recently, she had detected a bit of white around his temples. His tall sturdy frame remained forever youthful, and she still felt a lure in his blue eyes she couldn't explain. He was her faithful friend, companion, and lover. Jessica dreaded upsetting their recent tranquility. Caleb's visits north had softened him in ways she couldn't have, no matter how she'd tried in the first years of their marriage. What was on the reservation that gave him such peace of mind?

"I need some water," he said. "Let's go inside the house." He removed his apron, hung it on a peg, then followed her out.

They sat at the kitchen table, as they had so many times when something had to be decided on, when news came from family or friends, or when arguments had to be negotiated.

"What is it, Jessica?"

She glanced at the kitchen window, then back at his aging but still beautiful face. He held her gaze. "Ever since you got back from the city, you seem distracted. Are you ready to tell me what happened? Jacob has something to do with it, I suppose."

"Oh, for goodness' sake." She stirred in her seat.

"Just as I thought."

"It's not as you thought," she lied. "He showed up at the gallery. We had dinner that night and discussed Henry. He wants to have him in April. He wants him to experience the city."

Caleb rose, his full height sweeping the air up from the floor. She braced herself for his disapproval.

"I don't care what he wants. I'll be damned if I'll let *my* son have anything to do with the life your cousin or brother lead." He raked the strands of loosened hair away from his face, then turned his back on her to stare out at the open fields from the kitchen window. "How did he charm you this time?"

"Caleb, please. He has a right. He—"

"He has no rights. Isn't that what the adoption was all about?"

"Yes, but this is different."

He sat back down. "It's very different. Thanks for reminding me."

She let out a huff of impatience. "After all these years, you still think they haven't changed one bit?"

"I think he's putting on a good act. You think because he wears a fine suit, has a home on a hill, and drives a contraption on wheels that he's changed? He's only traded one set of weapons and bad habits for another."

Jessica sat, stunned. What did he know about Jacob? Was her husband still that jealous? "What are you talking about?"

Caleb continued. "I didn't want to tell you."

She closed her eyes and shook her head. "What is it?"

"The truth is, along with all those pretty furnishings, they've been dealing in the opium trade."

"I . . . I had no idea. How do you know, and for how long?"

He sat back. "The owner of the store on Market. He buys my turquoise jewelry."

She nodded. "Mr. Alby."

"Yes, Robert Alby. He and I have become well acquainted, and several months ago, he told me what is apparently common knowledge in the import business—J&W is one of those businesses making money selling opium."

Jessica lowered her head. Jacob involved in such a dirty trade? This couldn't be true. "How do we know this isn't just gossip?"

Clearly trying to temper his anger, Caleb glared at her. "Robert would have no reason to lie to me, Jessica."

"All right, it may have some truth, but why would they involve Henry? I'm sure he'll be quite safe." She didn't believe her own words and knew she couldn't allow Henry to leave her side with this new piece of information. Jacob had put her in an impossible situation. She'd have to learn more about this.

"I don't want to argue about this. It's too soon for Henry to know his real father. How do we keep Jacob from telling him? A day would be too much, but you're asking for a whole month."

Her husband didn't see the road ahead as she did. "He can't stay here to work beside you in the shop as Johnathan does. You know Henry balks at being stuck in a small town. Do we wait until he leaves on his own?" The thought of Henry out of her reach brought a lump of sadness to her throat. Her headstrong son was catapulting toward manhood and would soon be gone, and without her protection. Jessica saw the sadness come to Caleb's eyes.

He let out a breath. "I have to think on this."

"Jacob promised he wouldn't say a word about—"

"The boys are back from school," Caleb said. "We'll discuss this tonight." He walked out, leaving her with half a hope and a heavy heart. Jacob and Will were outlaws again, but in a different venue with different merchandise.

The chatter of her boys brought her back to homelife and the caring of her family. She donned her apron and took the remainder of last night's chicken from the icebox for their afternoon snack. Her heart and mind were torn between Caleb's need to remain the patriarch in his son's life and Jacob's need to know the son he had signed away at her request.

Jessica wrote to Jacob, explaining how they would wait a little longer to have Henry visit. She bravely inserted her concerns about his and Will's new trade. *Unless you can guarantee that you and Will have stopped such trade, I will not have Henry exposed to you and his uncle away from our protection.*

It was difficult to write, but she had to do it. Once the letter was sealed and posted, she waited for his reply on tenterhooks. On one hand, she had earned her husband's praise. On the other, she would hear Jacob's scorn.

Indeed, his letter was brief and defensive. He insisted he and Will had not been dealing in the trade she had suggested. He still wanted to see his son. He wrote, *Because I have no legal rights, I am counting on you to have compassion for my side of things.*

He knew exactly how to reach the soft side of her heart.

That afternoon, she and Caleb went back and forth like business partners scratching out a deal. While Caleb made his case against the visit, accusing Will and Jacob of dealing in the opium trade, Jessica continued to make her own case, sighting Jacob's denial of such accusations. The last word was Caleb's. "I'm the head of this household, and I say he doesn't go. That's final, Jessica."

Henry sat down in the chair his father had just occupied. "Father didn't look happy when I passed him just now."

"No, he isn't happy. We have to talk, Henry." Jessica had her boy's attention.

Crossing his limbs, her son prepared himself for another lecture on something he'd done to his brother, or his lack of interest in the homestead, or whatever he could imagine he had done wrong this time. It hurt her heart to see him act this way. Henry was not a farmhand. He never would be. Neither was he artistic. No, his busy mind debated, argued, and sized up every situation. She found it exhausting. Whenever he had to do a chore, he reasoned it could be done more efficiently by hiring a boy from town. "If time is money, then I cost Father much more than a younger boy who would be willing to haul manure for a nickel. Take it out of my allowance. Then everyone will be happy."

Caleb had no patience for Henry's reasoning, and Henry would end up not only having to clean the horse and cow stalls but forgo his allowance that week. "We all have our place here and our responsibilities," his father would remind him. Johnathan was more inclined to do his chores, for his reward was time in the workshop with his father, learning the art of silversmithing.

Just as Jessica was about to speak, Caleb walked in.

"There's no use in it," Caleb warned her.

"No use in what?" Henry asked. His back straightened. He squinted his brown eyes and brushed a strand of sun-kissed dark hair off his brow. He was a handsome boy, better looking than most of his peers. He didn't realize the girls who teased him were begging for his attention. It still confused him. Jessica loved him and Johnathan almost more than she could bear. She was grateful Johnathan wasn't in a hurry to go out into the world.

Caleb poured a glass of lemonade and gave it to his son. "Your mother's cousin, Jacob, wants you to visit him in April. I said no. The subject is closed."

Henry jumped up. "What?"

Jessica reached up and put her hand on her son's shoulder. He had grown several inches taller than her. "Sit down, Henry." Jessica met her husband's smirk with rolled eyes. "He'd like to show you the city and—"

Henry was back on his feet in a flash. "Honest?"

"Yes, honest," Jessica said.

"I told you, it's not going to happen. Go do your school work and forget we ever brought it up," Caleb said. "I need you here on the land."

Henry's shoulders slumped. "Pa, is that all I'm good for to you?"

Clearly chagrined by his son's statement, Caleb softened. "No, of course not."

The temperature in the room was heating up. To Jessica, it was another example of men having a hard time showing their true feelings. She puffed her cheeks in annoyance.

Downcast, Henry walked out of the kitchen and to his bedroom, mumbling just loud enough to be heard. "You can't keep me here for the rest of my life."

Caleb shifted his weight. "You were about to tell him. Why would you do that? I made my feelings clear."

"I know, but what about his feelings? He's right. We can't keep him here forever."

"No, but for God's sake, why are you taking Jacob's side against me? Why believe him and not me?"

Biting her lower lip, Jessica kept her tears at bay. "I'm not taking sides. I don't believe Jacob and Will are going to expose our son to danger. Do you believe they will? And how?"

"Don't be so condescending, damn it!"

She shut her eyes and let out a breath. "I'm sorry. I don't want to argue." She placed a hand on his arm. "Maybe we can have him stay for a week. If it seems odd or uncomfortable for him, he'll know and send us a telegram. If he's doing fine, then he can stay. He's not a child. He knows his own mind. You taught him that."

Placing his hands on his hips, Caleb looked up at the ceiling, then scratched his ear and folded his arms across his chest. "Let me sleep on it."

Before she could hug him, he was out the door. She stood very still. Her love for him was being tested. She longed to have him come back and tell her it was going to be all right, that they may disagree, but he still loved and respected her. After a moment, she turned to the pantry and took out what she needed to make dinner.

THE NEXT DAY AFTER SCHOOL, Caleb gave Henry the news that he'd decided, after much thought and consideration, to allow him to visit Jacob.

Henry's eyes darted around the floor. Jessica saw him calculating and making plans. She knew he was ready to start packing.

"I will send Jacob a letter," Caleb replied shortly.

Henry gave his mother a puzzled look. Caleb cleared his throat and walked out of the kitchen. "Don't start packing just yet, Henry. It's not for another month."

Hearing the front door close, Jessica hugged her son. "I didn't think he'd agree to let you go."

"I can't believe it, either." Henry whooped and picked her up. "I'll be living in the city!"

"Henry!" Jessica laughed, and sadness pricked at her heart.

JACOB RECOGNIZED THE ADDRESS ON the front of the envelope but not the script. Had Henry written himself to let him know Caleb's decision? He carefully opened the letter and went directly to the sender's name—*Caleb.*

Jacob,
I've agreed to let Henry spend three weeks in April with you.
I have no reason to agree to this, but he seems excited, and
Jessica is certain if we don't let him spend time away, he will
eventually leave on his own.
Let me be clear. If he comes back in any way altered from his
good, pure nature, you will answer to me. This is in no way a
time for revelation. Keep your word on that. Arrangements
will be made for you to meet him at the ferry station.
Caleb.

Jacob gave half a laugh. *My God, Cantrell, you're becoming more self-righteous in your old age.* His thoughts quickly went to Henry. *I will have my son with me.* He had to admit, he was a little nervous.

From his office threshold, he shouted, "Donza! Henry's coming in April!" He leaned against the doorframe, still holding Caleb's letter and smiling.

CHAPTER TWENTY-SEVEN

*J*OHNATHAN WAS STUDYING A PIECE OF JEWELRY AT CALEB'S workbench. The shop's natural light, along with the lit lamps, provided enough light for younger eyes, but it was Caleb's dream to install electric lighting someday. Johnathan turned the piece in his hands to see what needed to be done on the wide copper-and-silver wristband.

Several pieces of completed jewelry, small vases, cigarette and cigar cases, platters, and candy dishes for Caleb's customers were neatly laid out on shelves along one wall. Above the long workbench, beads and stones were in boxes near the small tools. Behind him were orders ready to be filled, along with the silver and copper that would shape the pieces. Caleb let Johnathan fashion some jewelry on his own, and he could see the thirteen-year-old was proud to be putting the finishing touches on a piece that might catch a fair price in one of the local shops.

Caleb picked up his own tool and resumed working on a match holder. It would be sent to the engraver as soon as he finished, then sent to one of his most valued customers—a wealthy woman who loved to give presents to her vast array of friends. She, along with many other patrons who appreciated his one-of-a-kind pieces, kept Caleb in business. It was enough for him to have been able to quit Higgins's factory several years ago and strike out on his own.

Like Jessica, he thrived in his artistic passion. Together, they talked about the future, which held the dream of building a center for artist seminars and instruction. If they could only agree on where the building would be and how they would teach their individual skills and techniques to their students. Jessica wanted it closer to the road, while Caleb thought of clearing more trees in the east end of their ten acres. Sometimes Caleb doubted his qualifications to teach, then he'd receive praise for his work. It would bring him around to the thought of sharing his talent to willing, paying participants. First, he would need electricity.

The fair-haired boy looked up at his father, his blue eyes a replica of Caleb's. "Why didn't Cousin Jacob ask me to visit?" he inquired quietly, then continued to hammer the edges of a square, abstract design he would later solder onto the bracelet.

"Your brother is older. Perhaps when you're older, he'll ask you."

"I guess so. Gee, he's only a year older, Pa." He tapped and tapped. "It's all right. I don't really like the city, to be honest. I'd rather go with you this summer up to the reservation." He slumped a shoulder. "I wish Mother wasn't so against it."

Caleb took a soft cloth in his hand and rubbed the match holder. "Well, I'd better not approach her with the idea again. I don't believe you could miss the fireworks it set off."

Johnathan squinted an eye and looked up at his father. "It was pretty loud."

Caleb touched the soft golden hair of his beautiful boy and smiled, then patted him on the back. "Your mother and I still love each other, don't worry. Arguing sometimes makes things clear between a husband and wife, even if it doesn't seem that way."

"But if you haven't spoken, is that the same as arguing?"

Caleb raised his brows. "Sometimes. Be gentle with that piece, John. The final touches have to be done with finesse."

Johnathan tilted his head. "Finesse?"

"Handle each piece delicately, with some thoughtfulness. Art is about being thoughtful, but not overly thoughtful."

"How do I do *that*?"

"Just don't try too hard. Let the piece become what it's meant to become. Do you understand?"

Johnathan became more pensive, then relaxed his hand and tapped in a different manner.

"That's right. Very good, Son."

When Johnathan stopped to take a look at his results, he asked, "Why don't you finesse Mother into letting me go with you?"

Caleb laughed. His son was more cognizant of his parents and their behavior than he had realized. "I guess that's a question I have no answer for, John. It's a very good question. I'll have to think it over."

Under his breath, Johnathan mumbled, "It's better than not talking at all."

"I catch your meaning. Don't worry, it will all work out. Your mother and I always get around to a solution. We have for many years, even before you were born."

Johnathan nodded in relief, then handed his father a tool in anticipation of his next move.

"Thank you," Caleb said as he received the exact tool he needed. "You're becoming very intuitive. Keep it up. It will serve you well." Caleb felt the warmth of love he had for his son. There was so much to teach him. His plan to take Johnathan up north to meet the Klamath people had been met with Jessica's stern refusal. He had argued that she was being overprotective, unreasonable, and fearful. "These are different times, Jessica. He'll be safe with me. You're letting your own experience with the Indians cloud your judgment."

No matter what he said, she would not bend. Her own argument was consistent. "He is too young." The back-and-forth went on longer than Caleb had wanted it to. By the end, he was worn out, and his silence was the only way he could gain his center of peace. It had been three days now, and they still were not talking.

Turning his thoughts back to the present, it gave him great satisfaction that one of his sons would follow in his footsteps and carry on the business. Although he loved Henry, Caleb couldn't forget that he was Jacob's biological son. He respected the path that would eventually lead Henry to where he should be, and in doing so he knew he had to let him go. He had to abandon his hope of the business someday becoming Cantrell *and Sons* Silverworks.

After some thought, Caleb decided to take his younger son's suggestion. He'd have to do some finessing. That night, after the boys were asleep, Caleb finally broke the thick silence.

"I've made a decision."

Jessica looked at him blankly, pretending not to understand.

He pretended not to notice. "Although I have my trepidations about sending Henry to the city, I conceded to let him go. In that vein, I believe you should allow Johnathan to come with me. It will be for the time Henry is away. He can miss a few weeks of school. This will teach him in a different way. I'll hire out the chores, so you will have little to do." He paused but wasn't going to let her interrupt his speech. "It will give you a well-deserved break. I've made up my mind. I'm taking Johnathan with me up north, or both boys stay home." His demand was made, but he felt more equipped to handle silver and stones than his wife.

Jessica's eyes widened in surprise. She stood from her chair and placed the half-knitted stocking on the table beside her. Tilting her head, she brought her lips inside her mouth tightly. Her hands were not on her hips. That was a good sign. Then her eyes misted, and her shoulders relaxed. Bringing her shawl around her chest, she wrapped herself in a hug. His heart softened. *Damn.*

"Very well. Take him with you."

Caleb shifted his weight. He hadn't expected this. "All right then. It's settled."

Jessica looked at him with her big brown eyes.

"I'll take good care of him. Don't worry." He stepped forward and brought his arms out, and she rushed into him. "I'm sorry you still have fear in you, sweetheart," he said as he cupped the top of her head with his hand. "You have to let the boys live their lives."

"I know." She sniffled. "I know."

CHAPTER TWENTY-EIGHT

April 3, 1906

$\mathcal{W}$AITING AT THE COACH STATION, JESSICA TRIED WITH ALL her might to stay strong. Henry was on his way to San Francisco, and it was as if her little boy had just learned to walk, and now he was waddling into uncharted waters without her. She bit her lip so she would not repeat, "Take care of yourself. Send a wire if you need us or if you get homesick."

Caleb was the opposite—calm and in control. He checked Henry's pack and looked at his tickets. "Once we're in Oakland, we can catch a bite to eat."

Henry's eyes lit up. "A restaurant in Oakland!"

Johnathan's mouth twisted, as if he was trying not to cry. The fact that her boys had never been apart added to her melancholy. The scene was almost too much for her. She put her arm around Johnathan's waist, who was now an inch taller than her.

The coach arrived, and after a motherly hug, Jessica, with Johnathan by her side, stepped aside to let Caleb and Henry board. Once settled inside, Caleb stuck his head out the window.

"I'll be back tomorrow morning," he reminded her.

"Are you sure he can ride the ferry alone? Then the omnibus? I just don't know."

Caleb looked exasperated, and she backed off. "I'll be brave," she told him.

As the coach drove off, Jessica took in a ragged breath and walked back to the carriage with Johnathan. "Let's visit Aunt June." A cup of tea with her aunt would soothe her aching heart.

HENRY ENTERED THE FOYER OF the impressive home of his second cousin. He had not seen this type of architecture close-up before. Along with taking the ferry ride across the bay all by himself and then finding the correct omnibus to take, this was another first of many new experiences he was hoping to have. He'd begged and bargained with his parents to let him do this without their or Jacob's help. His father had seemed relieved by not having to meet up with Jacob. Henry had the impression that his father didn't like his mother's cousin nor cared very much for her brother. It was of little consequence to him now. His own life was unfolding in front of him, and he was intent on grabbing every advantage that would offer a broader path to follow. The choices in a small town were limited, and although his parents' art took them away to the cities in the area, Henry was looking to make his own mark on San Francisco, and perhaps beyond.

A bit nervous, but happy to be here, Henry took in the wide dark wood trim surrounding the stark-white walls punctuated with the brightly colored fabric on the bench just inside the doorway. A woven piece of art hung on the wall depicting a tapestry of a city Henry thought might be a place down south. This was very different than anything he'd ever seen. It reminded him of a chapter in school on Mexican textiles and how they are made. What must the rest of this house look like? The terra-cotta tile under him looked inviting, and he wanted to take off his shoes and feel its texture. A woman dressed in a black-and-white uniform came into the foyer.

"I am Marie, the housekeeper. You must be Henry. May I take your coat and suitcase?"

Her thick accent was another layer adding to this new world.

"Yes, thank you."

"He's here, Jacob." A woman's voice from within the house could be heard, and soon Donza was standing in front of him. "How was your trip, Henry?"

Donza was taller than his mother. Her dark eyes, brown skin, black hair, and curvy body were exotic to Henry. She had large lips and big white teeth that gave her a generous smile.

"Good, thank you," he replied, then stretched his neck to look farther into the home.

"Come in, come in," she said. "Jacob will be down soon. He's just finishing up some business. It really never ends, but he has cleared his schedule for you."

Donza's accent wasn't as heavy as Marie's, but it still added to her exoticness. The housemaid took off with his things to a place he was yet to discover.

Henry hardly knew Donza. He had only seen her a few times at Uncle Burt's home. For reasons unknown, his parents stayed away whenever Jacob and Donza came to Clermont City.

Following her, he entered the living space, which was filled with yellows and oranges, greens and blues in designs that pleased him greatly. It felt joyful to him. A large couch was flanked by wood-framed cushioned chairs, square wood tables at their sides. A heavy rock fireplace on the wall in front of the furniture completed the room. Even with all the color, the room felt warm and inviting.

Henry took in every inch of the space. The heavy dark wood

trim continued into this room, accentuating the bright-white walls. The décor was a mixture of new and old worlds, the old world being mostly Spanish, which added a fullness to the lively space of colorful vases and rugs and pictures of ancestors he assumed were Donza's. Most impressive were the electric lamps with large bulbous glass shades dripping with glass lace. It was so different from the country farmhouse he'd grown up in.

"Welcome to our home, Henry," Donza said as she gestured for him to sit down. "We can wait for my husband in here. I hope your stay will be a pleasant one. Are you very hungry?"

Answering her, Henry said, "Father and I ate in Oakland, and Mother packed me some food."

Donza asked him a litany of questions about his school, his brother, if the ferry was on time, and how is the weather in Clermont City. He answered dutifully.

"Thank you for having me," he was finally able to say.

"It's our pleasure."

A little girl came bouncing into the room, breaking the awkwardness, Marie not far behind. She was a slightly built three-year-old. Her hair was dark and wildly unkempt. The little girl stopped in front of Henry, her light brown-green eyes like two round saucers.

"Are you Henry?" she asked.

Henry looked at the adorable child and smiled. "Yes, I'm Henry. Are you Jocelyn?"

"No!" she exclaimed. "I am *not* Jocelyn! My name is Linny!"

Marie rolled her eyes. She spoke calmly but sternly. "Linny, Henry wasn't aware of your nickname, and that was not the proper way to inform him. Please apologize."

Linny bowed her head and looked out from under her extremely long, lush eyelashes. "I'm sorry, Henry," she said, then stuck out her bottom lip, exaggerating a pout. She broke into a laugh, then ran out of the room, yelling, "I'm four!" Marie gave a cluck of her tongue and followed the girl.

"She's quite the little performer these days," Donza said. "She turns four soon, but she's decided she can't wait until her birthday and declares her new age to everyone."

Henry was entertained by his little cousin and wished she had stayed. He fidgeted with his tie.

"He shouldn't be too long now," Donza said, turning to look at the entrance of the room.

Henry nodded as he continued to look around and stir in his seat.

JACOB STOOD BY HIS OFFICE window, watching his son walk up the shrub-lined walkway. He could hardly believe how much the boy had grown. He could have sent his new automobile with a driver to collect the young man, but Jacob wanted to save that surprise for later. He'd learned from Jessica that Henry wanted to arrive all by himself.

This was his chance to show Henry who he was and what life could offer him. Caleb had had his chances, and from what he'd gathered from Will, he had done a fine job. Yet Jacob knew that Henry was not like Caleb and wouldn't settle for a simple home-stead. "Now it's my turn." He went downstairs.

"Henry!" he proclaimed as he entered the parlor.

Henry immediately stood to greet his cousin. "Cousin Jacob, thank you for having me." Before he could utter another word, Jacob's arms were around him in a loving embrace.

"Please, just address me as Jacob. You've certainly grown since I last saw you."

"Yes, it's been a while."

The young man's rigidity after the embrace reminded Jacob to stick to what was familiar to Henry. He had to calm down and continue the act of distant cousin.

"Well, I'll leave you two alone," Donza said.

Only days ago, Jacob was still having to convince her of the benefits of Henry's visit. Even up until last night before bed, the discussion had continued.

"I didn't think the two of you were that close," she had said. "After all, the Cantrells missed our wedding, and they were nowhere to be found at Jocelyn's christening. We barely ever see that part of your family."

"He's a good boy, and without my guidance, he would probably spend the rest of his life in a small uninteresting town or working tirelessly on his father's land. We can help expand his horizons, Donza," Jacob had argued. "And as for our wedding and the christening, I've told you time and again, Jessica is obliged to her husband, who, I imagine, doesn't want her to attend such functions. He's a man with little interest in the outside world, unless it's with the Indians up north. They certainly got under his skin."

"From what your mother has said, he sounds like a well-respected, reasonable man."

"He's . . . different." Jacob fumbled, eager to make his case. "That's beside the point."

"I'm angry that you will take more time to spend with a boy you hardly know than with your own wife and daughter." Before he could answer, she headed to her bedroom. "Never mind. The professor will keep me busy, and I will enjoy outings with my friends."

"As you always do, my dear." With that, Jacob watched the door close behind her. Nothing more was said on the subject. Just now her steely look reminded him of their impasse. He would deal with her later. It was time to be with his son. He had waited too long for this.

"Let me show you up to your room. I think you'll like the view," Jacob said.

He led Henry out of the parlor to a wide, divided staircase in the foyer. Henry stopped to look out from a large square window on the first landing. The late afternoon light shone through, bathing the landing with a soft glow. He commented on the well-groomed land. Jacob turned to answer him, and he took in his son's face. There could be no doubt that he looked like his father. Jacob took great satisfaction in it.

"Jose, our groundskeeper, is a very knowledgeable man. He lives on the grounds in a little cottage in back. You'll meet him. Many homes in this area have interesting gardens. You'll see more as we tour beyond here." The expression on Henry's face was full of anticipation, and Jacob's emotions rose. He took in a breath as he followed Henry up the next set of stairs.

They came to a room at the end of the hallway.

"And this is where you'll be staying. I hope it meets with your approval."

Henry went straight for another window. Jacob stood behind him, his heart full of nerves. He knew his son would enjoy the view of the spectacular city laid out before him in all its glory. Beyond was the bay and its sparkling waters.

"Gosh!" Henry said and turned around, surveying the spacious room.

Jacob had made sure it was just right. With its blue walls and dark trim, it looked elegant and up to the standard he wished to impart to his son. The bed, covered in rich linens of cream and blue, was surely larger than his one back home. A nightstand and lamp stood beside it. There was a generous armoire at one end of the room and a writing table at the other. Beneath their feet, a thick wool rug of oranges and blues covered the wide-planked wood floor. The artwork displayed on each wall was a mixture of different landscapes.

"I hope you approve, Henry," Jacob said.

"Yes, it's glorious!"

"And it's all yours for three whole weeks."

Jacob saw Henry's eyes land on one painting, in particular, of a landscape. "Do you recognize this one?" he asked.

Henry scrunched his nose and looked closer. "One of Mother's?"

"Indeed. I bought it from the gallery in the city. I love the way she—" Jacob stopped, as Henry had turned back to looking at the view.

"When can we go into the city?" he asked.

Jacob saw himself in Henry and longed to show him the world and guide him in his future, helping him to avoid some of the mistakes he had made. Then he recalled that, at one time, he'd thought this healthy and curious young man standing before him may have been one of his biggest mistakes. He swallowed hard against the bitter regret. "Why not tomorrow? We'll take a tour of the city, then to the offices to collect your uncle Will. He and I will treat you to a grand lunch at one of the finest restaurants in the city. How's that for a start?"

Henry smiled broadly, and now Jacob saw Jessica clearly in the boy. It took his breath away.

CHAPTER TWENTY-NINE

*T*HE NEXT DAY, HENRY WOKE WITH A SPARK OF EXCITEMENT. He had slept like a baby in the large bed. After a hardy breakfast, Jacob introduced Henry to his pride and joy—his new two-seater automobile.

"She's a Ford Model C. A doctor in the city owned her, but he had to return to Chicago." Jacob took a cloth from a hook in the stall and polished the side of the shiny black auto. He pointed to its features and then stood back. "Do you know what kind of trouble I would have gotten into if I'd had this baby back in the day?" He chuckled to himself.

Henry was astonished to be standing so close to such a machine. The large cushioned seats looked much more comfortable than his parents' carriage and certainly more comfortable than a saddle. A few people in Clermont City had one similar to this, but he had never seen one up close. Never in his wildest dreams had he thought he would ride in one.

"I'll keep the top off for today. Get in!" Jacob said.

The engine started, and Henry gripped the side of the door as the thing began to move around the stall and out of the entrance. His heart leapt in his chest as they drove down the winding drive and onto the dirt-packed street. The day was sunny, and he squinted to see the road through the glass shield in front of him. As they came closer to the city, the roads made for a bumpy ride, and Henry felt as if he were on a bucking horse. He was glued to his seat as the automobile whizzed down the hill. The warm breeze ruffled his hair, and the houses and buildings moved past him as if his horse were in a full gallop.

Once in the city, the thrill was overwhelming. Jacob darted around pedestrians, horses, bicycle riders, and carts. Henry became dizzy, looking up at the tall buildings as they passed one after another. He tried to focus on the chaotic dance playing out around him while Jacob drove, shouting, "Twenty-five miles an hour!" It was difficult for the young man to take it all in, and he finally just surrendered to it. He laughed, and Jacob joined him as the two reveled in the shared adventure.

Then Jacob drove up one of the steep hills, and Henry felt as if the auto might suddenly flip backward. He held on tight to the handle of the door with his heart in his throat. The machine seemed to defy gravity.

"Can you believe that most of this was flat at one time?" Jacob said loudly as the engine protested its task.

Henry shook his head in wonder as he felt his stomach rebel. This was no time to get sick. He wanted to prove to his cousin he could handle the city life.

Finally, they stopped safely in a place Jacob said was Union Square.

Henry exited the automobile with shaky legs. The impressive statue and stately buildings captured his attention. The statue in the middle of the square was tall and thin, like a giant finger rising out of the earth, and with what looked to Henry like a ballerina in a graceful pose placed on top. They walked around it, and he almost fell over looking up at its splendid detail.

"Gosh!" he exclaimed. Then he looked toward the giant building imposing itself on the landscape as it towered over all the rest. Before he could ask about it, Jacob spoke.

"That is the brand-new St. Francis Hotel. Would you like to have lunch there?"

Henry nodded. He was too overcome to speak.

"Well then, let's go to the offices and get your uncle!"

"Back down the hill?" Henry asked, his heart in his throat.

"Sure!" Jacob grabbed his shoulder. "Don't worry, it's safe enough."

Safe *enough* was not very reassuring, but they arrived unscathed, and Jacob parked the auto in front of J&W Imports.

The storefront of the import company had moved in recent years. It was still located on Market Street but closer to Union Depot in a recently renovated building. Henry saw some newer-looking buildings were followed by a row of houses with bizarre façades. It was as if they had been deliberately pushed together to provide room for even more structures. Some were quite fancy, as if dressed for a party with their colorfully painted exteriors. The whimsical homes contrasted the more serious stone-and-brick business buildings, and Henry wondered about the kind of people who lived within. *How interesting they must all be!*

J&W's showcase room was cool and dimly lit. Henry was in awe of the exotic furniture, textiles, and rugs. An impressive display of beautifully painted dishes was displayed at one end, and at the other stood a variety of vases and household accoutrements arranged in mock parlor settings. His neck stretched one way then the next as he followed Jacob to the staircase. They climbed to the offices on the second floor.

Jacob seemed proud to show off the place where he'd built his business. He turned a switch, and bright light illuminated the room. After his eyes adjusted, Henry surveyed his surroundings. It was simpler than he'd expected, with none of the colorful richness of Jacob's home.

Jacob stood by the large window. "I like my view of the bustling street below," he said. "Commerce."

Henry gave a slight grin. He knew little of that, but it sounded prosperous. The sleek wood furnishings and cabinets reflected the man who inhabited the space, a man Henry already admired for his good taste. He appreciated the style. It spoke to him of the efficiency he was drawn to. He could imagine himself in a similar office, but in law, not imports.

When it came to Will's office, Henry noted Jacob's hesitation. The two men were very different. Perhaps Uncle Will's office was not as tidy. Footsteps could be heard climbing the stairs. "Is he here, Jake?" Will's voice boomed from the stairwell.

"He is," Jacob replied. He and Henry smiled at each other.

"Well, look at you, young man!" Will embraced his nephew. "I think you must have grown a foot since I last saw you."

"It was only last Christmas, Uncle." Henry cheeks heated up.

"So it was. Sorry for not making it over more often. How is your mother enduring all this? She wrote to me saying your father is taking John up north with him."

"She's all right with it, I guess." He decided not to reveal the arguments it had taken for all this to come about.

"She's being very courageous, but she's always been a courageous person."

To Henry, she wasn't very interesting. She doted on him too much and was always wanting to feed him. Besides being a painter, he knew of nothing that required her to be courageous. He merely shrugged.

Will's office was more ornate and cluttered. Henry looked shyly away from a large painting with a risqué subject. The rich furnishings invited one to sit for a spell, appearing to be more of a meeting room than a workspace. A round table at one end with several seats around it looked like a card table. It wasn't a secret his uncle loved to play cards. A small painting on the wall caught his eye. It was one of his mother's watercolors, and his thoughts went to his home, then Johnathan. He wondered how he'd fare on his trip up north to the Klamath Reservation. Feeling a twinge of jealousy at Johnathan's adventure, he reminded himself that this journey suited him better.

"What do you think, Henry?" Will asked. "Not what you expected? Julia and I differed on how I should decorate my office, but as you can see, I won out. Her taste in décor is all over our apartment upstairs, though."

"It's very eke-le-tic," Henry said.

"Eclectic? Well, there you go! I am a decorator after all!"

Henry had nearly forgotten that Will and his wife were renting the upstairs of the building for their home, and now he was very anxious to see what an apartment home in the city was like. "May I visit you and Aunt Julia while I'm here?" he asked his uncle.

"Of course! Let me find out when Julia can arrange things with our cook."

"She still works in Chinatown?" he asked. Henry didn't share the opinions of his aunt and uncle and grandmother about Will's wife. Her efforts to promote healthy conditions in a seemingly hopeless situation baffled his family. Reports of violence and disease were constantly in the newspapers. Henry took his cues from his mother. "She's very valiant to be serving those who have trouble living a good life," his mother always inserted into conversations about Julia. He only knew Aunt Julia as a petite redhead who laughed without much provocation and who loved to talk about her cause "to uplift the poor from their wretched conditions." Henry had been in her company only a handful of times, but she had made an impression on him, not only for her spirited nature but also for her shabby dress. She stood out among his relatives like an urchin. His grandmother had commented once that she was at least clean. Deciding to form his own opinions of her and his cousin and uncle was one of the things Henry felt most grown-up about.

"Let's go to lunch. I'm starving," Will said.

CHAPTER THIRTY

*T*HEY RODE IN A HIRED CARRIAGE, MUCH TO HENRY'S RELIEF. Yet the hill was still as steep, and he held on hoping the horse and driver knew what to do. They stopped in front of the St. Francis Hotel. Entering through one of the gold-and-glass doors of the grand hotel, he felt as if he would burst with amazement, but he held back and straightened up, turning his head patiently as he took in all the splendor. No one knew him here. He could be a grown-up. He could be a wealthy city boy, or … He glanced down at his cotton pants and slightly worn shoes and grimaced.

Gold was everywhere, from the trim on the banisters of the sweeping marble staircases to the ceiling and chandeliers. Giant potted palms dwarfed him as he walked past them. The decorated ceiling held his attention until he nearly missed walking into one of the many wood-trimmed leather chairs in the lobby. The dining area with hanging golden cauldrons filled with draping ferns and gilded moss held its own rich ambiance, and Henry again found himself drawn to the ceiling. Its opulent glow came from enormous, brightly lit, crystal chandeliers.

The sharply dressed maître d' escorted the trio to their table as if he'd been expecting them. Quiet conversations created a humming sound. Henry felt as if he were in some sacred place, though his aunt and grandmother would have adamantly disagreed. His mind was soon changed as he looked around at the fashionably dressed patrons. He saw a variety of feathers, including the elegant peacock ones coming from a woman's hat and clothing. Some of the men wore bold striped ties, and their straw hats lay conspicuously on the tables. A few women held long elegant cigarette holders. A slight aroma of alcohol permeated the air like a spray of perfume through a cloud of tobacco smoke. His confidence waned in this place meant for adults as he trailed his cousin, who walked with an air of ownership through the restaurant. They sat down with no one giving the young man a second look.

Henry relaxed. The scene around him was impressive, and the ease with which Jacob and his uncle moved among the well-to-do guests told Henry that this was commonplace for them. Someday, he'd be just like them. The stories he'd managed to get out of his mother and Uncle Will, or overhear as a child about these two men, didn't seem to match their present-day personas. Today, they wore morning coats over buttoned waistcoats layered over high-collared shirts tucked into crisply pressed trousers. It was nothing like the rugged clothes he imagined they had once worn in their days on the trails. He adjusted his soft woolen coat and made sure he had closed the top button of his off-white cotton shirt. Then he smoothed his parted hair and cleared his throat.

Jacob smiled at him. "What say we get you some new duds while you're here?" he suggested.

Henry stopped fussing and smiled back. "Yes, I'd like that!" He looked over at his uncle, thinking of the stories of his and Jacob's past. They must have been exaggerations. How was it that these two men were ever on wilderness trails, and as he'd once overheard, gunrunners? Then he remembered his father's words just before he'd boarded the ferry. "If you can't tell me about everything you did when you get back home, then you know you shouldn't be doing it." *There's something I don't know.* Henry hated not knowing. His aunt called him a "busybody," and his mother told him he had an exasperating curiosity, but all Henry ever wanted was to know the truth about the world. Maybe he'd get to know the truth about Jacob and Uncle Will before this visit was over, some secret nugget about their younger days that he could take home with him. Uncle Burt would be proud, his great-uncle being the only member of the family who encouraged him to become a lawyer. Henry decided he'd make this a game. He'd have to ask the right questions.

A woman breezed by their table, taking Henry's attention away from his thoughts. She wore a flowing tight-waisted dress and a hat that took up too much space above her head. It was adorned with feathers and lace and long strands of pearls wrapped around a gauze-like fabric that billowed from all sides. He thought he even spied a small bird inserted in the brim. Her perfume lingered in her wake. When he turned around, Will and Jacob were looking at the curious boy with amusement. He shrugged his shoulders, and they laughed.

Will brought his napkin to his lap. "It's funny what women will wear these days, when the only thing a man wants to see is—"

"Will," Jacob said, low and sharp.

Will cleared his throat. "Well, let's see what looks good today." He opened his menu. "Do you like salmon, Henry?"

Henry nodded but was still preoccupied with his surroundings. He turned to his company. "The candleholders alone must be worth a pretty penny! Are they real gold?"

"They're not, but they're pretty good replicas. We get them in the store, and they sell out as fast as we put them on the floor," Will remarked, still looking at the menu.

"When can we see the rest of the city?" Henry asked eagerly.

"Impressive, isn't it?" Jacob asked.

"Yes, very!"

Two young women went by their table, and his attention was once again taken away. One of them winked at him suggestively, and he quickly turned back in his seat, his cheeks warm.

"You better be careful, Henry. Women fall quite easily for a handsome lad like yourself," Will advised. "It will get you into more trouble than you can imagine. Stay clear of women."

"Will, for God's sake, don't put ideas into his head," Jacob said.

Henry could feel his face become hotter. Embarrassed, he drank some of the water the waiter had poured into their glasses.

"Come now, let's talk about what we can do and see in these coming days. Do you like museums, Henry?" Jacob offered.

"Yes. I mean, those without lots of boring paintings in them."

"Bravo!" Will said, then once again turned to his menu. "What's this? The special today is swordfish? How the hell did they get that? I may have to try some. I hope it's fresh!"

Henry perused his own menu and saw his favorite—spaghetti and meatballs. Soon, his stomach was growling and his mind was on food.

"We could all do some exploring after lunch," Jacob suggested, "though I'm afraid you might fall in love with this city and never want to go home." He winked.

"I'll have to return to the office, I'm afraid," Will said. "You'll have to go without me."

"I thought Miss Stone was doing the ordering today. Did you get those orders from Canada squared away?"

"Yeah, but I still don't understand why the hell they want us to supply them with English tea towels!"

"I told them to buy from us. They'll still make their profit, and we'll make ours."

"That explains it. What about the silk from China? I had two patrons ask about it yesterday..."

Henry could only listen as the two men talked of business in the adult world. He couldn't wait until he was old enough to have something worthwhile to add to a conversation.

JACOB TRIED NOT TO STUDY his son, yet he wanted to watch his every movement, wanted to know his every thought. After they returned to the store with Will, he and Henry got back into the auto. Henry gave a noticeable wince.

"I'll drive like a little old man," Jacob said with a chuckle.

Jacob showed him more of the city, then up the hill again to some of the wealthier parts where stately houses bordered groomed streets. One house in particular caught Henry's eye.

"That one looks like a dollhouse," he said as they slowly moved along.

Stopping to take a better look, Jacob steered around to the other side of the street where the house stood. A row of hedges had recently been trimmed to reveal a cobblestone driveway and entrance to the house. It was still a grand lady. Jacob had passed it occasionally.

"Your mother lived here once. Did you know that?"

He watched Henry's eyes practically bulge out of his head. "Really?"

Jacob wasn't sure why, but he wanted his son to know more about the past, perhaps a prelude to the truth about his parental lineage. He was certain that Jessica had kept many of the years before Henry's birth a secret from the boy. Jacob loathed secrets. Although he carried his share of them, they were a burden to him now, and he had been careful over the years not to add more. His love for Jessica remained entangled in his mind. There was never a place to put those feelings. Somehow, he might reconcile them by getting to know his son.

They exited the auto and examined the house. Henry put his hand to his chin.

"I can't see Mother living here. Who was it with? Mr. Moore?"

"Ah, so she's told you she was married and divorced before she and your father met." Jacob wiped his brow. "What else did she tell you?"

"She didn't tell *me* anything. I heard her talking with Aunt June one day, and they mentioned Frederick Moore. Uncle Will told me later about him and the trial and Mr. Moore going to jail for manslaughter. Uncle Burt and I have discussed at length the differences between manslaughter and murder and all the degrees of murder. I find it very interesting, don't you? I'd love to know all the particulars of this case, but no one wants to tell me."

"The finer points of the law never were that interesting to me. This case is one for you to explore when you're much older, Son."

He'd called Henry *son*. Jacob reminded himself that a boy Henry's age was often called "*son*" by older men, but with his heart in a lurch, he decided it was time to return home.

"I've never come this close to a criminal's house, and one accused of murder, er, manslaughter!"

Jacob was relieved he hadn't minded or even noticed being called *son*.

On the way home, Henry's curiosity bubbled over. "Why did we stop at that house, Cousin Jacob?" he asked, raising his voice above the chugging of the auto's engine.

"Oh, I don't know. I thought you might want to see it."

"What was the trial like? Was Mr. Moore involved in criminal activities? How did he kill the man? How did he do it?"

Jacob pulled the vehicle to the side of the road where he could talk to his son. He let the sweeping territorial view be an excuse to stop.

"It's a beautiful sight, isn't it, Henry? With so much land to still be developed, this area will be even greater than it is now."

Jacob looked out onto the vastness of it, and he felt as if it represented the vastness of his son's life—open and ready to place his mark on it.

"What about Mr. Moore, Cousin Jacob?"

"Well, he got away with most of his cheating until the day it all caught up with him. I suppose you could say that the law catches up with wrongdoers eventually."

"But why did it take a murder to finally catch him and bring him to justice? It may have saved that man's life. It's not fair!"

"Henry, the law is on this side," Jacob said with his right hand open, "and fairness is on this side," he concluded with his left hand open.

"I don't understand."

"You're in good company," Jacob said with a laugh.

"Well, maybe I can help change that. I believe the laws need to be stricter! I want to bring order and justice to all the people!" Henry proclaimed.

"Good for you, Henry." Jacob patted his son's back. "I know you will succeed at whatever you set your mind to. It's the Stanford way."

Henry tilted his head. "You mean the Cantrell-Messing way?"

Jacob caught himself again. "Yes, yes, of course. Messing, Stanford, Cantrell . . . you're a part of it all. So, what does your father tell you about life, Henry?"

"Father says to be true to who you are, be kind and helpful to others, and always look for the artistic side in yourself no matter what you're doing," Henry recited.

Jacob grinned. "That's very well stated. I'd like to add to that, if I may?"

"Yes."

He had Henry's full attention, and he saw the years roll away. He swallowed the lump in his throat. "I would say be successful in everything you do, or pretend to be anyway, until you are. Success will give you a sense of self-worth, monetarily as well as personally."

"Were you successful on the trails?"

Jacob rubbed his chin. "That depends. Success can take on many meanings. I stayed alive, and that made me feel successful."

"I heard you and Uncle Will were gunrunners."

"Jesus, Henry, who told you that?"

"I listen. Is it just a family folktale?"

The expression on Henry's face told Jacob that his son was searching for the truth, and he couldn't deny him that. "Yes, it's true. I'd like to tell you that it was dangerous and wrong, but the fact is, your uncle and I had some pretty exciting times, and I'd never take back any of them." Jacob felt he had said enough. He changed the subject. "Well, young man, there is plenty in life to explore before you set your mind on one path."

Jacob turned the auto around and headed down the road and back home. "It's been a long day, and I don't know about you, but I'm getting hungry again. Let's get back to the house."

Henry agreed, and Jacob could see the wheels turning in his son's head.

That night at supper, Henry quizzed Jacob.

"What did you learn when you were young and in the wilderness, Jacob?"

"Ay," Donza chirped. "This isn't the best supper talk, Henry. Let's keep that discussion between you and Jacob for later, perhaps."

"I'm sorry," he said sheepishly.

"Donza is correct, but we'll get around to it, Henry," Jacob said and gave the boy a wink.

HENRY LAY IN BED THAT night thinking about his day. The movement of the auto was still in his system, and it made him restless. It had been unnerving to him at first, but now he was ready for more. He also wanted more information about his uncle's and cousin's adventures. He had a feeling his father might have been involved. The pieces were fragments, and his curiosity was left unsatisfied. His thoughts went to Frederick Moore, and he pretended he was the prosecuting attorney for the city. He launched into a brilliant speech of "justice having been awarded to the people of San

Francisco in this criminal case." He raised his arm from outside his covers in his declaration. "The world is now safer, thanks to such a worthy judgment from the jury!" he proclaimed in whispered drama. It was delicious, and he fell into a deep sleep while prosecuting the guilty and defending the innocent.

CHAPTER THIRTY-ONE

*O*NLY DAYS AGO, SHE WAS SAYING GOODBYE TO HENRY, AND now Jessica waved goodbye to Johnathan and Caleb, as she watched the stagecoach amble out of the station. The dust from the dry earth clouded the large, spoked wheels as the coach made its way down the street. It turned the bend and disappeared.

Walking back to her carriage, she was alone for the first time in many years. Heading home, she realized she had few responsibilities for several weeks. A familiar lightness entered her mind and body, one she recognized from long ago when she was young, before Caleb, before Frederick Moore, even before Jacob.

When she arrived home, a hired stable boy took charge of the horse and carriage. Jessica entered her home, clean from Hannah's work that morning. The homey scent of bread fresh from the oven greeted her. Alongside the bread, she found a tray of cinnamon cookies. *Oh, Hannah, you spoil me!* She could eat as much of both as she wanted. The cold beef and cheese from last night would make for a simple meal later in the early evening. A smiled crossed her face. She would sit on the porch and enjoy her own little picnic.

With only a slight stab of guilt, she grabbed a tall glass of cool tea and one of the cookies and headed to her art studio—her own standalone building next to Caleb's workshop. She had opened the windows earlier in the day, and a breeze had taken some of the heat out. Two commissioned paintings waited for her final touches. Three watercolors ready for delivery to the Talbot Gallery. Mr. Talbot's son, Geoffrey, only accepted her watercolor scenes. Jessica liked Geoffrey Talbot but sorely missed her friend and mentor. She felt she hadn't visited him as much as she would have liked. His peaceful death last year grieved her. He had been so instrumental in helping her become a prosperous artist. His wife was aged as well, and she knew Mrs. Talbot would soon be with her husband.

Today, her thoughts wandered to the day they rode up to Oakland together to visit the Gates Gallery. It had been her first real introduction to a city gallery where like-minded artists held monthly exhibits. The city had been teeming with activity, and it had excited her to no end. Thanks to Mr. Talbot, her dream of having her art in the Gates Gallery had come true. Though it had changed hands over the years, she was welcomed at every monthly exhibit, where she would display three of her pieces in the same theme. Lately, it had become more of a chore than a delight and with marginal profitability. She had let her membership lapse, and it had been a bittersweet choice.

Today, 1887 seemed like a lifetime ago. The art she did now was for a few galleries and commissioned pieces, which kept her as busy as she wanted to be. Dabbling in post-impressionist art was her new direction, and she loved the techniques she was learning. Realism had always been her friend and foe. This new technique was looser but still conveyed the truth in her art that she strived to bring forth. Teaching young artists in town was also something that enlivened her life.

Along with the Billingston Gallery, Jessica brought in enough income to keep her bank account full and add to the household budget. However, her dream of showing in large galleries in New York City, Chicago, and her hometown of Hartford, Connecticut, had fallen short. So far, her entries had only been accepted in small galleries in Boston and one in Hartford. Shipping her best pieces to them on a regular basis, however, made her proud to share her work with those on the East Coast, especially her birthplace. A friend of her mother's had recently written how surprised she was to see a local girl's artwork make it into a gallery in busy downtown Hartford. Jessica smiled. "A local girl" at her age!

The heat in the studio stopped her from pressing forward with her work. Jessica touched her watercolor brushes, then scanned the squares of paint arranged by color on one table and her tubes of oils on a smaller table near her easel. Glancing around the studio, she saw what needed to be done.

Less inspired than she thought she would be, she moved outside into the warm air. Suddenly feeling a surge of energy, Jessica decided to walk down to the river. The field would be open and hot, so she stopped by the house to get her wide-brim hat and another cookie. Besides a few hired hands for outside work, she was alone at the homestead.

Jessica strolled serenely to the waters with her snack and her memories. The memories of her kidnapping, even after all these years, still remained in her, tainting the place she'd once loved without apprehension. The place where memories collided. Where she'd first felt feelings for Caleb and knew he might feel the same. The picnic above the river's edge where he'd tried, unsuccessfully, to kiss her for the first time. The walks they'd shared there, the discussions of the future before they'd married.

Then, Blue Heron taking her from her life, and the day she had to say goodbye to Jacob after their long journey to get her back home again while their child, her beautiful Henry, grew inside her. The world would never look the same. The innocence of life had been grabbed from her that day in May with the shocking force of a man grabbing her by the waist and fleeing with her to unknown regions. Now the river had come to symbolize the strength she had and the courage she would carry with her. The sharp edges of her remembrances had worn down, but today she felt them more acutely. She was alone, and it stirred up some fear. She talked to herself about the safety of her surroundings now, and the feeling vanished.

Waving a fly away, she sat on the bench Caleb had made many years ago and listened to the world at the river's edge. Looking east, she contemplated the dense forest now. Perhaps a barn for instruction and seminars would fit well there. Smiling, she looked forward to Caleb's reaction at her agreeing with his plans. With a deep breath, she found her peace.

She thought of her husband and son now on the reservation, a mysterious place to her. It felt as if Caleb had another life away from his home and family. The feeling invaded the sultry afternoon. It always disturbed her to think of him finding something, or perhaps someone, to feed his soul beyond what she could give him. When he returned from the reservation, refreshed yet somewhat sad and contemplative, it took him days to come back to his life with her. How long would it take this time?

Today, she wanted to bury those thoughts. Her own attachment to Jacob gave her little justification for her jealousy. She gave a soft laugh and wondered how she was going to resist the temptation to travel into San Francisco to see how Henry was getting along.

CHAPTER THIRTY-TWO

*W*ATCHING HIS SON, WHO WAS BESIDE HIMSELF WITH excitement, Caleb smiled. He recalled how excited he'd been when his own father had taken him to new places.

"Father, when does the train go through a tunnel?" Johnathan asked, his blue eyes brighter than ever.

"It won't be for a while, Son."

"Oh. Will we see the mountains soon?"

"Johnathan, we've barely left the station."

"I know, I know, but how long will it take to get to Red Bow's after that?"

"We've been over this before, John. It's going to be a long trip, so you might as well settle in and enjoy the travel. It's part of the journey."

"Well, all right." He sat back but not all the way. "I bet Henry will be sore about not coming with us!" he chirped. "He's missing all *this!*" His hand flung to the window as the landscape went past them.

Caleb unfolded his newspaper. "I think your brother may be too taken with the city to give it any thought."

"I can't wait to swim in the lake."

"It'll still be quite cold, but you're welcome to try."

"What do you think Ma is doing without us?"

Caleb wondered the same thing. He had a feeling she would visit Henry at some point. It disturbed him that she would not leave her son—or Jacob—alone. His jealousy sat with him like a spoiled child, always nagging, never satisfied. Another question from Johnathan took him out of himself.

"Are we going to have a ceremonial dance?" he asked with a scrunched nose.

Caleb handed his son part of the newspaper. "Here . . . read!"

AFTER THEY LEFT THE TRAIN, Caleb and Johnathan took another stagecoach to a small outpost near the Klamath Reservation. The father and son walked the rest of the way, about a quarter of a mile. Before entering the village, Caleb decided they would camp for a few days in the woods nearby to give Johnathan a real taste of the wilderness. Their own acreage was too familiar to his son.

After a few nights, however, the boy had had his fill of the howling coyotes, threats of bears, and the relentless mosquitos and ants, not to mention the giant buck that just about made him jump out of his skin when he went into the woods one evening to relieve himself.

As they headed into the village, Johnathan could barely contain his curiosity. "This is a village of houses. Where are the teepees? Can we go inside one? I hope so! What will we eat?"

"John, we'll get to all that soon enough. Let's find my friend first." Caleb thought he had schooled his sons on life on the reservation, but apparently John's views were mixed up with those of his schoolmates' narrow views of Indians. Caleb hoped this visit would enlighten him and he'd pass his new knowledge along.

Caleb's reunion with Red Bow who was once named Strong Bow, Soaring Feather's eldest son, was heartfelt. They were like two brothers coming together after a long absence.

Johnathan soon peppered Red Bow with more questions. Knowing they wouldn't have a proper visit unless the boy was busy, the men released him into the care of Red Bow's neighbors, Sows Seeds and Kaley Sanders. Their children, along with others around his age, had gathered in anticipation of Caleb's arrival.

"He's a bright boy, Caleb," Red Bow said. "He looks so much like you, I thought I had been sent back to another time. You were older than he when we met, but still a young man."

"He may be my image, but he won't imitate my life if I have anything to say about it." Caleb watched Johnathan reluctantly follow one of the children.

"Yes, the young ones have it easier these days, but I still worry for mine."

They sat on benches at a wooden table outside of Red Bow's modest timber home. The scents of spring grass and green-leafed black cottonwoods mingled with the freshness of the lake's clean waters. A firepit for cooking was in the middle of the open area in front of them. The hills in the distance suddenly reminded Caleb of the time he'd crossed from Colorado to Oregon. He absently rubbed his scarred shoulder. A sweet breeze took the memory from him, whisking it back to the time where it belonged.

The community buzzed with activity. The other wood houses were similar to Red Bow's, with a low and long structure. Beyond the home was a shop, and Caleb hoped Red Bow would share his latest silverwork with him. It was Red Bow he'd first learned the craft from. Back in those days, Caleb was eager to take in as much knowledge and skill as he could. Besides felling trees for the tribe's lumber mills, he worked hard to learn the craft of silversmithing.

"Each time I come up here, something new has been added." He pointed to a larger building with a sign on it. "I see the medicine man has his own clinic now."

"Yes, we are very grateful he works well with your government's medicine man."

Red Bow looked in the distance then came back to Caleb. "I never will forget the time you walked into the reservation."

Caleb said with a half laugh, "I had no idea where I was. I was barely nineteen and starving."

Beatrice came out of the house with her arms laden with food. "Did someone say they were starving?"

Caleb was very pleased to see Red Bow's wife, and he rose to embrace the woman. How little she now resembled the young robust white woman who had decided to marry an Indian man. Her thinner frame and the creases in her face revealed her hard life, but her eyes were cheerful and bright, and her contentment was plain to see. He couldn't help thinking of Jessica and the life she would have had if she hadn't been rescued from the renegade Indians. Jacob crossed his mind as well. He resented that he not only owed Jacob his life, but Jessica's, too.

Beatrice stared up at him. "You've come back to us, Caleb. You look very well."

"It's good to be here. You are also looking well, Beatrice." He helped her place fruit, flatbread, dried meats, and goat's milk on the wooden table.

"He's his father's son!" Beatrice exclaimed, seeing Johnathan playing in the common area with the other children.

Caleb smiled with pride and yearned for Soaring Feather to see him. He would present the boy to his elder mentor—Johnathan would be meeting a real warrior.

Beatrice settled in and asked Caleb how he was doing in his world.

"I'm doing well. I'm quite content. Life, as you know, Beatrice, has its hardships. I endure."

She nodded in agreement. "As we all do."

"I am glad to return to this village. It brings me peace."

"There is always a place for you here, Tall Wheat."

Caleb smiled. He liked his Indian name given to him many years ago when he had stumbled onto the camp after escaping his life as a gofer to a band of outlaws. Sitting across from Red Bow today, he felt gratitude for this beautiful place near the Klamath Lake and the friends he had here. After finishing a bit of bread and cheese, he asked about his mentor Soaring Feather.

"I want to show off my son to him," he said with pride.

Red Bow lowered his head. "Yes, our father would have been very pleased with you, Tall Wheat. We knew you were coming, so we waited to tell you. It's been four months now. A bad cough. His lungs could not breathe. One day, he walked to the lake and washed his face in the cold water. I followed at a distance. He was not steady on his feet. He returned to his home, and I left for mine. The next day, when his helper found him, his spirit had already left his body."

Caleb felt the past fly into his mind. His first impression of the Klamath chief had been a mixture of fear and awe. He sat in a large teepee on a low wooden bench, a fur robe over his shoulders, his long, skin-wrapped braids draped on his chest. His voice had been soft yet strong when he'd asked Red Bow, "Who have we here? Where does he come from?" After proving himself as a strong worker and ready learner, the tribe under Soaring Feather's approval took Caleb in, until the day he had to leave and seek out his own home and his own tribe. Those were some of the best years of his life, and now he yearned to have one more visit with the "father" who'd taught him so much.

Tears welled in Caleb's eyes. He let them drop down his cheeks as he grasped Red Bow's outstretched arm. "His spirit will live inside me forever. I feel your loss, my friend."

"The village feels it, too, but we have been a great comfort to one another. We celebrated the life of a good, brave, and wise man."

They chewed slowly on the food Beatrice had brought, and after a long silence, Red Bow asked about his other son.

"And what of your son Henry? He is not with you."

"Henry decided he'd rather spend time in the city with my wife's cousin and brother."

Red Bow nodded. "He is on his own quest?"

"I suppose, but it isn't one I approve of. It was Jessica's idea."

"Ah, there's a story behind your words—I can see it in your eyes. We will talk tonight when the darkness hushes the land and the stories come out of us more easily."

"I'm afraid this story is not one that comes out of me easily in any light," Caleb replied.

Red Bow nodded, and they talked of other things. "How is the tribe getting along?" Caleb asked.

"We have lost two elder members since my father's passing. We were without a strong leader for a time. The government was our only leader, and we quickly had our elections. I was named to succeed my father for our village. Feeling the weakness of our position was hard. It was a confusing time. I and others were able to help our people through that time. Within these borders, we are a strong tribe again."

"I'm sorry for your losses. I know Soaring Feather is proud of you, Red Bow. I am proud of you also. Our government's interference in Indian affairs has always troubled me."

"*Your* government, my friend." Red Bow cocked an eyebrow. "But the land is good, and we have little trouble here with other tribes. We make the most of it. We have done well with logging and other enterprises. I have become a businessman instead of a silversmith. But I still make jewelry when I have the time. Beatrice sells it for me in town. It is good to keep it going. I find pleasure in it."

Caleb ached with nostalgia for days gone by. Time was a thief who never looked back.

That night, Red Bow, Beatrice, their three sons, and several of their neighbors sat in a circle around a large stone firepit. The house was better suited for company, but Red Bow wanted to give Caleb's son a taste of ceremony. The elders drank the hearty wine while the children drank fresh berry juice. They all enjoyed the banquet of food the tribe's women had prepared. Rabbit stew, fresh vegetables, baskets of nuts, baked bread and cakes topped with fruits. It was a time of plenty with the spring harvest. They all sat on animal pelts around the low flame of the fire, telling stories of the past, including Caleb's time with the tribe. The familiar faces cheered Caleb. They chanted, "He was kind and a good worker. He was different and had a hard time learning the language. He nearly lost his life when a tree he was felling went the wrong way. He and Meadow were good together. The children loved to braid his long blond hair. He learned the art of silver crafting. It is good he has made a living from it."

With the mention of Soaring Feather's niece, Meadow, Caleb's heart lurched. He didn't see her tonight or the last time he had come to visit. She had been his steady companion when he joined the tribe. He'd wanted to take her with him when he decided to leave the village, but it was forbidden and he knew it. The parting was bittersweet, and he held a special place in his heart for her. He hoped he could see her while he was here.

Caleb went to sit beside Johnathan. "I heard you had some matches of strength with a few of the boys."

"I handled the bow as well as you taught me, but they are all so much better than me. And some of the games with the hatchet and knives were hard." He lowered his head. "I felt foolish."

Red Bow's youngest son, Jay, a boy the same age as Johnathan, spoke. "You did well, Rushes," he said. Then, in a whisper, Jay added, "Those boys are getting ready for their quest, and they have been practicing for hours each day."

"Rushes?" Caleb asked.

"It's the name they gave me. I guess I rush too much. I have to take more time to think before acting."

Caleb patted his back. "It's a good lesson to learn." In fact, it was a lesson he was forever trying to teach both of his sons. Maybe others would have to teach his sons now. His journey as a father felt as if it was coming to an end. It saddened him, and at the same time, he knew there was much more to experience with Henry and Johnathan. He liked seeing his son through the eyes of his Klamath family.

To Johnathan's delight, a teepee had been erected for him and Caleb to stay in. It was filled with pelts and warm blankets. That night, the sound of Johnathan's gentle, rhythmic breathing told Caleb his son was sleeping soundly. He himself had a harder time falling asleep. He had to admit, he missed his bed. *You're getting soft, Cantrell.* He brought another pelt underneath him. He thought of Henry and how he was on his own quest—different than a tribal quest but a quest all the same. What knowledge would he take from his visit in the city that he could use as he grew into a man? In Caleb's opinion, not much. Then his mind wandered to Meadow. Red Bow said she would welcome him tomorrow.

EACH TIME HE SAW MEADOW, his fondness for her and her beauty grew. She was unlike the women he had known. Her waist was not bound by corsets. Her curvaceous figure held its own shape. Her dark hair was not drawn up in a neat bun above her round face. Instead, it was allowed to flow freely or in long braids. She had a glint in her almost-black eyes as if a light shone from the inside of her, peeking out from her pupils. Although she had grown taller since her youth, she still only came up to the middle of his chest. Each time he saw her, he wanted to pick her up as he had when she was a girl and hug her until she cheerfully begged him to put her down. Those days of abandon were behind them, and he now greeted her with guarded respect. Tonight, he wanted those days back, and he wondered why.

She had become a widow with two children. Her husband had been killed by a lone army soldier who had fled from his ranks. It was said, in his fear, the soldier had shot the unarmed Indian before he could even speak or defend himself. Since then, she had remained alone but surrounded by her people. Her sons were young men now. She was a grandmother, yet in spite of the title, she remained as youthful as ever to him. They stood in her doorway.

"Hello, my Meadow," Caleb said.

"Hello, Tall Wheat." She placed her hand in his. "It is good to see you." They embraced, and she led him into her modest dwelling, a two-room home filled with adornments reflecting a lifetime spent among her people. They sat on the soft sheepskins in front of the open fire, its clay-and-mud surroundings giving off a blanketing warmth. There they talked of the past and of the present, leaving the future to itself. The lust he'd once felt for her began to surface. He longed to touch her, to caress her smooth skin. Did she still want him? She made supper for them, and they ate well in comfortable silence. With a cup of wine each, they went back to the sheepskin and woven rugs, blankets and pillows stuffed with horsehair. Caleb felt at home.

"Tell me about your homestead," she asked.

"It's grown. It's about four times the size of your cabin."

"Ay! That is something. And your business?"

"That too has grown. I love what I do, and I have your uncle Red Bow to thank for that. I have much to be thankful for from all of you."

Her smile was welcoming, and he felt a twinge of guilt for being with her like this. He told himself she was different. Their relationship was different. It didn't belong to the outside world. The sun was setting and the village quieting. The crack and pop from the burning wood filled the room. The aroma of it filled Caleb with nostalgia.

"I must go," he said. He unlocked his crossed legs and stood with a moan.

She looked up, and he offered her his hand. They laughed at their bodies not being so agile as when they romped the forest together and played in the lake on hot summer days or sat for hours in each other's company without the pain on rising.

"You will stay with me tonight."

He laughed and cupped her face. "Is that so?"

"Yes, it is so. Beatrice will care for your son. Each time you come to see us, to see me, we part as friends. I want it to be different this time. We will part as lovers."

Caleb felt his growing need to lie in her arms and feel her smooth body next to his.

"You were always a bossy one," he said.

She became serious and took his hand and brought him to lie down on her bed in the other room of her cabin.

The smell of her flesh, the touch of her hands on his body sent Caleb into another realm. He made love to her as if he were a youth in his sexual prime.

CHAPTER THIRTY-THREE

San Francisco—April 17, 1906

$\mathscr{T}$HE DAYS WERE PASSING TOO QUICKLY FOR HENRY. HE HAD been shown the city in all directions and still wanted more. Jacob spared no expense on his new clothes or the places they dined. Today, he would spend time at J&W Imports. Henry would help with paperwork while he took care of other business.

Jacob left the building, handing him over to Miss Stone, the secretary. Henry followed the older heavyset woman to her small office. She went to her desk and handed him a stack of thin yellow papers and asked if he would organize them alphabetically by the names of the companies. Henry stared at her as if he were being asked to wash the floor.

"I don't know if this is what my cousin had in mind," he said.

"Mr. Messing?" she called out into the hall.

His uncle came into her office. "Yes, Miss Stone? Is Henry here asking to take over your job?"

She smiled broadly, then looked at Henry. "I think he'd rather be doing something else."

"I see." Will squinted one eye and smirked. "Jacob thought this would be good for you. I think he's trying to show you all sides of the business. But this is not a man's job, and I have something better in mind. I have a pickup this morning. Won't take long, then we can go get some pastries. I've been dying for a peach Danish!"

Henry's excitement for this new adventure dwindled when he found himself at the foul-smelling docks of the city among a few unsavory sorts. They had straggly beards and shabby clothes and stunk of rotting fish, body odor, and alcohol. Henry took a few steps back and brought a finger to his nose. He suddenly felt unsafe. One of the men handed Will a thick paper bundle tied with a string, which he quickly tucked into his coat. In exchange, his uncle gave the man a small wooden box. Then the men hurried off down the planked pier and into a rickety boat. Back in the carriage, Henry watched Will, who said nothing of what just happened. This wouldn't do.

"What was that?" he asked.

Will chuckled. "The other side of business. Nothing to be concerned about. I know Jake wants you to see the life of success and the advantages it can offer, but this is the real side of success, and it isn't always pretty."

Henry nodded. "What did he give you, and what did you give him?"

Taking a flask from his coat, Will unscrewed the cap and took a quick swig. "I do a little trading and selling on the side."

"Oh." Henry looked out the window as the carriage made its way back into the city. The smell of the men had gone, but not the smell of alcohol.

Will smiled, and Henry saw a different side of his uncle. "Why did you take me along? That didn't look legal."

"Sometimes, my boy, one has to deal outside the law to get ahead," Will said with a chuckle. "Besides, I get bored with everyday life. Need a little excitement once in a while."

"Does Jacob know?"

Another chuckle, and Will peered out the window. "Nope. He's far too clean and civilized for that now. He's got plenty to hide himself, though."

The bitterness in Will's voice startled Henry. "Are you mad at Cousin Jacob?"

"No, of course not. I love him like a brother. Doesn't mean we don't disagree like brothers."

"Did you disagree on the trails?"

"We sure did. If it weren't for a matter of life and death, we'd still be out there discussing going east or west." He laughed and shook his head. "Rescuing your mom was the toughest time between him and me. Thought we'd be done for sure."

Henry's pulse raced. "How? Why?"

"Now don't you get me talking about all that. Safe to say, it all turned out fine in the long run for us, and someday you'll have to figure out if it did for you, too."

"For me?" Henry asked.

The carriage stopped in front of J&W Imports. Without answering Henry, he hopped onto the side of the street.

"I think we'll have to take a rain check on that Danish. Maybe tomorrow. Come in and wait for Jacob. I need to take care of this." He patted his coat pocket and disappeared into the store. Henry followed and watched as his uncle climbed the stairs to his office. Confused and disheartened, he sat on one of the display chairs and waited for Jacob to return.

Henry said nothing about his unusual morning with his uncle. He had a dirty secret, and it weighed heavily on him, putting a blemish on a near-perfect visit.

CHAPTER THIRTY-FOUR

April 18, 1906—5:12 a.m.

*H*ENRY WAS ROUSED FROM SLEEP BY A SHAKING THAT HE thought was Jacob at the foot of his bed. He looked up from his drowsy haze into the dusky light of dawn to find no one in his room. The movement became greater, and it made him dizzy. He was jolted from his bed, the hard floor hitting his face. The artwork and the lamp crashed around him. The whole room swayed like a boat caught in a storm.

He stumbled toward the door, struggling to keep his balance. The door swung open wildly, then shut again with a mighty slam. His heart was pounding out of his chest as he grabbed its knob. One of the hinges let loose, and the door fell haphazardly across the threshold, trapping him in. Parts of the ceiling came down on his head. He heard Jacob's voice from the other side of his nightmare. Henry shielded his eyes from the window's glass shattering with flying shards. The shaking stopped with such suddenness

Henry felt it as if he were still moving. An eerie silence followed. Then movement outside his room.

Henry shoved the door aside and stepped into the hallway. Jocelyn came running down the hall and into her father's arms, her forehead bruised and bloodied. Marie, still in her nightcap, came rushing behind her while tying her robe. "Ay! An earthquake!"

Jocelyn whimpered, and Jacob examined her, finding only the cut forehead. He handed her to Marie, whose outstretched arms scooped her up. "Where is Donza?" he asked.

Henry looked confused. "Isn't she with you?"

Jacob gave him a sidelong look. "She must still be in her room, too scared to come out, I imagine. Henry, go outside with Marie and Jocelyn. Watch your steps."

Henry gingerly guided Marie down each stair as she held tight to a whimpering Linny. As he passed the window on the stair landing, the beautiful sight of the city was replaced by a thick, forboding gray, and he was sure it wasn't the fog.

The main floor was in shambles, and he carefully made his way through the fallen debris and glass as he continued to help Marie with Linny. The three of them were finally outside when another jolt forced them to the ground.

"I want Mama!" the little girl wailed.

Marie rocked her as she sat on the front lawn keeping her balance through the wave of the earth beneath them. When it abated she said, "We are safe. Go help Mr. Stanford with his wife."

Henry went back inside. He called for Jacob and heard his reply upstairs. Carefully he went back up to find Jacob by a door down the hall. "Jocelyn is fine. Marie has her." His words went unnoticed as Jacob pounded on the door and shouted for his wife to answer him.

"Donza, for God's sake, let me in!" Jacob turned to Henry. "I'll need a hammer to get these hinges off. Get Jose. Tell him we need help. Hurry!"

After a gingerly descent, Henry quickly went for the shed, which was attached to Jose's cottage. He saw that the small house had some exterior damage but was still standing. Jose was coming out, clutching his arm, blood running down his sleeve and onto his trousers.

"Mrs. Stanford is trapped in her bedroom. We need to get the hinges off the door."

Jose pointed with his chin to his work shed. "On the right wall as you go in. Look for a small crowbar. Where are the others?"

"Marie and Linny are in the front."

Jose hurried past Henry.

Flinging the door open, Henry immediately surveyed the shed. Finding a crowbar, he ran back to the house. On his way, he noticed Donza's window was broken, the shards of glass hanging from its frame. His heart raced as he reached Jacob. They pried the hinges off the jammed door and lifted it out of the way, revealing a wardrobe lying on its side, blocking the threshold. After some maneuvering, they finally got it out of the way, only to find a gruesome discovery.

Donza's body lay facedown in a pool of blood. Jacob gasped as he gingerly turned her over. A shard of glass stuck into her neck, and her face was bruised and swollen.

Jacob lifted Donza's limp body. "Grab the bedsheet."

Acid rose in Henry's throat. He didn't want to ask if she was dead or alive.

He pulled the top sheet off Donza's bed. It was surreal to be standing in a woman's bedroom—possibly a dead woman's bedroom—removing a sheet from her bed. He couldn't move and wanted to collapse and bury his face in his hands. Then Jacob's voice startled him into action.

"Henry! Damn it, I need your help!"

Jacob wrapped her body, then he and Henry cautiously made their way downstairs, the weight of Donza's body adding to their clumsy descent. Past the tumbled mess that had once been the neat interior of the home, they brought her to lie down just outside of the foyer.

"Get me the cushions off the bench," Jacob instructed.

Henry did what he was told, and they placed her body on the soft layer. Jacob knelt beside his wife, feeling her pulse.

Henry felt tears slide down his face. "Are you going to take it out of her neck?"

Jacob didn't respond as he tried to find her heartbeat.

Then Jacob spoke. "If I remove it, she'll bleed more. Her pulse is weak, but I think I felt something. We need to get her to the hospital. Where's Jose?"

"He's hurt, too. I think he went to find Marie."

The sweet sound of sirens coming closer to the house had Henry wanting to cry out with relief.

"Make sure they come down our road—don't let them pass us by!" Jacob ordered.

Henry ran as fast as he could, skidding on the gravel driveway but righting himself each time. He was about to flag down the ambulance driver when he saw Jose had already stopped them. A man's attention was on Jose's arm. He had sat the groundskeeper down. "You've lost a lot of blood." Henry heard him say.

Winded, he asked, "Are you the doctor? We need help at the house!"

"Son, everyone needs our help right now! This man, Jose is it?" Jose nodded. "He needs my attention right now. I'm Dr. Perez."

Henry heard the doctor speak Spanish to Jose, and Jose nodded weakly.

"Yes, sir, but there's a woman who is barely alive up there!" Henry heard his voice shake.

After wrapping Jose's arm, Dr. Perez grabbed his medical bag and told the ambulance driver to wait.

The doctor and Henry and Jose went back to the house, and Marie came running to them with Jocelyn in tow. Marie took Jose around to the terrace to sit down as Henry led the doctor to Jacob. Jacob sat beside his wife, his face ashen with grief.

"I'm a physician, sir. Is this your wife?"

Jacob looked up at Henry and then at the doctor. "This was my wife."

Henry let out a muted sob. The doctor quickly examined the body. He made the sign of the cross, then took out a pocket watch from his vest. "Time of death, 5:52 a.m."

Jacob lowered his head as the doctor wrote in a small notebook and then asked Jacob questions about the deceased. Henry could see his cousin answering with little emotion. He sat down helplessly and placed his head in his hands, waiting for Jacob to be done with the doctor.

"Do you know of any others here who might be hurt?" Henry felt a slight nudge, and he was taken out of his stupor. "Are there any more casualties?" the doctor asked. Henry shook his head numbly.

"Then I'll be leaving. I'll send the coroner over here as soon as I can, but I don't know how long it will take. I suggest you cover the body well with more than a sheet." He asked for them to look away.

Henry heard the sucking sound of the shard of glass being removed from Donza's neck. The fluids in his stomach rose, and he vomited onto the grass. He felt embarrassed and wiped his mouth on his sleeve. He realized he was still in his nightclothes.

"You folks stay put for now. It's dangerous to go anywhere. I'm sorry for your loss," the doctor said, adding, "God help us all!" Wiping his hands on the sheet and grabbing his medical bag, he rushed out of the house.

Jacob stood and covered Donza's head. "Get me a blanket."

THE GROUP SAT IN SILENCE on the back terrace. Marie was able to put Linny to sleep on a makeshift bed under the eaves. Jacob looked out into the distance at the flames coming from the heart of the city. Marie brought bread and wine for everyone and reported that the damage in the kitchen wasn't too great. It was something to be grateful for in this sudden tragedy. Henry sat watching his elders as if to take his cues from them. In a flash of acute dread, it occurred to him that his family back home might be in trouble. Could they have felt the quake? Was the whole world destroyed? He had to find out. He'd walk to the ferry if he had to.

Jose bowed his head in prayer.

Marie began to sob quietly into her handkerchief. "My poor Mrs. Stanford and her poor *chica.*"

Linny began to whimper, and Marie went to her. Jacob didn't move and continued to stare off into the distance.

Henry felt acutely inconsiderate, but he had to tell them he needed to go home.

"You can't go!" Marie shouted.

Jose chimed in, "Look." He pointed toward the city. "We can see the fires from here. No, *chico,* you stay put like the good doctor say. And we will need your help here."

Slumping into a chair, Henry accepted his fate. He would have to wait. He looked at Jocelyn, sitting in Marie's arms, a blanket wrapped around her, sucking her thumb. She looked back at him with watery eyes.

"I'll stay and help," he said, giving her a wink.

In return, she took her thumb out of her mouth and produced a wet smile. "Where's my momma?"

Henry looked at Marie. She shook her head. "Your momma is in heaven, little one," she said.

Linny stuck her thumb back in her mouth. Henry was heartsick for her. He was torn between this family and his own. He decided to do what his father taught him in tough situations—wait and see what develops.

CHAPTER THIRTY-FIVE

Clermont City—April 18, 1906

*J*ESSICA TOSSED AND TURNED. IT WAS NO USE. SHE COULDN'T sleep. A frightful feeling nagged her, filling her with anxiety. Something was wrong. Reaching for her golden watch on her bedside table, she heard the sound of the birds' first chirpings. She looked out the window. The dark gray sky gave a bit of light as she held the pretty timepiece to the window. Wiping the glass front, she squinted to see its hands. Four o'clock.

She left the bed and donned her robe. The bathroom was cold, and after she had finished, she hopped back into bed and brought the quilt and wool blankets around her. The warmth made her drowsy, and she fell asleep.

What seemed like only minutes later, she was woken by a shaking. The bed shimmied across the room, and she held on to the headboard as the whole house felt like it was coming apart at the seams. The crashing of objects to the floor and the creaking of beams made her petrified to leave the bed, even if she could. Jessica feared the shaking would never end, then it stopped as suddenly as it had begun.

Jessica cautiously reached for her robe and slid out of bed. Entering the parlor, she surveyed the damage—an oil lamp in ruins on the floor, its contents seeping into the wood, a few paintings hanging askew, candles on their sides, the liquor cabinet's door ajar with a few broken bottles inside. The smell of alcohol and kerosene permeated the air. For what she could see, all the windows were intact. The kitchen was in shambles, with flour, broken pottery, and dishes strewn on the counter from cabinets forced open by the shaking.

Worried and anxious about her boys, she quickly cleaned up the kerosene oil and liquor. The rest would have to wait. With her stomach in knots, she hurried to get dressed. While doing so, another shaking had her holding on to the bed post. Soon she was headed to Ben and Sally's home, telling herself everyone was fine and this was just a small quake and a bit of excitement. The predawn light on the path seemed ghostly, and she hurried to get to the Loggins' home. Sally came rushing from the house to meet her.

"My Lord! Are you all right?" Sally asked, out of breath.

"Yes, but my house is a mess!" Jessica answered. "What about you two?"

"Ben's checking on the barn and animals. Our house is the same. I'll be cleaning for the rest of the day." She wiped her brow.

Jessica chided herself for not checking on her own animals. She knew it would've been Caleb's first thought. Assured her neighbors were safe, she headed to the barn. The animals were excited, but she managed to calm them before she saddled up her mare and road into town.

AN ACRID ODOR FROM SOMETHING burning filled the air as Jessica made her way down the main street. A loud boom sent her horse into a skittish dance. Flames came from where the sound resonated. She pulled hard on the reins and was able to get her back on course. As she approached the main street, she saw more flames shooting from one of the houses. Several people shouted as a bucket brigade formed. The fire seemed untouched by the splashes of water. Other voices rose in panic as she made her way to her aunt's and mother's homes. Everyone was outside, children were crying, dogs were barking, and shouts of men giving orders surrounded her. In the faint, growing light, she could see the damage to homes, broken windows, toppled chimney stacks, and even a few fallen trees, but no other fires. She steered clear of the cracks in the road. The sharp cry of a siren broke through the chaos, and Jessica felt some relief. The town's fire department was a good one.

Finally, she got to her mother's home and ran inside. The house was empty and just as messy from the quake as her own. She would have to help straighten it up later. She brought her mare around back to the stables. Checking on their horses and the condition of the stable, she was satisfied the animals would be safe. Entering the house, she saw Hannah on her knees in the parlor, cleaning up broken glass.

"Hannah!"

"Jessica!" They grabbed each other's arms. "Your mother and aunt are in the kitchen," Hannah said. "Your uncle is about to leave for the newspaper offices. He says the *Gazette* might be getting news of surrounding areas."

Jessica went into the kitchen, and her mother and aunt jumped up and wrapped their arms around her. "Thank the Lord!" said her aunt.

"We were worried sick!" her mother said, wiping her eyes with a handkerchief.

"I'm fine." She let go of the women. "Uncle, do you think this is widespread or just our area?"

"That's what I'm going to find out." Before leaving, he warned the women not to go outside and to hunker down under the kitchen table for safety if there was another quake. Just then, the house shook, and they all held tight to one another. Hannah screamed from the next room. Running into the kitchen, she sobbed. "That's the third one already!"

The women went to work cleaning up both houses. Hannah with June and Jessica helped her mother. They felt several small quakes but managed to finish most of the cleaning. Finally, Burt returned home. Jessica and Bethany went to see what the news was. He was flushed and smelled of smoke and kerosene. He sat down at the kitchen table and rubbed his chin. "Ladies, please sit. I'm afraid I have bad news."

Jessica's pulse raced in fear. She kept standing.

"San Francisco got the worst of it," Burt said. "A telegraph came direct from the mayor's office that the city is in chaos and the mayor hasn't gotten the full scope yet. The eyewitness said all was lost."

Bringing a hand to her stomach, Jessica let out a sob. June was in hysterics. Bethany looked shocked. Hannah put her hand to her mouth and let out a cry.

"I have to get Henry! I have to rescue my son!" Jessica was heading for the door.

June cried as she prayed for the safety of her loved ones. She whispered, "My granddaughter."

Jessica stopped herself. She knew she would have to remain calm and focused. Caleb would do that, and she would have to imitate his strength.

"Are Caleb and Johnathan safe?" she asked her uncle.

"Yes, I would think so. It's too far up north, but to be honest, no one knows much right now."

"I'll ride to Oakland and then get on the ferry. I'll try to telegraph you as soon as I get a chance."

The group looked at her, all wide-eyed.

"You will do no such thing," her mother commanded. "We will have the sheriff or a posse of men go and find them."

"I'll take you," Burt said. He rubbed his chest. "Let me catch my breath, then we can be on our way."

Jessica looked at her aunt. They both knew Burt's heart problems had gotten worse, and he would be in more distress having to travel.

"No, Uncle Burt. I'll get one of the men in town, Mr. Harper or his son, Ralph. Don't worry, someone will help me."

Having secured the lie, she gathered the needed provisions from her aunt's pantry. It would be several hours before she reached the docks of the Oakland ferry. With her mother's coat for added warmth and the unknown looming ahead, Jessica left the house. What would she see when she got there? She'd taken a map from her uncle that showed her where Jacob lived—the same district in which she'd once lived. Although the years had softened her, she now felt a calling to resurrect the courage and determination she'd once possessed.

Chapter Thirty-Six

*O*NCE SHE ARRIVED IN OAKLAND, JESSICA SECURED HER HORSE at the blacksmith's stable before walking to the ferry. She looked over the waters and saw the orange-and-crimson horizon with black smoke rising up to the sky. The air was hazy, and she brought her handkerchief to her nose.

Weaving around pockets of clamoring people, she felt the acute buzz of excitement. Bricks were in heaps in front of many of the buildings, blocking the way. Broken wooden façades were being collected by men. She spied women inside the stores, cleaning up. The damage made her heart sink. How bad was it on the other side of the bay? Praying for her son's safety, she knew she had to cross those waters—and soon.

The ferry station was crowded with those like her, desperate to reach the city, but the ticket office was closed and the sheriff was turning people away. "I'm sorry, but there's no ferry going into the city."

"But my son is there! How can I reach my son?" Jessica tugged at his sleeve, pleading as he passed her.

"I'd suggest you take the roundabout way," the sheriff said. "Or maybe one of the fishermen will take you across." He shook her hand off and continued through the crowd.

Farther down the dock, she spied a stout man with a captain's hat, standing next to a fishing boat. He waved and announced that he would take passengers to the city for a price.

Jessica looked at the bobbing vessel. "Is that thing even seaworthy?" she asked no one in particular.

A man pushed her aside. "I'll pay!"

Jessica was forced back as others shoved to get to the dock. She caught the captain's eye. "Please," she mouthed.

"I can take about ten of ya," he said. He shouldered his way past the small mob, grabbed Jessica and another woman by the elbows, and helped them into his boat. "It'll get you there, ladies," he said. "My cousin lives just inland, and if he's not lying under a pile of rubble, he can help get you into the city. I'm Captain Westermane, but everyone calls me Manny."

"That's generous of you, Captain Westermane," Jessica said. The other woman nodded between quiet sobs.

Soon, eleven people, including Jessica and the captain, were on their way.

The rocky waters of the San Francisco Bay made Jessica queasy. Sitting on a wooden seat, the smell of rotting fish encompassing her, Jessica held tight to the worn trim of the boat as she looked straight ahead at the bobbing shoreline, trying desperately to talk herself out of becoming seasick. Before too long, smoke clouded the air with an acrid smell. Her mind went from the stink of the boat to the peril that lay ahead of her.

As the boat tipped and swayed, the captain shouted, "She's an old steamer, but she's a good gal!"

If the shock of the earthquake wasn't enough to send her head spinning and her heart pounding, this watery journey, filled with the sounds of retching and moaning, was about to undo her. Jessica took several deep breaths and focused her thoughts on Henry.

As the city of San Francisco drew closer, Jessica noticed that they weren't going into the dock near the ferry building but much farther down the shore.

"Why aren't you docking at the ferry landing?" a man called to Manny, who was steering his boat through the choppy waters.

"Not allowed to!" he shouted without looking back. "Not to worry, sir, we're almost there."

After much maneuvering, Manny brought his vessel into one of the slips by a gray, weather-worn dock. Relieved that this part of her journey was over, she was helped by another passenger onto the bobbing landing deck. There were several other similar fishing boats bobbing alongside them, and it looked as if they, too, were being used to transport people, but these passengers were leaving the city. Weary-looking souls clung to children and their belongings. Was this a sign of what was ahead of her?

The captain's shouts brought her back to her own circumstance. "Joe!" Manny called to one of the other captains. "She's not too bad this morning. Just watch the southwest current. It's troublesome!"

"Thanks, Manny, will do! I suppose you'll be in it many more times today? I hear the whole of the city is fleeing!"

Manny took off his hat and placed it on his heart. "God bless us all!"

Hearing the exchange, Jessica became acutely alert, and her adrenaline pulsed through her body. She was ready to find her son. Where could he be if everyone was leaving?

The small inlet district was almost completely destroyed, and what was left standing was on fire. Walking into the neighborhood, she witnessed the results of the quake. It was much worse than Clermont City.

After walking for about a quarter of a mile, she and a few of the other passengers arrived with Manny at his cousin's house. The stables were long and filled with horses. A man who introduced himself as Lorne escorted Jessica and a few other people to a small buggy with a cart attached. They all took turns paying Lorne and Manny. If this was a sign of things to come, Jessica hoped she would have enough money to get to Henry. They got into the back of the cart.

Jessica felt acutely alone as she watched the two men turn around and head back. The boy at the reins clicked his tongue, and the horses whinnied and the carriage lurched. They were jerked back, and she held on tight to her satchel. Soon, the horse found its rhythm, and she swayed with the others as they went deeper into the smoke and chaos. After a while, the boy stopped the horse and turned to his passengers.

"This is as far as I go."

Grumblings turned to angry shouts. "How are we to get into the city? I paid for transport to downtown! I want my money back!"

Jessica had no time for this. She lifted one end of her skirt and tucked her satchel under her arm as she made her way down from the carriage. It was an awkward exit, and she nearly tumbled to the ground.

Looking about, she found herself among scores of people on foot, carrying their belongings in boxes and sacks. She saw housewares, bedding, pots and pans. Moaning and weeping, stoic and dazed, they passed as she watched in horror. Coughing and retching echoed around her as the refugees made their way out of the city to patches of land free from the threat of falling debris and fire.

Her eyes darted through the crowd, searching for the face of a loved one. No one looked familiar. So many injured, some fallen on the side of the road, skirted by the surge of humanity. No one stopped to check if they were dead or could be saved. The smoke accosted her lungs, and she began to cough uncontrollably. Jessica quickly found her handkerchief and, like so many others, covered her mouth and nose, tying it tightly at the back of her head.

The air was warm and thick. The view of the city shocked her. It was unrecognizable. The fires roared in many places as bucket brigades lined the streets. The sun had risen looking like a red-orange ball in the sky. It seemed more like dusk than late morning.

Fighting to figure out the way to get to Jacob's with the landscape so altered by the quake, she lifted her skirts higher and made a perilous trek to Market Street and J&W's offices. The deeper she got into the downtown area, the more desperate the situation looked. Jessica had to walk on all types of debris covering the streets. There was a mixture of quiet shock on most faces, crying women with children and babies in their arms, men shouting orders, dogs barking, and the helpless moaning and wailing of those in need of help. It penetrated her heart with sorrow and fear. She wanted to help, but it was a stew of misery, and she had to stay focused on her mission.

After trudging through the gray cloud of disorder, she came to J&W Imports. The façade of the building had fallen on the sidewalk, blocking the entrance. To her great relief, the building wasn't on fire. Jessica shouted up to the second floor. "Will! Jacob!"

She went to the back alley. The broken glass and fallen bricks impeded her way, but she managed to get under a window and shout again for her brother and Jacob. Climbing up the fire escape would be impossible. The first step was too high off the ground. Again, she called up to them. There was no answer. As she was ready to give in to her despair and begin her trek to Jacob's house, she heard her name and looked up. A miracle! Will was at the window.

"Jessica!" he shouted down to her through the shattered pane. "What the hell are you doing here?"

"I came to get Henry!"

"Stay there. I'll be right down."

She watched him come down the fire escape, a large thick package tucked under his arm. Jumping to the ground, he nearly lost his balance and the package. He righted himself, and she ran into his arms. "I have to get to my son!" she said in tears. Her next words were, "Thank God you're safe."

"I'll take you up to Jacob's." Grasping her hand, Will led her onto the main road, where scores of men were navigating and inspecting the wreckage.

"Where's Julia?"

"She's around here somewhere. She said she had to help, and I couldn't stop her. I'll come back for her later."

With tight lips, Jessica answered with a solid nod.

To her surprise, the residents on the top of the hill had come out to look at the damage down in the city with a spectator's curiosity. Was the city so divided between the haves and have-nots? The rich lived in houses that seemed to stand up to the quake. It gave her some relief that all might be well with Henry. With a puffing breath, she made her way up the steep hill beside her brother. She coughed into her sleeve. Her handkerchief was inadequate at filtering out the heavy smoke.

When they finally came to the top, Jessica glanced back and saw the full scope of destruction. Her breath hitched, and she made the sign of the cross, then she caught up with Will as he strode ahead of her.

"Where is his house? Are we close?" she asked, panting. Her lungs tightened and her legs weakened. "Will, I have to stop and catch my breath!" she called to him.

Will turned around as if he hadn't noticed she had stopped. He ran back to her. "Here, lean on me."

Her head was swimming as she steadied her breathing. She sat down on the road. Unladylike to be sure, but she had to rest. Spurred on by her determination to reach her son, she took Will's outstretched hand, and they continued on.

The curved driveway leading up to Jacob's home was never a more welcome sight to Jessica. Another few yards and she would be with Henry. She pulled her handkerchief down and looked beyond the neatly hedged path, where she saw a beautifully crafted home, a manicured lawn, and flower boxes artfully placed around the outside, all surrounded by a blossoming hedge grove. As she got farther onto the property, she saw some of the damage to the house. It was standing! When she reached the front yard, the reason for her journey came running to her.

Henry embraced his mother. After witnessing the heart-wrenching scene in the city, she could not have been more grateful to hold her son tight. Pulling away, she examined him and noticed he was doing the same with her. Her heart swelled. He was whole and safe.

Will wiped his forehead with the back of his hand as he patted Henry on the back.

"Jacob is in the house," Henry said to Will. "Marie and Jose are with Jocelyn in Jose's cottage out back."

Henry went stiff and bowed his head. Jessica sensed there was more. "Is everyone all right?"

"Donza is dead."

Tears welled in her son's eyes, and she embraced him again. He pulled away first. "Jacob placed her in the house, wrapped in a blanket. We didn't know what to do. We're still waiting for the coroner."

Will took charge. "All right. Henry, stay here with your mother. I'll go inside and see to Jacob."

"Come around to the terrace, Mother. I'll get you a glass of water."

Jessica realized she was exhausted and mighty thirsty. "Yes, thank you, Henry."

Henry led her to the terrace, and she sat heavily on a padded wrought iron garden chair. The blanket he placed over her lap felt warm and inviting. She could wait now that she had found her son. She took in a breath. The air was lighter up here, and she thanked God for that. Her thoughts went to Jacob and the loss of his poor wife. The nightmare of this earthquake had revealed another tragedy, this one too close to her family. Henry returned with a glass of water, and she drank it down.

"Henry, sit with me. Tell me what happened."

Her son couldn't sit. Leaning against the terrace wall with the city on fire in the distance, he told her what she wanted to know.

"Oh, dear." Jessica placed her hand over her chest. She could feel the pumping of her heart. "I'm so sorry you had to go through this. We need to go home."

"Mother, I was afraid and still am, but I'm not a baby. Jocelyn has lost her mother, and Jacob his wife. I need to stay and help as much as I can."

Incredulously, she looked at her son. "I need you back home. I don't know if your father and Johnathan are safe or when they'll return."

Henry nodded and turned to face the city.

Jessica saw the back of a tall man instead of her son, and she knew this experience would change him forever. Like her own experiences, which had punctuated her life and stolen her innocence, so, too, would her son's life be seasoned by this event. She wanted to weep for his lost boyhood. Mostly, she wanted to take him home to the safety of Rail River Acres.

CHAPTER THIRTY-SEVEN

*H*earing footfalls behind her, Jessica turned to see Jacob walking onto the brick terrace. His face was pale, and he looked hastily put together. Her brother followed behind. She stood and walked to him. They embraced without a word.

He came away from her, his hands on her forearms. "You are a marvel. What a mother won't do for her son."

"I'm so sorry for your loss. Henry told me what happened. My God, Jacob, how terrible!" Her throat tightened, and she feared she would begin to sob. Jessica barely knew the woman, yet to see Jacob in pain was as if she had lost a loved one herself.

He wiped his eyes. "Will told me of the carnage in the city." He ran his hand across the day's growth of beard on his chin. "I can't believe this."

"I can't either," she said. "The whole city is in shock."

Jacob turned to Will. "Where's Julia?"

Will shook his head. "She couldn't and wouldn't leave. Helping others is her life's work. I just hope she looks after herself."

They all agreed. In less than a minute after Will's statement, another shaking rattled the landscape, and Jessica braced against Jacob. He held on to her, and soon it stopped.

"Damn!" Will said. "I need to get to my wife. Enough is enough. I'll get her back here even if I have to drag her!"

"And Henry and I must get back home," Jessica said.

"You're not going anywhere," Will said to her.

The sharpness of his statement jolted Jessica into a dire reality—she might have to stay the night, at least. Searching Jacob's face, she saw his resignation.

He turned to Will. "Take my auto."

"Jake, it's worse than you can see from here," Will informed him. "We had a time just on foot. You can't get that machine through the wreckage. I'll get back as soon as I find Julia."

Jacob relented. "Whatever you need. Just get back safe."

He gave his cousin a bear hug. "I always have, Cuz."

AFTER WILL WAS OUTFITTED WITH food, clean clothes, a blanket, and water, he left back down the hill. The pack he carried, along with a rifle and ammo, sent Jacob back in time. He reassured himself that his cousin still had the trails in him and the skills to survive.

Soon after, the clip-clop of horses coming up the drive brought Jacob to the front of his home. The coroner's carriage had arrived. It was mid-afternoon, and the heat was rising in the house. He helped the driver place the body in the back of the covered coach and quietly said his goodbye.

Standing at the top of the winding gravel drive, he watched the rocking carriage weave its way down and away from him. He'd been told she would be in the icehouse for now, along with the other bodies. Jacob winced at the thought of her body among so many strangers, yet he also realized the practicality of the situation. His mind and heart were a tangle of emotion and logic.

He walked back to the house, where Henry and Jose were cleaning and restoring his home. Jose's arm was still wrapped tight, but he refused to rest and was making do with one arm. Jacob felt that to even lift a broken or upturned item right now seemed almost disrespectful to his wife. How could he think of repairs to a home she had touched with her style and taste from her own heritage while her body lay in an icehouse? Before he could form another thought about Donza, a crushing blow of guilt hit him. He had fallen out of love with her several years ago, and now she was gone. Had he unconsciously willed this horrible outcome? Running his hands over his hair, he looked up at the darkening sky. *No*, he decided. *If I had that much power over circumstances, I would be with the woman I truly love.*

Putting his loss aside, he went to find Marie and his daughter. Sadness shook him like the trembling of the earth—the poor child had only him as a parent now.

CHAPTER THIRTY-EIGHT

WITH JACOB'S ASSISTANCE, MARIE PLACED JOCELYN TO SLEEP in a nest of blankets in his study. She stayed with the child while Jacob went to the kitchen, where Jessica continued to tidy up the room. It looked almost normal again.

"Thank you," he said to her back as she looked out the window. Startled, she turned to him, tears streaking her face.

"I didn't mean to sneak up on you," he said.

She wiped her cheeks on the apron she wore. "No, it's fine. I was lost in thought."

Jacob wanted to reach out to her, but he couldn't move. He longed to have her in his arms.

"Would you like a cup of tea?" she asked. "I was just about to put the kettle on. How is Jocelyn?"

"She's sleeping. I don't think she understands her mother is truly gone. Thank heavens for Marie." He sat down at the long wooden worktable. "My daughter is in shock, and there is nothing I can do to help her." He put his head in his hands.

Jessica lit the stove and prepared the teapot for the hot water.

"Can you stay a little longer?" he asked. His voice was raspy and the words seemed to stick in his throat.

She brushed away a few stray strands of hair escaping her bun. "I want to, but I need to find out if Caleb and Johnathan are safe, even though your father said they probably were. I can't just leave it at that. Everything is turned upside down."

"I know. What of our elders?"

"My mother and your parents are fine. Like most of the houses, it's a matter of cleaning up. Hannah and the neighbors were helping. Clermont City wasn't as hard hit."

"That's good. I know my father's heart can't take much. Was he in much distress? I'm sure my mother is beside herself."

"Everyone was fine." She didn't want to let Jacob know his father's heart was acting up.

He nodded. "Thank you."

They took their tea in silence, holding each other's hand.

IT WAS A RESTLESS NIGHT for everyone. Will had not returned, and the smell from the fires and the sounds of upheaval filled the hours leading to dawn. Late last night, she had fallen asleep in her petticoat huddled on the settee near the fireplace. A heavy blanket over her weary body. On rising, Jessica's throat felt prickly and she coughed. The smoke from the city permeated the house. She headed to the kitchen. Her dreams came to mind. She was lying by the campfire after her rescue from the Indian camp so long ago with Jacob just feet away. Why she had brought that memory into her sleep she didn't know, but it left her with a profound feeling of fate working its way into her life. Why was she here with Jacob at this most grievous time? What favor was she to return to him for saving her life from the fate of the Indians? She swept it to the back of her mind. There was only today to think about and how she and Henry would get home.

Before donning her dress, Jessica went to the back door and shook it out, dust and debris flying everywhere. She pinned her hair in place and felt halfway decent. Deciding everyone could use a good meal, she searched the pantry for fixings. Only three eggs in a basket remained intact. She found a slab of bacon and milk in the icebox. Biscuits and gravy would have to suffice.

Henry, Jacob, and Jose came in from their night in Jose's house. The upstairs of Jacob's home was still haunted by Donza's gruesome demise, and it was decided Jose's cottage would better suit the men. Marie and Joselyn slept in the study downstairs.

Once the men were seated at the table, she served coffee and breakfast. Marie came in and made some porridge for Jocelyn, then returned to the study with the warm bowl. Jacob nibbled at his food, Henry and Jose ate with gusto, and Jessica politely cleaned her plate. She had been famished.

"Jacob," she began quietly. "I was thinking. Henry can stay here if you need him."

Jacob looked up from his coffee, which he had been staring into for the past several minutes. His hair was disheveled, and his two-day-old beard covered his chin and upper lip. The look in his eyes broke her heart, and the thought of leaving him grieved her.

"No," he said. "I want Henry to be with you when you travel back." He raised his hand at her protest. "I know, I know, you can take care of yourself. You made it here without help. It was without my knowledge, though. Knowing how bad it is, it would cause me greater grief to let you out there alone."

Jessica shifted in her chair. Henry's puzzled expression made her uncomfortable. "You're very kind, Cousin," she said. "But you are overly concerned for me."

Jacob gave her a dark look. He turned to Henry. "Your mother has never allowed me to love her as I wish to."

"Jacob." Jessica darted up from her seat. "I will take Henry with me as you like, and rest assured, we will be safe. For now, I think a nice cool bath and shave might help you considerably."

A slight shake of his head told her he was beyond worrying about decorum. He was beyond the thoughts of keeping secrets deep inside. She worried he might not be in his right mind. He left the dining room, and she heard the door close to the downstairs washroom.

"Is he going to be all right, Mother?"

She put her cup down. "Yes. He's still in shock. As soon as your uncle Will arrives, we will make our way home. He and Jacob need to take care of this situation without us in the way."

Henry nodded. He rubbed the back of his neck. "Um … is it all right that I feel ready to go home?"

"Of course it is. I will tell your father and brother how helpful and brave you were."

"I didn't feel brave. I just did what came to me. It was awful."

Jessica placed a hand on her son's back. "This will pass, and we'll look back on this tragedy as a time we were called to be someone we didn't know we were." She wasn't certain of her words, but she was deeply proud of her son. How long would it take for the city and surrounding area to find normality again? Sadly, that included Jacob and his little daughter. A part of her wanted to stay and help him through his sorrow and help little Joselyn as well.

Later that day, Will arrived with Julia. They were dirty and exhausted, smelling of acrid smoke as if they had been fighting the fires themselves. Jessica wouldn't be surprised to learn Julia had. Relieved to see they were all right, she prepared a bath for her sister-in-law and washed her clothes. Marie offered her one of her dresses while Will cleaned up at Jose's. Then Marie went back to taking care of Jocelyn, who was now in the parlor asking questions. Marie was gently answering them as Jessica made her way to the terrace, where she waited for Will and Julie and Jacob.

A soft breeze dispersed some of the smoke, and the view below was startling. She wondered how she was going to brave another journey through the wreckage of the city.

Jacob and Jessica listened to Will and Julia's account of the damage. It was beyond belief. News had gotten around about the area most struck by the earthquake, and by Will's account, Caleb and Johnathan had most likely been spared any real danger.

"Jake, we'll have to find another building. They might have to tear ours down," Will said. "The ceiling mostly held, but we've had some damage to the merchandise. Fortunately, we were spared a fire."

"You can repair and continue on," Julia said to Jacob as she leaned over to him and clasped his hand in both of hers.

Jealousy pricked Jessica, and she was surprised by it. "We are ready to go home," she announced. "Henry may have to leave his new clothes. We will need to travel light."

"I'm sure it couldn't have affected Caleb and Johnathan," Jacob said. "And Caleb is very capable of taking care of things. Won't you both stay a while longer? It doesn't sound safe. Let's talk about this, Jessica."

Will gave Jessica a curious look. "Is that what you want, Jess?"

She slowly replied, "I suppose—"

"I think I'll check on Jocelyn," Julia said and excused herself.

After she was gone, Will spoke. "Jess, you can return home once the roads are safe again. The ferry was operating but not on schedule. We'll hire a boat. You said your horse is in Oakland? You'll need to hire a rig for you and Henry. Do you have enough money? If not, I can give you what you need."

Looking at his cousin, Jacob stroked his beard. "Did you get to the bank?"

"Um . . . no. I had some cash in my office." Will stood abruptly and walked back into the house.

Watching her brother leave, Jessica rose, letting out a puff of air. "It's refreshing to know I can count on him."

Jacob came to stand by her side, their bodies nearly touching. "He's always got ready cash, and I don't know where it comes from. He can't be having a constant winning streak."

The closeness of his body was arousing, making his words drift over her. Will was ever a worry, but it didn't matter at the moment. She decided it would be too risky to stay to comfort Jacob. Tomorrow she and Henry would leave.

CHAPTER THIRTY-NINE

*T*HAT NIGHT, THE DISTANT NOISES MADE JESSICA UNEASY. THE day had been filled with sirens, and the trembles caused by large booms coming from the dynamite ignited to stop the spread of the fires had everyone in the house on edge. The random flames gave the sky a soft orange-yellow glow as she stood on the terrace. Holding her wrapped shawl around her with one hand and carrying a lantern with the other, she walked onto the lawn. April in the city was still cool, but tonight the air carried a thickness to it, trapped by the clouds of smoke. The fires still threatened to come their way, and it unnerved her. She thought of Caleb. Did he know? Was he on his way home? And what would he think if he found her gone?

A shadow of someone on the terrace startled her. She raised the lantern to see Jacob.

"What are you doing out here?" he asked.

"Same as you, I suppose."

They sat on the cold wrought iron chairs. The cushions, damp from dew, had been set aside. Jessica shivered and thought of the warm bench on her porch. In the near silence, the distant voices rose up. Shouts, sometimes screams, were a reminder of this life-changing event.

Jacob rose and offered her his arm. "Let's go inside where it's warm. A glass of port?"

Sitting in the parlor, which was cleaned and rid of debris, Jessica sipped the wine. Jacob was looking cleaned up as well. His handsomeness flared up her love for him. She brought her hand to her chest and sighed.

"Caleb will surely be heading back once he's heard the news," she said.

Jacob gave a small smile. "My wife will never come back."

"Oh dear. I didn't mean to—"

"I know what you meant. As long as we talk about Caleb, nothing will happen between us."

"You just lost your wife, and you're thinking of us?"

"I don't know what to think. I want to hold you, Jess. I need to feel your comfort."

She set her wineglass down. They rose, and she stood on tiptoe as he took her waist and drew her into him. Pressing their bodies together, Jessica felt as if she had never left his side. The years of separation didn't matter. His strong arms embraced her, and she let him place his hand on her chin, lifting her mouth to meet his. He kissed her tenderly, and his mouth was warm and tasted of the port wine. The scent of his body brought warm and inviting memories, but she knew this was wrong.

Regretfully, she slipped out of his arms and turned her back on him, wiping her mouth. He brought her back to him. They stood in each other's arms for a while, then they returned to sit together. His mouth found hers again, and he caressed her lips with his. The passion ignited in her was almost too much. They took it no further, but she felt as satisfied as if they had just made love and as guilty.

STIFF AND YAWNING, JESSICA WOKE, curled up in Jacob's arms. They were still on the sofa. She scrambled away, nearly falling on the floor. Jacob roused. He, too, was surprised.

He rubbed his eyes and chin. "We must have fallen asleep." He brought his legs around and sat up. "I slept too well."

Jessica stopped straightening the skirt of her dress and re-pinned her hair. "Hmm, me too." She puffed air out of her nose, her shoulders relaxing. "I'll make us some coffee."

No sooner had she entered the kitchen than she heard Henry, Marie, and Jocelyn coming from their beds. Her heart trembled. How close she had come to having to explain the unexplainable. Will and Julia entered through the back door. They and Henry were staying at Jose's, who had left to be with his family southeast of the city.

"Good morning" wasn't the greeting today. Instead, everyone asked how the other was and how they got through the night. Jessica couldn't look at Jacob, but her night had been one of security and warmth.

After a breakfast of porridge, biscuits and gravy, apples, and raisins, they all resumed the clean-up effort while Will went in search of housing for him and Julia until their apartment was liveable again. He also promised to bring home food supplies.

Good to his promise, he arrived late in the afternoon having secured a home outside the city for him and his wife and a burlap sack containing carrots and potatoes, a chunk of salted pork, flour, eggs, and a bottle of milk. Jessica and Julia prepared the evening meal. Marie took care of Jocelyn, who whimpered for her mother when she wasn't crying aloud. Jessica told herself they would leave the next day.

JESSICA AND JACOB HAD ONE last visit. The house was quiet, and everyone was asleep. They went out to the terrace where the air, although close, wasn't as stuffy as inside.

"It's hard to see you and Henry go. I've gotten very fond of him. He's a good boy." Jacob gave a small laugh. "I mean, young man. He certainly proved his grit through all of this. And his kindness. You've raised him well." He brushed his nose. "You and Caleb both."

"I was hoping you would see he is a product of both his parents."

"Don't rub it in." Jacob raised a brow at her.

"Jacob . . . when is the funeral? Have you heard when they can bury the bodies?"

"Will's been working on it. I haven't the heart. Look at me— I'm making love to you less than a week after my wife dies. I'm a confused child!"

"We didn't exactly make love."

"It was to me. Whenever I touch you, I feel I'm making love to you. Donza and I grew apart years ago. I miss her as my daughter's mother and as the good woman she was. It's a tragedy I can't quite grasp." He turned away. "In all honesty, I didn't think of her as the woman I would grow old with."

"It may have been a premonition."

"Oh, my dear, you do love to put things in their proper place. Nice and neat. Just like us."

"It's my way of coping, Jacob. Don't you see that?"

"I do. Now I do," he said with sincerity.

"Give it time. You will sort through all this. It's not your fault. As for Jocelyn, don't let me be a stranger to her. Don't let your parents or my mother be strangers to her either. Come see us. She will need family."

Jacob put his head in his hands. "Donza's family," he whispered.

"I tried to send a telegram, but I'm not sure if it made it to Sacramento."

Jessica knew he had his life to contend with, but Will would be by his side. Her thoughts turned to Henry and the strange conversation they'd had yesterday about her brother.

"Mother, I think I saw something that might explain why Uncle Will has the money to secure a home and pay for other things, like food and our passage home."

She hadn't thought much of his words until she'd looked him in the face. "What is it, Henry?"

"Well, he took me down to the docks one day, and I saw him trade something for a paper bundle. I think it was money."

"Henry, tell me everything you saw."

After her son had told her more about the side trip Will had taken him on, Jessica was furious. Making an effort to remain calm, she explained, "It's none of our business, Henry. Thank you for telling me, though. You did the right thing. No use in carrying around the burdens of your uncle's misdeeds. He has a bit of a problem with staying on the right side of the law. Since he was a young man, he's always sought out . . . well, I guess you could call it the adventure of doing something he knows he isn't supposed to be doing."

Henry's expression had worried her. She knew he loved his uncle, and his loyalty between the truth and Will had been split.

"It's all right, Henry. You can still love him, but I doubt he'll ever change his ways."

"We should tell Jacob," Henry said.

Jessica thought about that and shook her head. "Maybe. For now, we have other things to be concerned about." She'd left her son to his own judgment, promising herself she would discuss the subject with him again once they were safely home with Caleb and Johnathan.

"Jess?"

She turned and saw Jacob staring at her. "I asked if you'd like a refill," he said. "You seem to be somewhere else."

"Sorry. I was, actually." She accepted another pour and took a sip. "Henry told me something that might explain Will's cash flow."

"Please don't tell me." Jacob sighed. "I don't want to know."

She knew he wasn't telling the truth. She told him what Henry had revealed to her. Jacob cursed and slapped the rock wall.

"I knew it, but I didn't want to think about it. I'll wring his damn neck! I'll cut him off from the business!"

Trying to calm him took some doing, but Jessica managed to talk sense into him.

"Deal with it later, Jacob. There can be no trading of any kind at this time. Will is far from the tables and the docks."

"Jess, I need you more than ever. We'll telegram Caleb and let him know you're safe, and I'm sure he and Johnathan are fine and back home. Please . . ."

Leaning into his shoulder, she rubbed his back. "I wish it were true. I'm sorry, but I have to go home." It brought tears to her eyes and a lump to her throat.

They straightened, and he cleared his throat. "Yes, you must do that. I'll be fine. Just a moment of weakness. Forgive anything I've said to you these few days. I'm not rational."

She smiled with a nod. "I know. I love you and wish you the best."

"I love you, too, Jess. Be careful tomorrow, and if you can get word to me that you and Henry are safe, I would greatly appreciate it."

"I will be careful. Don't worry. You have enough to do here."

"How am I going to do all of it?"

She took his hand and touched his face. "You will manage. I am sure you will. Remember who you are, Jacob. That man out there on the trails still exists inside of you. Courageous and free and intelligent. Caleb has taught me that we follow a path in life that is meant for us and us alone, and at the same time we all are on the same path."

Jacob winced. "I don't think advice from Caleb is helpful right now. And what the hell does that mean?"

Jessica smiled. "Sorry, and I'm not sure. It brought me comfort. I guess everything happens for a reason."

"You and I happened for a reason. Hell if I know why. My wife died for a reason? She left her child for a reason?"

"Don't get angry."

"I am angry!" He stood, defiant.

Jessica looked into his watery eyes. He softened. She went to him, and he embraced her and wept.

The next day she and Henry said their goodbyes and left for home. It took them two days to journey around the broken city and find a place to stay overnight. Then the boat ride in choppy waters to Oakland. Her horse was still at the farrier's, and she decided to put Henry on the coach, and she would ride home alone. It was a brave decision given she had not let him out of her sight the whole trip. She needed the time alone to prepare for home. It was a strange and familiar feeling.

CHAPTER FORTY

Rail River Acres, Clermont City—May 1906

*C*ALEB SAT AT HIS WORKBENCH MAKING A NECKLACE HE'D promised to send to Meadow. Jessica walked in and commented on the fine job he was doing. Then she said, sighing, "I can still smell the smoke."

Since returning home with Johnathan, Caleb had seen a difference in his wife. She jumped at the slightest noise and cleaned the house more often than it needed. Her art was no longer her focus. Concern for their sons took all her attention. She woke in the night, clinging to him and crying. It was subsiding a little, but now her words deflated his hopes that she would heal from her experience and her mind would be at peace.

His own experience had been upsetting as well. He couldn't get home fast enough once word had traveled to Red Bow about the quake. He and Johnathan had tried to get into San Francisco, but the waterways were a confusing mess, and no one was allowed to cross into the raging chaos of the city.

He put his tool down and placed the necklace aside. "Yes, I've heard that said in town among those who were there. I'm sorry, sweetheart. The peace of the river will help clear the memory. Let's walk down together." As he said this, he wondered if she had found her peace there.

While Henry had shared his experience in detail to his brother and father, Jessica had kept most of what she saw and experienced to herself. It was hard for Caleb not to suspect something had gone on between her and Jacob. He held no illusions that their love had not diminished. His own love for Meadow was testament to how long and far-reaching love could be. Again, his love for Jessica was tested, and his jealousy was still strong within him. He contemplated the difference between their love and his feelings for Meadow. One was lovely and pure, while the latter was hampered by the past and passionate greed. Those interfering thoughts had closed him off for too many days since they'd reunited.

"How can I help you?" he asked Jessica.

She shook her head. "Time will help."

Caleb coughed. His chest had been tight lately.

She rubbed his back. "I'll brew up some medicinal tea for you tonight. You really should see the doctor," she said.

He waved her off. "I'm fine. Let's walk in peace now. I'm worried about you."

"I know. I'll be better soon. Clermont City feels as if it will rise out of this and be as good as ever. San Francisco, I read, has begun their resurrection in earnest. Will writes that J&W is getting orders in again. Their new venue seems even better than the last one." They walked for a while through the low grass of the field. The warmth coming from the brownness of it gave off a most aromatic smell to her. So many feelings flooded back to her. Today they would be good ones—summer on the horizon, her boys playing and laughing and her husband by her side. "I'm still so sad that the Billingston Gallery was destroyed. I'm glad I got most of my paintings out the week before. My loss is nothing compared to Jilly's. Poor dear must be a wreck."

"I know you lost a few paintings, but there's more to this tragedy than the lost art."

She stopped. "I agree, but you, of all people, should recognize the value of art. An artful city full of life was all but lost." Her voice cracked. "We need comfort along with practicality."

"Yes, I've tried to comfort you, but . . ." His shoulders lowered. "What about you and Jacob? How well did you comfort him?" The question had been percolating in him ever since she returned. Her agitation from his question made him more alert. In his experience, he knew guilt created anger.

"I did what I could. I wanted to get home mostly. But, Caleb, what kind of human being would I be if I didn't comfort a loved one who just lost his wife?"

"It's not the fact you comforted him. It's in what way you did."

"You needn't worry about it. Trust me, it was a terrible time."

Wanting to find his home with her again or learn his fate, he asked, "Are we still husband and wife?"

She stopped and looked him in the eye, then answered directly, "Yes."

He took her hand, and they walked along the edge of the river. He felt a bit sheepish, but he had to know. A sense of relief came over him. He waited for her to ask the same question of him, but she spoke on a different subject.

"We can build our new building there," she said, pointing to the eastern stand of forest.

"Oh?"

She smiled. "Yes. I think your idea is good. We need to build something . . . something for the future."

Caleb's heart opened, and he knew all would be well.

CHAPTER FORTY-ONE

July 1912

$\mathcal{S}$UMMER WAS IN FULL SWING AT RAIL RIVER ACRES. HENRY and Johnathan worked at harvesting the ripe fruit and vegetables to sell to the local stores in town. In the fall, Henry would return to Santa Clara University, where he was studying law, and Johnathan would be taking on a more managerial role in the silverworks business. John had a mind for figures as well and intuitive hands when it came to the art. He worked alongside his father in all aspects, including teaching. Caleb's silversmith building stood proudly among the backdrop of the forest, and though it began with just one or two students in the summer, he now had schools in several surrounding towns who taught his program to their students. His days were filled with the silversmithing he loved and sold, along with teaching young men the art he had mastered.

These days, Jessica split her time between her artwork, teaching, and helping Hannah and Sally with canning the harvest. It was a busy season, and Rail River Acres was a buzz of activity. Jessica hadn't visited her mother and aunt for many days. The town had gotten back to normal after the quake, and her life was as full as ever.

When she saw her uncle climb down from his coach, she rushed from the kitchen to greet him, hoping he had brought her mother and aunt with him. To her disappointment, he was alone, and a grave expression hung on his face.

"Uncle, this is a surprise." Jessica hugged the large man, and he smelled of the spice-scented soap he used. It warmed her heart. She admonished herself for not visiting him and her mother and aunt as often as she should.

"Jessica, my dear, I'm afraid this is not a visit. I have sad news."

Holding her arms around her waist, she waited for the words to come from her uncle while her mind raced. *Who? What? When?*

He looked down at the ground, then back up at her. "My dear wife. She left us this morning."

Jessica clutched her chest. "No." Shaking her head, she couldn't stop repeating no.

His bearlike arms wrapped around her, and she sobbed into him. Coming away, she took the handkerchief he offered. She wiped her eyes, which wouldn't dry.

"She had a cough a few days ago. It went into her lungs. It happened so fast." His last words broke.

"I'm so sorry, Uncle. I knew she was fragile, but I . . . Oh God, what will we do without Aunt June?" Her tears flowed.

"Your mother will need you, Jessica. I promised to bring you back with me. I hope I can keep my promise."

"Oh, yes, of course. I will pack an overnight bag. Come in, Uncle. Let me have Hannah gather the boys and Caleb." Jessica brought her weary uncle to sit on Caleb's old leather chair. She quickly got him a glass of cool water. Hannah came out of the kitchen.

"Mr. Stanford, what a pleasant—" She turned to Jessica, whose eyes were surely an indication of something unpleasant.

Jessica grabbed Hannah's arm. "June passed this morning." The women embraced and wept. "Fetch Caleb and the boys to come inside. I will let them know. I must be in town for several days. I hope you can manage here while I'm gone."

Hannah nodded. Wiping her face with the back of her hand, she went to corral the rest of the family.

Jessica sat with her mother, who looked thin and pale as the organist played the loud solemn notes of a funeral. The Clermont City Church was filled to capacity on a sweltering day in July—her aunt's favorite time of year. A sniffle from Henry and a quiet sob from Johnathan had Jessica wanting to put her arms around her older children and comfort them. Farther down the row, ten-year-old Jocelyn, now officially called Linny, wept into a handkerchief while Jacob comforted her. The years after Linny lost her mother, June had embraced her granddaughter, and they'd often visited each other. Caleb sat to Jessica's right, and his arm rested around her shoulder.

Last night, Jessica had not been able to hold back her sadness as she lay in his arms. "She was a mother to me," she'd cried onto his chest, wetting his flesh under her cheek. His soothing touch as he'd stroked her hair and hummed a deep, steady note while rocking her gently had helped to calm her. She'd thought of the loss Jacob would feel, and the well of grief rose again to start her sobbing. Finally, in the late hours of the night, spent from her outpouring of emotions, she'd fallen asleep.

Today, she came to a more reasonable agreement with her grief. After nearly losing her aunt during that damp and dreary winter, Jessica felt she'd had her longer than anyone had hoped. It was a blessing she was now more grateful for.

At the reception, an array of June's signature dishes spread out in a feast of food and drink. Hannah and Bethany had worked to make sure her love of cooking and feeding others was on display. Will and Julia helped, as Julia could never keep from offering her services and always wrangled her husband into joining her. Jessica knew her brother needed to keep busy as well. His quick wit and devil-may-care attitude were absent, reflecting the heavy grief of the day. Jessica approached Jacob and hugged him. They walked outside, away from the crowded house filled with mourners.

"She was the thread that held us together," Jacob said as they came around the house to June's neglected garden. "I wish she had known how much I loved her."

"I wish she had, too."

Jacob wiped away a tear running down his cheek. Sardonically, he replied, "Well, thank you for that."

"Jacob, you'll have to come to terms with your own grief. To me, she was my heart's home. I confided in her. She gave me strength and understanding, yet there was one thing I could never tell her—I loved her son, and we had a child together." She stopped to pluck a wildflower growing by the garden gate. The smell brought her back to her aunt kneeling among her vegetables. Her heart ached. "She loved Henry and watched him grow. I have to know that was enough."

"I suppose you're right. I do have to face my guilt. I thought most of it had left me long ago, but now I'm afraid it only went into hiding. I love you and my son. That's that. I put her through a lot of worry. I wish I had written to her as I traveled." He stepped onto one of the dirt paths, running his hand through his newly cut hair.

"I wish you had written to me." Jessica felt the unfairness of bringing the subject up. "I'm sorry, that was unnecessary."

"You're right, though. I'm sorry. I did what I knew how to at the time, and avoiding you was what I could do to keep sane. After losing Donza, my world changed. I knew who I was again. I think it took a tragedy like that to wake me up. I'm not a businessman, or once an outlaw or even a man who is in love with a woman he can't have. I'm more than even a father." He gave a small laugh. "I don't know how to explain it, Jess, but I found forgiveness for myself, past and present, and in that I found myself."

"Jacob, that's profound and quite wonderful." She took his arm, and they walked back to the house. "I feel as if I have had the same experience. It's taken me a long time to forgive myself. I'm not sure I have completely."

"You have nothing to be forgiven for, and I won't listen to a word to the contrary."

"Yes, sir," she conceded.

They were able to find levity on this sad day. It gave Jessica a comfort she had not expected to receive and more unexpected from the person who gave it.

Caleb greeted them at the door. Jessica unhooked her arm from Jacob's. He went inside, passing Caleb.

"Before you say a word, we are cousins. He's lost his mother, and I've lost a beloved aunt," Jessica said.

With a nod, Caleb put his arm around her, and they walked into the house. "Your mother wants to return home. I offered, but . . ."

Bethany had warmed slightly to Caleb over the years, yet she still remained skeptical of her daughter's husband. She occasionally reminded Jessica how much easier life could have been if she had married someone of her own status.

Jessica gave a wry smile. "Hannah will take her over and stay with her."

As the crowd thinned, leaving only the immediate relatives, Austin and Laura, Sophie and Carl were the last to say their goodbyes.

"Uncle, please let Carl and me know if you need anything at all," Sophie said. Her boys were living in Los Angeles and had claimed it would be too far for them to travel at this time. Billy was in seminary in Utah—a shock to everyone—and Franklin was working at the University of California in the Arts department. Carl nodded his agreement, then brushed a bit of food off his protruding belly. Austin gave a handshake to Burt, and Laura gave a hug.

"We can't imagine what you are going through, brother," Laura said. "But we are here if you need us. Remember, my club meets every Wednesday at my house. Other than that, don't hesitate."

"Yes, thank you, Laura. Thank you, Austin, for the …spirits," Burt replied his last word out of Laura's hearing.

The house was quiet after Jessica and Linny cleared the dishes and cleaned the kitchen. Caleb and the boys rode back to Rail River Acres, Caleb noting that their work would need to resume the next day.

"I'll borrow one of Uncle's horses and be along later this evening," she told them.

Caleb gave her a kiss before leaving and said in her ear, "Don't be long."

She smiled and took in his gentle blue eyes. He and her sons would be home, waiting for her. The thought gave her strength.

The parlor held an air of solemnity as Jacob came downstairs after saying good night to his daughter. Jessica sat alone. Her uncle and niece had retired upstairs, and her mother, with Will and Julia, had returned to Bethany's home. It was good to have everyone in town and settled in for the night. The one person who always brought the family together with her Sunday suppers was gone, and yet, this was what she would have wanted more than anything—her house full of family and friends. *Oh, Auntie, we will all miss you so much.* The house and kitchen were put back together, and that felt good to Jessica. As it was in the old days after her aunt had cooked a fine meal, Jessica would help clean up and make things ready to welcome June's baking and cooking once again. Tonight, Jessica breathed a sigh of relief. The difficult day was over.

"Let me fix you a drink," Jacob said as he went over to the nearly depleted side cart.

"Just red wine for me," she answered.

With drinks in hand, they sat without a word for many minutes. Jacob was the first to speak. His words were filled with the tiredness she felt. "Father and I were talking just now. Will and I have to return to the city tomorrow. I'll take Father with us. I want him to live with Linny and me."

"He agreed?" she said in surprise.

"Not the living with part, only to come with us for an extended stay. Once he sees he is better off near us, I think he'll agree to the move."

"He and my mother are close. I don't know how she'll do without him."

"Bethany is your problem."

Jessica raised her brows. "I didn't look at it like that. I love my mother, but Hannah and the rest of us will have our hands full without June." She managed a faint laugh, and Jacob returned one himself.

THIRTEEN MONTHS LATER, BURT DIED, leaving the family grieving once more over the loss of another of their beloved members. Henry took it especially hard. He and Burt had a special relationship.

"I will make a great lawyer in his name," he claimed that night after the funeral.

Jessica smiled at her son. She was sad for her loss, but his as well. The big gentle man in her life, who'd always treated her as a daughter, had left a giant hole in her heart.

"He'll be looking down on you and smiling at your success as he holds on to Aunt June's hand," she had said to him.

Henry had let the tears stream down his cheeks.

"I miss him, too," John said.

Bringing her other son into the fold, she thought how wonderful it had been for her aunt and uncle to experience her children and they to in turn spend time with Burt and June. The fact that Henry was their nephew and their grandson entered her mind. She shivered.

"What is it, Mother?" Johnathan asked.

"Oh, just a chill."

"Did someone walk over your grave, as they say?"

She raised her brows. "Perhaps, John. Perhaps."

Part Three

CHAPTER FORTY-TWO

Clermont City—October 1918

*C*ALEB AND JOHNATHAN WERE READYING FOR THEIR JOURNEY to the Klamath Reservation. In the years that followed their visit when John was thirteen, Caleb and his son had helped build a school and a new community house. This would be their first visit in several years. Red Bow was getting older and not in good health. Caleb needed to see him.

While John's brother, Henry, pursued the law, John continued to follow his own calling in silversmithing and teaching the craft. He had also become a strong advocate for Native tribes in Northern California. Anxious to share news and updates with the tribes in Oregon, he was looking forward to this trip.

Much had changed on the homestead. The old barn had been repurposed into Jessica's school and day-long art retreats. Their land had become a contemporary art haven, and they thrived on it. Henry lived in San Francisco, while Johnathan had a small home of his own in Clermont City proper and traveled often for the nonprofit advocacy work he did. Jessica marveled at her sons, each helping society in their own ways. She wished her aunt and uncle had lived to see the boys grow into their manhood.

Today, she was focused on her husband and younger son. A pandemic was sweeping the world, and the two were bent on visiting the Klamath people.

"I can't bear it." Jessica wrung her hands. "Of all times, Caleb."

At forty-eight, Caleb stood tall and proud as always. His blond hair was streaked with white and plaited into one braid that ran down the length of his back. He reflected the Native culture in his art and had absorbed it into his being. Clermont City knew him as the bohemian artist on the hill, yet he garnered respect wherever he went for the help he'd given in the town's recovery from the earthquake and the programs he was instrumental in developing for those in need. Their town had grown to over ten thousand, and not everyone living there had a chance to make a decent living. Now the Spanish flu was slowly invading.

"We'll be fine. We'll cover our faces and wash our hands as we're told to do. The train will be running as always, so I see no indication we can't travel," he recited.

Knowing she could not argue with her stubborn husband, she shook her head and retreated to the kitchen, where packs of food waited for them to take along on their journey. So many trips, so many trails. It seemed to never end. Caleb had become like a warrior in his life, wanting to prove his worthiness. Throughout the years, she had come to accept his ways, his travels, and his solitude, but today, she was beside herself with worry.

"Mother, trust the spirits that guide us there. We will be safe," John said as he put his arm around her shoulders. He was a beautiful man, so like his father. She took his hand and kissed it.

"Your spirits have never comforted me, and they do not today, John. But I will pray that you will not fall ill or bring that terrible sickness back with you."

Henry had come in from San Francisco to wish them safe travels and comfort his mother. He also wanted to make sure she and Hannah would stay vigilant in their efforts to ward off the flu. He was becoming a bit of a worrier and caregiver toward his mother whenever he heard his father and brother were both leaving town. He also wanted to see her before he wasn't allowed to travel, as the sickness was in the city and spreading, and quarantining was becoming the rule of the day.

When the hour arrived for Henry to take his father and brother to the train station, Jessica heaved a sob and hugged her son, then kissed her husband goodbye.

"I'll return to you as always, sweetheart," Caleb reassured her.

It was all she ever had—his love and confidence. He always came back to her.

Sixteen-year-old Jocelyn sat with her father in Jessica's parlor, taking refreshment and talking of the awful toll of the pandemic.

"My teacher says we might not be able to attend school until after Christmas," Jocelyn said as she bit into another cookie.

"You sound a little too cheered by that news," Jessica remarked with a smile.

"I would *love* to stay home and do nothing all day!" She stretched her body as if lounging on a chaise.

"There will be no chance of that, young lady. I've already lined up a tutor for you," Jacob was quick to reply.

Sitting straight again, she lamented, "Father! That isn't fair!"

Jacob exchanged a mutual smirk of understanding with Jessica. "Wouldn't life be wonderful if everything was fair?" he said.

"Thank you for coming to stay the weekend with me," Jessica said. "I hope it won't be long between visits."

Jacob tilted his head. "We shall see. I will miss your visits as well."

"Yes, Auntie Jessica! You have to see what I've done to my room. Father let me pick out all the coverings, curtains and all. I painted it a . . ." She brought a finger to her mouth. "What's the color again, Father?"

Jacob rolled his eyes. "I think it was cotillion pink?"

"Yes! Oh, don't you love the name? And it looks so lovely! Marie says it suits me very well. When my friends are allowed over again, they will be sore with envy!"

The energy of the spirited girl tired the adults, and by evening, Jessica was ready to have a quiet moment with her father.

The bedrooms upstairs were ready for the weary travelers, and Jocelyn went to hers almost immediately after dessert, her big brown-green eyes barely able to stay open. At last, she had worn out.

"Sleep well, my darling," Jacob said.

"Good night, Linny," Jessica said.

After the kitchen was cleaned, Hannah retired to her rooms on the other side of the house.

Once they were alone, Jacob and Jessica went to the porch with a glass of wine in hand, Jacob carrying the bottle.

"That sweet girl is always a balm to my spirits, Jacob." Jessica made herself comfortable on the cushioned sofa.

"As well as mine . . . most of the time. She's a handful. She goes from talking incessantly to complete silence for hours, sometimes days, at the merest slight. This age is very confusing."

"It is, but she'll get through it."

"Yes, but I'm not sure I will!"

They laughed and felt the ease of their relationship.

"How are my brother and Julia?"

"They were having some problems for a while. Not being able to have children has been difficult, as you know. Julia does more social work than Will would like. She's had to curtail it, though. This damn flu has affected everyone."

"That must be a very hard thing for her to do. She's a strong-willed woman."

"Years back, when I found out Will was indeed dealing in opium, she's the one who convinced me to stay with him and continue the business. Her strength of will helped me through that time. I nearly cut him off completely. We're better now, of course. He's mellowed with age, and I think he's completely stopped drinking, although the card tables still call to him."

"Well, he wouldn't be Will if he didn't gamble." She leaned back and took a sip of wine. Thoughtfully, she said, "I didn't know about him dealing in that awful trade by himself. I thought for a while it was the two of you making money on the side."

Jacob shook his head sternly. "Oh, no. Not this time."

"Yes, what a relief to find that out. I couldn't stand it if you were still being unlawful."

He squinted at her. "I can't get rid of my reputation after all these years, can I?"

"That's funny, but I guess not."

"Clear your mind of any wrongdoing on my part. I've been straight as an arrow for years. And now my partner is, too, thanks to Julia."

"Cheers to that." She held up her glass, and he followed suit. They both drank to it. "I'm worried about Caleb and John getting sick. As you can imagine, they wouldn't take my advice on not going. You men think you're invincible!"

"Caleb, Will, and I . . . we braved a lot when we were young. We were up for anything—rough and ready! What makes you think we would change just because we're getting older? I admire Caleb for doing what he does, even if I think he's not right this time. I know it's put a burden on you, and I hate to see that."

"Living with him hasn't been what I expected. He's a solitary man in many ways. I sometimes wonder why he decided to marry."

"He fell in love . . . with you."

"And I fell in love with two men, both unreachable in their own ways." She put a finger to her chin. "Or are all men unreachable? Perhaps my high expectations were my downfall in all of this."

"Why, I think you've finally got it!"

They laughed, trying to temper the noise lest they wake Linny and Hannah. Talking until past midnight, they finally made their way upstairs. In the hallway, before entering their rooms, Jacob kissed her good night.

She stepped away and whispered, "I think that was the most respectful kiss I've ever received from you."

He smiled. "Oh . . . if only we were alone."

She patted his chest and went to her room. "Good night, Jacob."

"Good night, Jess."

UNLIKE OTHER VISITS, JESSICA BECAME emotional saying goodbye to Jacob and Linny. She wasn't sure when she could go into the city or if they would be able to travel to see her.

"Stay well, my dear," Jacob said to her.

"And both of you stay well, too."

Jocelyn lifted her skirt just past her ankles as she went down the porch with her heavy suitcase in hand. Turning, she said, "I want to be just like you, Cousin Jessica! I love your style. Write to me!"

Jacob turned to Jessica. "That dress you're wearing is what all the girls are looking at now, so I've heard. I can't give in to Linny wearing the new fashion just yet."

Jessica lifted one of the many sheer layers of her long straight-cut dress. Then she put a hand to his arm. "Be open-minded now, Pa." They chuckled, and he gave her one last kiss on the cheek.

Hannah was in the kitchen making lunch when Jessica walked in and sat heavily at the table. "Oh, Hannah, what will become of us in this terrible time?"

Hannah put the kettle on and sat by her friend. "We'll not let that sickness come into this house. I have plenty of bleach and soap!"

Jessica laughed and wrinkled her nose. It was what she had smelled ever since the start of the horrible, spreading flu. She sat back, her heart full and aching. She took a deep breath. She would have to stay strong. Caleb would want her to do so. But in truth, what she wanted was to curl up in their bed and sleep until they came back to her, safe and healthy. She felt her cheek. Was she getting sick? It was cool as the first day of spring.

Hannah brought her out of herself. "You might have to forgo your next retreat. It will put you at risk with all those artist types." Under her breath, she said, "Some are not the cleanest."

She replied with a light laugh and raised brows, knowing Hannah disliked a few of the more free-spirited artists. She realized that life was about to become very different for everyone.

Chapter Forty-Three

On quick inspection of her husband, Jessica was appalled by what she saw. He was thinner and seemed almost feeble as John helped him walk from the automobile to the front porch.

"My God, Caleb!" she blurted out, then turned to her son. "John, take him to the back bedroom. We'll have to quarantine him there. Are you all right?" She felt her son's forehead as the three moved together, getting Caleb to the back room. It was hot. He jolted away from her hand.

"Mother, do not touch me. Stay clear!" John shouted.

Gasping, she stood back with her hand to her mouth, watching her son guide his hunched father into the room and close the door. Rushing to the phone, she called their doctor.

With a white cloth tied securely around his nose and mouth, gloves, and a heavy cotton garment over his clothes, Dr. Mitchell examined his patient. "He will have to remain here. Clermont

General is full. I will send a nurse to come and look in on him. She will bring the necessary medicines. You will have to take care of him, but you must wear face coverings, gloves, and a garment over your clothes. Thoroughly wash your hands after coming in contact with him. Wash your gloves and garments, too. Disinfect the area around him often."

Jessica listened closely to the muffled instructions coming from behind his mask. His prescription included quarantining her son, too. He would stay in a different room. "It's the young who are suffering most," the doctor said, "but I've seen all ages affected by it."

She and Hannah had their orders, and the house became a bubble in which life outside had no meaning. Jessica's only thought was to nurse her husband back to health and hope John would fight, for he was also infected. Her mother was given strict orders to stay home. Jessica would have to rely on the goodness of Bethany's neighbors to check in on her, for Jessica could not leave her home until her husband and son were healthy again. It was a formidable situation, and she prayed for the courage to see it through.

With great care not to become ill themselves, the two women took shifts giving medicine, placing cool cloths on Caleb's body and forehead, and feeding liquids and bland, soft foods. John rallied after three long weeks. It was a great blessing Jessica would forever be grateful for, yet her husband worsened. He wasn't the best patient, and she was not the best nurse, but together they managed, as they had done so many times in their marriage. This time, it was for life or death.

She stood by the sun-drenched window, watching her husband. The sunlight on the bed made him look almost ghostlike. He still captivated her heart, and she was saddened by his present state, but in a strange way, she felt, for the first time, she truly had him all to herself.

That night, she couldn't sleep. She went to his bedroom door. Peeking in, a mask covering her nose and mouth, she found he wasn't there. Quickly, she made her way down the hall to the bathroom, but he wasn't there, either. He was not in his favorite room, nor in his study. It was a balmy night for late December. Was he well enough to sit on the porch? A spring of hope bubbled up inside her. The porch was empty, and a chill traveled up her spine.

She walked around the house with the light of the moon as her guide, hoping to find his figure somewhere in it. She saw only the dark shadows of the barn and his workshop, along with the gleaming shrubs and trees. For a brief moment, she was taken back to the moonlit night when he had proposed to her at Clermont City's Summer Ball outside of City Hall. Her heart fell into her stomach as she realized that the beginning of their lives together seemed like only yesterday, and now the end was looming over them. She began to cry out his name as she feverishly searched the property. The yelps and shrill cries of coyotes coming out of the land made her shiver. Suddenly, she remembered the day he had said to her, "Jessica, when it's my time, I would like to die by the river. This land and its beauty are a part of me. I want it to take me home. Bury me there."

She recalled being upset, telling him not to talk that way. "You have years ahead of you."

He had given her a loving look and smiled. "Remember what I said."

Jessica now stood in the middle of their land under the lonely moon. She slowly made her way over the knoll and down to the river, her legs feeling unreliable under her body and her head pounding with the beat of her heart.

A flicker of lights caught her eye, and she ran to find John leaning over a wrapped lump. Caleb? The candles danced, and the scene looked surreal to her. She wondered if she might be dreaming. John rose. She threw questions at him. "What are you doing? What is this? Where's your father? Caleb? This night air will—"

In the light, she saw her son's face, stoic and stricken.

"Mother, he may still carry the sickness. Don't touch him."

Her son's words were far away as she slowly brought her hand down to Caleb's face.

"Mother!"

She gasped at how cold his cheek felt. Kneeling, she tucked the heavy Indian blanket closer to his body. She recognized the blanket—it was one Soaring Feather had gifted him many years ago. Bending over Caleb's body, the years of loving him overpowered her, and she wailed without restraint. She raised her head and ran both of her hands around his face, now wet with her tears. She felt him listening, and she talked to him of her love and respect for him. The clouds shaded the moon. The flicker of candlelight reminded her of the Indians dancing around the firepits. The sound of warriors chanting filled her head. *He dances with us,* she heard softly in her mind.

"Truly . . . truly," she whispered.

Startled by John's touch, then comforted by his embrace, she and her son sat by the body of their beloved husband and father as long as they could. The moon escaped the clouds and lit the ground. The candles continued their dance.

They gently covered his face, and Jessica stayed with him while John returned home to retrieve the pine box Caleb had made for himself several years ago. John told her he had hidden it under his workshop, away from her. Jessica wasn't surprised, but it added to her already firm belief of him, and she talked to him once more.

"You were never mine to have. You never belonged to me." She wept with a bowed head, her loss so complete.

John drove the coffin over on a flat cart with a single horse. Together, they lifted Caleb's heavy body into the box, and John nailed it shut. There would be no church service or cemetery burial. The pandemic had seen to that. No, he would be buried by the river where he'd asked John to help him lie on this winter night.

"Henry and I will dig the grave. I will send word to him as soon as I can."

Jessica nodded. She said a prayer for Caleb's soul and then slowly walked away.

The sound of the river's trickling, a spark of light as the moon lit its gentle waves, and the soft shushing of the trees all seemed to welcome his body into their realm, yet his spirit would soar somewhere beyond to a place she hoped she'd someday reunite with him. For now, she had to let him go freely as her heart broke in two.

IN THE DAYS AND WEEKS that followed, Jessica navigated the tides of her sorrow. Will was by her side as soon as he could manage to get out of the city, which wasn't for several weeks. Jacob couldn't risk the journey with Linny and sent Jessica a long letter expressing his sympathy and love. Johnathan took over the silversmithing company his father had labored over since he was a boy. It was his business now, and he felt an obligation to keep it alive with the high standards Caleb had honed for all those years. He had become as good as his father at the art, and Caleb had even told him that he had exceeded him in many ways.

Jessica leaned on her sons and brother until she felt she could no longer keep them from their lives. With Hannah by her side, she would find another trail to follow, one that would lead her out of her grief. Her art would take on another layer of her life—a life spent with Caleb.

Henry took it upon himself to settle his father's estate. Jessica was more than happy to let him do so. As the pandemic raged, she knew it would take some time before all was done, but time didn't matter to her. She was able to sustain herself financially. It was the ups and downs of her emotions she found more difficult. She often took a cup of tea with Aunt June at her kitchen table, and it soothed her, if only in her imaginary visits.

CHAPTER FORTY-FOUR

San Francisco, 1920

*T*HE WORLD WAS SLOWLY COMING BACK TO SEMI-NORMAL AS the flu began to loosen its grip on the country. It had been nearly two years since Caleb's death, and Henry Cantrell was still sorting through his father's papers and settling accounts. Since he could do little to no work during the pandemic, and his own work was double-fold once things began to pick up, Henry had placed it aside. Now he was determined to have done with it and close the estate. The small strongbox was the last of it.

"Now, where's the key to this thing?" He looked through envelopes with no success, then searched a few boxes without finding it. He went to the secretary outside his office. "Miss Hughes, do you have a pair of scissors or a screwdriver handy?"

"Scissors, yes, but not a screwdriver. I'll ask the maintenance department, Mr. Cantrell."

He went back to his office, and eventually there came a knock. "Come in."

Miss Hughes handed him a large screwdriver with a red handle. "Is this what you wanted?"

He ran a hand over his groomed hair. "I suppose this will do. Here's the problem. Can't find the key to this darn thing."

She tilted her head down to the lock. Her hand reached up to her hair, and she pulled a long pin from the middle of her rolled-up bun. Sticking the pin in the lock, she wiggled it. Nothing happened. She tried again, and a click was heard. Placing the pin back in her hair and wearing a satisfied smile on her face, she left the room.

"Thank you, Miss Hughes."

"You're welcome, Mr. Cantrell."

Henry chuckled as he brought the box around to sit in front of him. Opening the lid, he found several documents and personal items. He set aside trinkets to look at later, and then he read the documents—land deeds, business permits, and the like.

One document stood out among the rest. He read the official paper with disbelief. He sat back in his chair, shock rushing through him. *This can't be!*

In anticipation of her son's mood, Jessica had Hannah bake his favorite pastry. Freshly brewed coffee waited on the tray alongside the plate of apricot scones. Puffy clouds swept across the robin's-egg-blue sky. Jessica viewed the scenery from her kitchen window. It was a familiar view, yet each time, it felt new, this land she had observed with love for so many years. She could almost hear herself calling the boys in for their meal or bath time, cherished memories of a daily routine. The window also framed the early days of wondering, hoping, and anticipating without giving in to fear.

After Henry's call that morning, she'd found herself again needing to row in the rough waters with confidence and bravery. He hadn't told her the particulars, but she knew why he was coming to see her.

The late afternoon was warm, and she felt a flush of heat. Lifting her bobbed hair off the nape of her neck, now heavily streaked with gray, she wiped the sweat away. The loose pale-blue dress she wore draped easily over her body. She was glad the days of corsets and tightly ribbed clothing for her were gone. She adored the new fashion not yet accepted in proper society, but what did she care for society these days? Some people judged her on her style of short hair and loose clothes as improper for a woman of her age. She had learned to let the judgments of others roll off her back and fall to the ground, where she would cheerfully walk over them. The freedom that came with age had found her, and she embraced it fully, though soon, the past was about to rear its head, a part of life she'd thought might not catch up with her. *How foolish of me.*

Could she tell him only what he needed to know to satisfy his curiosity? Perhaps it would be enough, perhaps not. She turned away from the window. *Oh, Caleb, I wish you were here.*

She braced herself for what was to come.

CHAPTER FORTY-FIVE

*P*ULLING UP TO HIS CHILDHOOD HOME, HENRY'S MIND filled again with all the questions he had tried to put aside as he traveled from San Francisco to Clermont City. He examined the trees he had climbed and played under as a child, the sound of the river he'd explored endlessly, and the field in which he had created all sorts of adventures. It all seemed guilty for hiding this terrible secret. Even the sweet smell of the air breezing into his automobile was suspect. The old barn, now a gallery and artist retreat for his mother's students, looked as if it, too, had held something back from him for all those years. Even the building in the east field, where his father's teaching had been cut short by the pandemic, was also entangled in lies.

He stepped onto the front steps and gave a brief knock, then walked in.

"Mother?" Henry's strong, clear voice rang out from the now larger screened-in porch. The porch that had served as a play area for him and his brother, Johnathan. It was a place where he'd discussed with his father the weighty subjects of life, from a young age all the way into manhood, and where he'd had his first kiss at age thirteen with Missy Leighton. The creaky noise of some of the floorboards spoke to him of a past that was not as it had appeared to be. Jessica came in from the kitchen, holding a tray of refreshments, and he quickly helped her with it. He placed it on the table. They sat down on the white wicker chairs with the flowered cushions. Henry touched the pillow on his chair and remembered his father complaining one day about how they weren't masculine enough for his most favorite room in the house.

"Henry, how's work? Are they ready to make you a partner? Have you spoken with Johnathan lately? I just don't see enough of my boys these days," Jessica rattled on as she poured him a cup of coffee.

"Mother, it's too hot for coffee. Do you have something cooler?" He paced the floor.

"I have some lemonade in the icebox, but I don't know how cool it is. The repairman said he couldn't make it today. I'm afraid I called him too late."

"In this heat? How could you let that slide? Where's Hannah? Isn't she supposed to take care of all those details? I swear she's not much use to you anymore. We need to get you a real assistant. Someone younger."

"Henry, you talk as if my life is out of control, for goodness, sake. Hannah is having a well-deserved day off, and the repairman will be here tomorrow."

He looked thoughtfully at his mother.

"What is it, Henry? What do you need to talk with me about?"

"Mother, I found this in some of Father's things." He handed her the adoption certificate.

JESSICA TOOK IT FROM HIM and felt an ache of foreboding in her chest. She pretended to read it over, but she was well aware of its contents. She handed it back to him. Her body felt cold from within, and she reached for the hot coffee.

"Where did you find it? I haven't seen it for many years. As you know, your father was a private person and kept his own affairs separate from mine."

"His own affairs?" Henry answered incredulously. "This isn't his *own* affairs! Tell me what this means!"

A sting of sadness and regret filled her now. She had anticipated this day would come. She began her prepared speech. "When two people love each other, it's hard to—"

"It says that Caleb Cantrell adopted me from Jacob Stanford!" he shouted. "Tell me if this is true, and if it is, how did this all come about?"

Jessica saw the attorney coming out in Henry in an attempt to protect his client, a young and innocent version of himself. She wished she had told him years ago and suffered the consequences when Caleb was by her side. Her grown son stood before her wanting answers, and yet to her, he was the little boy she loved and wanted to protect.

Henry sat down on the edge of the chair, his hands clasped over his knees. His face softened, and her heart ached. "Mother, please tell me the truth. I have a right to know, and no matter what, I'll still love you and Father, but I must know what happened."

Tears formed in his eyes. She was trapped. The truth needed to finally come out to the one person who was at the center of it all.

"You know I was kidnapped, and Will and Jacob found me. Well, in my time away from your father, and being close again to Jacob... When I was rescued, your father took it upon himself to adopt you. It was the only reasonable thing to do at the time. You didn't need to know because Caleb was a devoted father to you. Let me get you some cool water."

"Mother, sit down."

Slowly, she sat again, her insides trembling.

"Mother, I'm not a little boy. You can tell me."

She quietly responded. "Jacob and I have been in love for a very long time. It's been a difficult relationship, but there was nothing to do but have your father adopt you."

"You broke your marriage vows for him? Good God! Your own cousin?"

The son who couldn't be satisfied with half answers, who needed information and every detail of that information to give his life meaning, was asking something of her she didn't want to give. How could she avoid the truth and make it right for him? It was something she'd asked Caleb many times in the months leading to his death. His answer was always the same. "Tell him the truth and let him figure it out."

"First of all, your father would not appreciate your tone with me, Henry. It's not easy to tell you this, and it certainly isn't easy to tell you that Jacob is your natural father. Before you judge any of us too harshly, promise me you'll keep your mind and heart open. Love is a powerful emotion."

He tilted his head. "I can't promise you anything."

Jessica clasped her hands in her lap. The years of holding on to the secret were over. A weight was lifting, but she felt as if her skin had been peeled from her body and she was exposed down to every last nerve.

His jaw went slack. Rising, he peered out onto the land, his profile in stern concentration.

"We were in love long before I met your father, and that's what I want you to know. Sometimes, love can't be limited by what society and—" She stopped talking. He wasn't listening. A heavy silence surrounded them.

"*Cousin* Jacob?" he whispered. She knew it would be difficult for Henry to comprehend that the man he had come to know as a friend and mentor was his father. He ran his fingers through his hair and paced the floor, then suddenly turned to her.

"Your own cousin? What were you both thinking? And all this time, he never said a word to me! Who else knows? Does Johnathan? Does Grandmother know?" He slapped a hand to his forehead. "My God, Grandma! How can I ever face her again? Uncle Burt and Aunt June? This is some kind of awful conspiracy against me! Did you ever intend to tell me?"

His tall handsome figure loomed over her. "Henry, calm yourself. No one knew but me, your father, and Jacob. I told John only a few days ago, and your uncle Will knows."

An audible moan came from Henry.

"Try not to make sense of it, Henry. It has never changed the love or legitimacy of you in any way. I knew it was time to let you know, but unfortunately, you found out ahead of me. It wasn't as if you had a terrible childhood because of it. Be reasonable now." Her excuses seemed childish to her, and she took in a breath and released her defensiveness. "I'm truly sorry. Please come sit down."

He walked back into the house, and she followed.

"I have to go. I have several cases to review tonight," he said and went for the door.

"Henry, don't leave like this. I want to help you understand me and why this—"

"Mother," he interrupted calmly. "I haven't been a lawyer for very long, but I know that whenever a client wants to help *me* understand *them*, it's apparent they have a guilty conscience and they're hoping I can carry some of their burden. Well, I learned quickly that I can't do that for them, and I won't do it for you, or my father, or Jacob."

Jessica felt the weight of his words upon her heart. The truth might take her son from her.

"I love you, Henry, and Caleb loved you, and Jacob is so happy to have you in his life. Don't throw all of this away. Please keep your heart open."

"What would Father say if he were here?" Henry asked, his breathing labored.

"Henry, I know this is a shock to you. Sit down and take some deep breaths."

"What would he say, Mother?" he shouted.

Jessica stood back and wished she had Johnathan here with them. He was most like Caleb and would have offered some balance to a very unstable situation. He was the one who could reason with Henry. They were different in their personalities, and their lives had taken different paths, but John could always settle his brother down whenever Henry's frustration took hold of him.

"I think—I believe—he would tell you the same. That is, not to throw away the past, but perhaps to incorporate this into your life."

"I'll talk with you later, maybe next week. It's getting busy at the office."

The coldness in his words brought tears to her eyes. She dabbed them and dropped her tense shoulders in surrender.

"All right, Henry. When you have the time, I'd love for you to talk with me about your thoughts and feelings, how you're coping."

"Don't patronize me, Mother. You know damn well how I will be *coping* with this."

Jessica decided to let him vent his anger. It was the least she could give him. She felt that she had done enough for one day. The years of holding in her secret were over, and she felt light-headed from the weight of this burden having been lifted from her. Her guilt remained, however, and now it was also her son's burden to carry.

"Good night, Mother."

"Good night, Henry. I love you."

THE ROAR OF HENRY'S 1914 Franklin sedan's engine as it rumbled down the gravel road competed with his own thoughts. He pulled the large auto over to the side and cut the engine. Looking at the land where he'd grown up, he let the memories flow. The grass, browned by the summer's heat, gave off its heavy scent like sun-warmed hay. The part that wove between the tall trees as it expanded into the field was greener and held its own heady scent, sending him whirling back in time. He got out of his vehicle and walked over to the clearing.

Henry approached the banks of the Rail River and stood still as its quiet, easy flow calmed him. He sat down by his father's grave. The ground was warm, and he heard his young voice calling out to his brother.

"Johnny, let's go swimming! I'll race ya in!"

He could feel the excitement of catching his first fish after trying for what seemed like hours, his father's expression full of pride.

"I knew you could do it, Henry. You just needed to be patient," Caleb had said.

My father Caleb, not Jacob. He was still grieving the loss of the man who had taught him to be true to himself. Now that advice seemed shallow, considering what Caleb had kept inside him. He ached to talk with him and get his side of the story. An intense anger suddenly consumed him. He got up and grabbed the first heavy stick he could find, then threw it as hard as he could against the nearby tree. It splintered as it came off the mighty trunk, and Henry winced as the shards lashed back at him.

"Goddammit!" he shouted. "Damn you, God! Damn you!"

He sat down in defeat. The powers that be had him licked, and he was helpless to fight them. He wanted desperately to apologize to Caleb for any and all the trouble he had caused him, starting from his conception. Henry's thoughts were a scramble. He cringed with embarrassment and shame when he thought of his mother and Jacob together. All those years of knowing Jacob, whom he had trusted and admired, seemed tainted. The man who had shown him a different way of seeing the world outside of his own back-yard. The man he'd helped grieve over the loss of his wife after the earthquake—an event that had sealed a bond between them. The next person he had confided in when he had fallen in love after he had told his mother. He loved this man, but how could he ever face him again?

Henry reasoned this was why Caleb had never shown any fondness for Jacob, but then, he hadn't shown much affection for the rest of his mother's family outside of Aunt June and Uncle Burt. Still, it explained why, as a boy, he never saw Jacob and his family but spent time with Uncle Will and then Will and Julia. His mind cruised over the years after the earthquake. His mother had visited the city more often. Were they continuing their affair? He also concluded that the story his mother would tell him would be fraught with guilt, and he decided not to talk with her about this ever again. It would become his responsibility now, but the burden she had bestowed on him was great. His life would never be the same.

CHAPTER FORTY-SIX

*J*ESSICA REACHED FOR THE PHONE AS HENRY SPED DOWN the driveway. Her son's anger rattled her. Her hand shook as she held the receiver in one hand and the base of the phone in the other. *Oh, my dear son.* Soon, Jacob was on the other end of the line.

"Jacob, it's me. Can you talk?"

"Yes, what is it, Jess?"

"Henry. He found the adoption certificate going through Caleb's papers. He just left. Oh, Jacob, he was very upset." After a long pause, she asked, "Are you there, Jacob?"

"Yes, yes, I'm here. It was going to happen one way or another. I hoped the two of us would tell him together. I wanted to wait until you weren't in such grief, but time slipped by."

"He's more than upset. I'm afraid he'll never speak to either one of us again."

"Nonsense! I'll talk to him. Will and I have some business to discuss with a few of our vendors this week. I'll invite Henry to supper next Wednesday. That will give him time to think this over. Now, please don't upset yourself too much. I'm worried about you. Henry is a grown man. For Christ's sake, it isn't as if we abused him. He had a wonderful childhood."

"That's what I told him. It didn't help. We're not seeing this in his shoes. It's a terrible blow, though I wish he could see—"

"See what?" he interrupted. "No matter how you slice it, we're guilty as charged by our son, the lawyer."

"I want him to know I did this for him." Jessica began to weep and then cough as she brought a handkerchief to her mouth.

Jacob exhaled in frustration. "Listen to me, Jess, don't get yourself tied in knots. We will get through this together."

"Yes, of course we will." She wiped her tears and blew her nose. "Thank you, Jacob. Thank you for being my rock these past few years. I don't know how I could've—" She choked on her words.

"All right now, let's be strong. This isn't the end of the world."

Jessica felt it was the end, for clearly, a great chapter of her life had closed with Caleb's death, and now the past threatened to swallow her up. She hung up the phone, hoping Henry and Jacob would find a solution that involved her son's forgiveness.

Making herself a cup of tea, she sipped it slowly as she walked down the hallway to face the door of Caleb's study. This addition had been his place to work on new designs in solitude. She hadn't opened the door since his passing. Henry took care of his father's affairs, and she admonished herself for not securing the document that had brought her son such anguish. She had put too much responsibility on Henry, and her guilt and grief were multiplied. She coughed into her handkerchief again and felt her lungs heave into her rib cage. Her breathing was labored as she steadied herself and swallowed another sip of the warm brew. Placing her hand on the knob, she turned it with deliberation.

Like a vacuous tomb, it opened to reveal a room no longer of consequence without its occupant. The faint smell of his tobacco hit her with longing, and she closed the door. She ached for Caleb to be seated at his desk, looking up at her with his blue eyes, softened by age. The man she loved was no longer there.

CHAPTER FORTY-SEVEN

*T*HE YOUNG LAWYER TURNED TO SOMEONE HE COULD TRUST and who might bring some sense to the situation, but Henry found it hard to get the words out correctly, though once he started, he found himself rambling.

"I decided I couldn't keep this to myself. I can't talk to Mother."

Will took off his spectacles and brought the short glass to his lips. Henry took a sip of his ginger ale.

"I'm sorry that one of us hadn't told you before you found out this way. I truly regret that, Henry. Don't lessen Caleb's role in your life because of this."

"Of course not. I just want to understand how or why he would allow it."

"He loved your mother, that's how."

Henry lifted his mouth up at one corner.

"Understand this, and put aside the young lawyer in you, if you can. Understand that we all had an important part to play in your life, and whether it was Jacob or Caleb who gave you your beginning, here you are, alive, healthy, and making your way as an attorney, though I still can't understand for the life of me why."

"Yes, Uncle, I know you wanted something different for me, but like you said, here I am. Maybe you should have been a lawyer. You seem to have a knack for summation."

"Respect for your elders, Henry, don't forget." He smiled. "Yes, here we all are. I'm sure it was very hard for your mother to acknowledge this."

"She tried to explain it to me, but I guess I didn't want to listen."

"Henry, life is a great big mess, and we're lucky if we can hold on to those we love long enough to reach some peace with them. Don't let her suffer."

"So, you're saying let bygones be bygones, and I should just embrace the love of my family and ignore the deceit and lies at my expense?" Henry shook his head in disbelief.

"The deceit and lies in your honor."

Henry stepped away from his uncle and refreshed his glass. Looking at his uncle's drink, he asked, "I thought you quit that stuff?"

"You're right, you're right. I shouldn't be drinking. Just a few now and then. I appreciate your concern, Henry. You're like the son I never had."

Henry lifted his hands in surrender. "Please, Uncle Will, I don't need any more fathers!"

Will laughed out loud. "No, you do not, but you get my meaning."

"I do, thanks," Henry said with a smile. "But seriously, how will I ever face Jacob again?"

Will drained his glass and filled it with ginger ale. "I don't know, but you will, and it might bring some peace to you both."

THE HILLTOP RESIDENCE WAS AS beautiful as always, and the lights that flickered inside gave Henry a warm feeling. The curtains hadn't been drawn yet, and he saw inside the familiar home he knew so well. The many visits here had Henry saddened now. His life had suddenly changed so dramatically.

Stopping his automobile in front of the entrance, he lost the courage he had mustered on his drive from his modest apartment in the city. Jacob's invitation had quickly become ashes in his little stove, but after a day of thought, he'd decided he had to be brave. He considered what it must have been like for a man to give up his own son because he had fallen in love with the wrong woman. He contemplated what he would do if he and his fiancée, Jeanine, had to give up a future child of theirs. Jeanine McCullen was the love of his life, and he couldn't imagine what he would do without her. His mind was in a tumble, and the pit of his stomach ached. He wasn't sure how long he sat in front of the house until a knock on the window of the car startled him.

Jacob opened the car door and leaned in. "Don't you want to come inside?"

"I . . . I was going to come in." The first words he spoke to Jacob since knowing he was his real father felt stiff. "I should let you know I can't stay long."

He looked up at Jacob, and the two locked eyes. He exited and followed Jacob to the house.

The study in which so many talks of his future had taken place felt smaller to Henry. His hands were damp, and he welcomed the cool glass of water Jacob offered him. They sat quietly for a moment.

"How is Jocelyn?" Henry asked.

"She's still as well as when you saw her a few weeks ago. We're going to the theater next Thursday. Would you like to join us? She'd be thrilled."

Avoiding the invitation, Henry nervously continued. "I'm glad to hear she's well. And you? How have you been?"

Jacob gave a slight chuckle. "Henry, is there something we should talk about?"

"I've . . ." He cleared his throat. "I've learned that you are my father." He could almost see his words hanging in the air, and he saw a sadness in Jacob's eyes as the man took in the statement.

"Henry, you did nothing wrong. Your mother and I—"

"I don't want to discuss you and Mother in the same sentence. I don't even want to imagine. I mean, Christ!"

Jacob rubbed his neck. "All right, I understand."

The room was quiet again, and Jacob went to the small bar. "Would you like a drink, Henry?"

"No, I'm fine with water, thanks. I don't want to confuse my senses any more than they already are."

Jacob made his drink and sat down in the chair opposite his son. "What do you want me to tell you, Henry? I'll give you any information you want."

Henry looked straight into Jacob's eyes. "Why? Why did you act so damn recklessly?"

Jacob swallowed his sip of bourbon. He coughed a bit and wiped his mouth. "Didn't expect that, Henry."

"I wanted to ask my mother the same thing, but she gets so emotional these days. She started with, 'When you love someone' and all that shit. I need to know why, not because of this feeling or that feeling."

"Look, this isn't that black and white, my friend. Let's take the right or wrong out of it. What would you like from me, Henry?"

"Honestly? I want things to go back to the way they were before I found out."

Jacob smirked. "Me, too, but I don't see why we can't continue to be friends. Allow me to say something here, will you?"

Henry looked at him, afraid he might reveal more than he was ready to hear, but he nodded for Jacob to continue.

"I was young and sure-footed. I thought, with half a brain, I could succeed at anything I set my mind to. Most of the time, that worked in my favor. Sometimes it worked against me. In this situation, the latter was the case. Your mother convinced me that it would be better for you and everyone involved if we did it her way. I agreed, having less than a stable life to offer you. Caleb brought you up right, Henry. He was a good father, and I'm not sure I could have done any better. Know this—I always loved you. In my heart, you were always my son, but someone else was raising you, and I'd agreed to let that happen. I couldn't just step in and take over. Can you see how impossible it was for your mother and me? Mostly, can you forgive us?"

Henry looked away as his eyes watered. "I don't know how to make this work," he said hoarsely.

"Henry, we're friends, and that will never change. Please understand that I did try. In the beginning, I tried."

"Uncle Will said you wanted us to be a family."

"Yes, yes I did! But I was too late. Your mother and Caleb . . . well, they had John on the way."

"I guess my mother is a stronger character than even she knows."

"Love is a strong character, Henry."

"I doubt I'd compromise my integrity for a woman, even Jeanine."

"You have a good woman there. You're lucky you're free to love her. Society says it's fine for the two of you to marry, have a family and a good life. Not everyone gets to have that. I wanted your mother, but for us, it wasn't possible. We made our love work and spent too many years apart."

Henry rolled his eyes.

Jacob stirred in his seat and scratched his forehead. "All right, just let me have it. I know you must be angry as all hell."

Henry didn't know what to say. In truth, he had nothing but the ultimate respect for Jacob. The strangeness of this moment overwhelmed him. He felt hot, and he gulped the water, hoping it would turn down the heat welling up in him.

"I have to go," he said as he set his glass down and went for the door.

"Henry, this is the time. You decided to come here. I can take it."

Henry looked back at Jacob, and for a moment, he was caught in a space between anger and hopelessness. He could walk away and hide his feelings, continue the lies, let the deceit sit between them without his acknowledgment. He could carry on as if nothing had happened.

He spoke with only a few constrained words. "I respected you." His mind flooded with anger, and suddenly, he felt unstoppable. "Yes, I respected you, and it sickens me to think of what you and my mother did!" He was shouting now. He wanted retribution. "My father was and always will be Caleb Cantrell, and nothing you can say or do will ever change that! You were both heartless to him, and I want to hate both of you for doing that to him and to me! You were selfish! So damn selfish!"

Jacob nodded and took a deep breath. Letting it out, he said, "Yes, I was selfish and I'm sorry, but don't judge a person until you've walked in their shoes."

Henry felt the heat rise in his face. "Oh, you can be sure I will never walk in your shoes!"

"Fair enough. So far you haven't. I suppose that's a good start."

Henry suddenly regretted his outburst. "Jacob, I'm angry, I didn't mean to imply—"

"Of course you did, and well deserved on my part. Now, where do we go from here?"

Wrung out from his outburst, his heart thudding against his ribs, Henry sat down. "I don't know. I don't want to think about it. I just want to live my life."

"No one's stopping you." Jacob stuck his hand out to his son. "Let's find peace with this."

Henry looked at the gesture. "That's it? We'll shake, and everything will be forgiven and forgotten?"

"God, you're as stubborn as your old man!"

"I am my father's son," Henry said proudly.

"Yes, you are."

Henry stood as tall as Jacob, and all that came between them now were the years gone by.

"Let me see you out," Jacob offered, breaking the stalemate. "We'll talk again soon."

Henry went for the door, then turned around. "Give me some time."

"I'll wait to hear from you. Don't let it be too long."

Henry gave a jerk of his head and left.

Driving back to his apartment, he let the tears flow as he wiped his eyes to see the road.

Chapter Forty-Eight

*H*ENRY KEPT BUSY. EACH TIME HE REACHED FOR THE PHONE to call his mother, he quickly returned the receiver to its stand and walked away. His heart wasn't in it.

As the sun began to set over the bay outside his third-floor apartment, Henry buttoned his white shirt and pulled a tie around his neck. This evening, he was meeting his brother at the ferry dock, and they were having dinner at a restaurant in the city. His brother had suggested a weekend visit to his small home in Clermont City, but Henry declined, knowing he'd probably have to see his mother.

The dinner was mostly filled with small talk and getting caught up on each other's lives. When the brandy and dessert arrived, Henry felt his brother had something to say to him about the matter of their mother and her cousin.

"Well, John"—Henry waved a fork—"what do you think of the news of me being a bastard?"

"Henry, you're not a bastard," John said. His blue eyes, the color of Caleb's, reflected the same compassion. "I feel rotten about it, to tell the truth." He played with the cloud of cream on his plate. "It's . . . very disturbing, to say the least." Placing his utensil down with smooth deliberation, he looked at Henry. "We are still brothers, and nothing has changed that."

"Half brother, half second cousin."

John furrowed his brow as if realizing the connection for the first time. "You are my full brother, no matter what anyone says."

"I feel the same way, John. I won't be talking to Mother or Jacob again, so you and Will and Grandma are my only family now."

"Oh, come on, Henry. You can't just cut them out of your life. Especially Mother. She'll track you down!"

John laughed at his own statement while Henry just gave a smirk. "Why should I have them in my life? They betrayed me."

John tilted his head. "I know. They betrayed both of us."

The brothers sat in silence until the check was handed to Henry. "Put it on my account," he said to the waiter.

The waiter gave him a quizzical look. "Sir?"

John held back a laugh.

"Never mind," Henry said, reaching into his pocket. He tore off a few bills from the several he had and handed them to the waiter. "Keep the change."

The waiter gave a quick assessment of the money and stalked off, clearly offended. Henry sat back in his chair and smiled. "Someday."

"You'll get there, Hen."

"What about you, John? Is Father's business enough for you? Working with the Indians? Is that enough?"

"Yes, it's fulfilling for me. Amy and I will be married next spring, and . . . well, I'd like to have land and a family." John stood and put his simple blue cotton coat over his soft cream-colored shirt and dark trousers. Like Caleb, he usually wore a bolo tie with turquoise inlay. His longish blond hair matched his father's.

Henry was always trying to buy his brother smarter-looking clothes, suggesting the new style of haircut for men, or explaining how bolo ties were simply not the fashion, but John seemed happy with what he had and gracefully refused his offers. It occurred to Henry that his brother was content with his life. Something moved him. Would he ever find peace? His search for material comforts drove his career, but what about his heart?

"You need to forgive them," John said as they left the restaurant.

Henry didn't reply, and they walked to his auto, then drove back to his apartment.

"Now, where am I to sleep in this stuffy flat of yours?"

Henry smiled and pulled a Murphy bed from the wall. "Voilà!" he said with an outstretched arm.

"A secret bed!" John laughed. "Does Jeanine know about this?"

Henry slapped his brother's back. "No, and don't tell her. She'd make me sleep on it when I snore too loud."

"When are you two sinners getting hitched?"

"When I can afford a decent home."

"Ah, Henry, Jeanine would marry you tomorrow."

"I know, but she might not be very happy living in a bachelor apartment for a year or two . . . or three."

"Remember, our grandparents lived in a cramped apartment above an Italian restaurant in downtown Hartford while Grandpa climbed the ladder of success. Uncle Burt and Aunt June lived the same way. Will and Jacob grew up in a grand home with plenty of advantages, but they were taught how those circumstances didn't happen overnight."

Henry shook his head. "Uncle Burt said he and Grandpa Thomas and the grandmas stuck together through thick and thin. Heck, I feel as if Grandma and Burt and June were all one grandparent to me." He scratched his head. "It was hard to pull the wool over any of them."

Taking a long pause, Henry realized his veins were filled with the blood of good, hardworking people, no matter the circumstances of his birth. Then he wondered aloud, "Why didn't Jacob and Will take advantage of such privilege?"

John shrugged. "I guess they wanted to carve out their own destinies, like our father. They didn't want to settle for what was handed to them. Like you. Father handed you a thriving business, and you decided to do something very different. You're your own man, and I'm proud of you, Henry, as is the rest of this family."

Henry took a deep breath and let it out. His mind felt freer than it had since his discovery. He nodded to his brother, who in turn gave him a broad smile.

HENRY SAID GOOD NIGHT TO John, and shortly after his head hit his pillow, he saw the irony in his life. He'd bedded Jeanine before they were married, sneaking her into his flat at night and sneaking her out in the wee hours of the morning. *But she's not my damn cousin!* His anger at his mother and Jacob lessened, and it disturbed him. His craving to despise them, to hurt them, had been palpable at times. Could he deny them his approval? Have them arrested for incest? Create a scandal? His mind reeled. His heart quickened, then broke. He couldn't hurt either one of them. His love for his mother and Jacob was too strong. Before falling asleep, he made a vow to himself that he would find peace in his life, and that meant coming to terms with his birth.

CHAPTER FORTY-NINE

May 1921

$\mathcal{O}$N THE KNOLL IN THE BROAD FIELD OF RAIL RIVER ACRES, Henry stood beside his nervous and excited brother. A tall arch of branches covered in spring blossoms horseshoed over them as the tension grew, awaiting the bride's entrance onto the field. The guests mingled softly.

Henry looked over at his mother seated beside Jacob. They held hands and looked as if they were the proud parents. He ached to have his father there seated beside his mother. How proud Caleb would be of his younger son, his true flesh and blood.

Henry erased the worn-out feelings of betrayal and grief. His mother caught his eye and smiled. It had been many months since he'd seen her or even talked with her by phone. Without thinking, he smiled back and broke the wall he had built up between them. It wasn't completely gone, but it wasn't as solid as it had been.

Jeanine sat in the row behind Jessica, and when he looked over at his soon-to-be wife, he had to chuckle to himself. Her head was tilted, and her expression was warm. She had noticed that he smiled at his mother. He knew she and his mother would be a force to be reckoned with once they got together. It brought him a deep feeling of comfort, filling the void of emptiness he had been experiencing since the day he found out the truth. This was a new chapter in his life, one of many.

The oohs and aahs waved over the seated attendants as the bride made her way down the path to the arch and her waiting groom.

JESSICA BROUGHT A HANDKERCHIEF TO her eyes. Amy was a dear girl and would make her son a good wife. She truly felt she was gaining a daughter rather than losing her son. Her mind went back to the time she'd walked in the low, damp grass of Rail River Acres on that sunny October day to meet with her own groom. How in love she'd been, how free she'd felt to have this beautiful, wonderful, complicated man waiting anxiously for her. How different she was from when she'd married Frederick and endured that hardship and abuse. She'd walked with confidence toward the life they would build together, the difficulties they would overcome, the problems they would solve, the victories they would celebrate, and the love they would make with their bodies and souls. It had all been ahead of them, as it was now for her son and his wife. She released a gentle sigh. Jacob squeezed her hand, and she was with him again. He smiled at her and winked, unaware of the years she was reliving, the years she had lived without him.

Then she caught Henry's eye. He was smiling at her. She smiled back and nearly spoke aloud to him. *I love you.* She nodded, as if to say she accepted his acknowledgment.

"I now pronounce you husband and wife."

The cheers rose as everyone stood. The couple hurried down the grass aisle as rice flew up around them. Henry stopped in front of his mother and stuck out his elbow. "Shall we?" he said. Jessica felt her legs go weak and her heart fill her chest so that she might burst out in a great sob. She took his arm, and together they walked to the house, where a reception waited.

THE FESTIVITIES WERE WINDING DOWN as the couple bid the well-wishers goodbye. Jessica noticed Henry and John talking to each other as if in a consultation. They both looked over at her. John came over and embraced his mother.

"Thank you for this and for . . . everything."

His embrace was warm, and she wanted to linger in it. With the rushing thought of wanting to keep him to herself, she reluctantly let him go. He and Amy hopped into his secondhand auto and sped off to their honeymoon, where a cabin waited for them on the scenic Lake Tahoe. She watched them go as Henry approached her.

"Mother, will you walk with me to the river?"

Tired and a bit melancholy, she gladly accepted his arm, and they walked quietly through the grassy field. The path to the river was wide and neatly trimmed.

Jessica broke the silence. "Oh, how you and John loved to play in this field."

"It wasn't a field, Mother. It was a battleground, a ship on the high seas, a wild ride on great stallions, and so many other worlds."

She laughed, loving how her boys had let their imaginations run wild on long days when they hadn't a care.

They sat on the bench overlooking the river and, in the near distance, Caleb's grave.

"I want to tell you something," Henry began. "I want to say I'm sorry for my actions when I found out about you and Jacob. It was childish of me."

Jessica turned to him, the breeze playing with the light-pink tiers of her new dress. "No, don't think that. It was not childish. I'm so happy we are talking again. That we can be, well, friends. You had every right to feel betrayed."

His chest rose and fell with a sigh. "I still feel betrayed. I have my days."

"Of course. I know it will take time, if it ever will feel right to you."

"It's more than that."

"What then?"

"Caleb was my father, yet he knew I wasn't his son. Did he love John more than me?"

Another crack in her armor brought up her sorrow. She knew the truth.

"I will tell you this—Caleb may have loved John slightly differently than you because I think he felt John was a part of him in a way you were not, but he loved and cared about you just as much. You need never doubt that. He never indicated to me that he didn't love you, and you know your father was a very honest man."

Henry rubbed his chin. "He was that. I miss him so much."

"So do I." Jessica cleared her throat. "How are you and John? What was that little discussion just now?"

"We're fine. He's so different from me, but I think we manage to find common ground."

"Good, that's what I want to hear . . . and?"

"Mother, the other thing I wanted to talk to you about, what John and I have been discussing." He stood up and looked out onto the river, its flow gently running past. "It's Caleb's inheritance from his grandmother's estate."

"Oh?"

He turned to face her. "It's still a large sum. Collecting interest, I suppose, but I'd like to invest it for you."

"Now, please don't go trying to run my financial affairs. I have Mr. McNeil to do that for me."

"John says we should break it up and—"

"What? I don't even have one foot in the grave!"

"He means each of us taking a part of it to invest for you and, well, for our own futures. There're great opportunities out there now that the war is over."

She gave a smirk and raised her chin. "I see." Rising, she felt the warm air flow around her, nurturing her, the river and trees guarding her. "Money always seems to turn people's heads, and I can see my sons are no different."

Tearing a blade of grass from the banks of the river, Henry wrapped it around his finger like a ring. Jessica was taken back to the time when he was little and did that same thing. Where had her innocent little boy gone?

"We will talk about this when the time comes for me to settle my will in the future," she said. "As of now, I feel confident in my own investments." Before her son could argue, she turned and swept up the bank and onto the field. "I'm still in my prime!" she announced.

"Yes, ma'am."

Henry joined her, and they walked back to the house, chatting about the wedding and guests and how soon there might be another such event.

"Don't let time fly by. Marry and settle down," Jessica said.

"I'll think about it," Henry replied.

She took pleasure in their reunion, yet her heart told her to be wary of his request to handle her estate. Leaving it to the future, she shook the displeasure of it out of her head and let this beautiful day embrace her once again. As they walked closer to the house, she saw Jacob coming toward them, and her heart leapt in her chest. *After all these years.*

CHAPTER FIFTY

Clermont City

After pouring the strong-brewed tea she knew her mother preferred, Jessica slid the plate of scones in front of Bethany as she sat down. The autumn light was bright and the sky a deep blue, a perfect day to slip away and take a moment with her mother. Now that the bustle of John's wedding was over and Jessica's summer seminars completed, she could relax until the next round of students and more commissions for her oil paintings.

"Mother, how are you and Miss Tilton getting on? I haven't heard from you in days."

Her mother brought the fine china cup to her lips and took a cautious sip. Tilting her head, she returned it to the matching saucer. "Fine, just fine. She's a good housekeeper and companion. Thank you for hiring her for me." She fingered the rim of her cup.

Jessica had come down from her sanctuary for more than just a visit. She checked her breathing and noticed it was shallow. Taking a breath, she relaxed her shoulders and stomach. Her nervousness didn't go unnoticed.

"Dear, is there something bothering you? I hope you haven't been running yourself ragged with instructing and painting along with all your other chores. Hannah is getting on in age herself. You need a Miss Tilton, the both of you!"

Giving a short laugh, Jessica mused that her mother still thought she had a house to run and children to feed and a husband to care for. "Mother, the housekeeper and groundskeepers take care of the chores. You know I have no more responsibilities in that way, nor does Hannah."

"I suppose." Her mother turned away and looked outside.

"Now, I have to ask, is there something bothering you?"

She saw her mother rub the back of her neck. How unusual. This woman was always so confident and outspoken. "I have some . . . news."

"Oh?" Jessica sat back. She couldn't imagine what news her mother could have, except perhaps she'd decided to take up knitting or one of her clubs had nominated her to chair a charity. Mother was good at organizing such events even at her age. "I'm all ears."

Taking her napkin and wiping the corners of her mouth with great demure, her mother's cheeks turned pink. "Well, you know your father's rival, Mr. Hawthorne?"

Jessica searched her memory of the man. "Yes, the thin, balding man? I thought they were also friends. I recall him and his wife coming to a few of the parties you and father gave. My God, that was another lifetime ago."

"Yes, it was indeed a friendly rivalry." Her mother smiled a most peculiar grin. Her cheeks became pink.

"Mother?"

"After your father died, he was a great help and comfort to me. His wife, too. And when poor Miriam died of the influenza, I wrote to provide some comfort to him. One thing has led to another, and he's decided to come visit me . . . maybe make a move here."

A silence followed.

"Jessica, close your mouth before you catch a fly."

Jessica looked wide-eyed at her mother. Who was this woman? She reached out and placed her hand over her mother's. "You're nearly eighty." Although her mother wasn't ill or infirm, she didn't want to think of her taking an interest in men.

Bethany withdrew her hand and played with her napkin. "Oh, now don't go making more of this than it is. We're just two old fogies in need of some company and . . . companionship." There was that blush again.

Her mother's news almost took away her own nerves. Perhaps this was a new day for them both.

"I had you all wrong, Mother. I'm thrilled you've found another chapter in your life."

"Yes, that's right. A new chapter. We're never too old. Well, he and I are very old, but we will sit on my porch and watch the sunsets, drink wine—he loves chardonnay, like me—and that will be that."

"Wonderful!" Jessica replied with a clap. She cleared her throat. "Speaking of new chapters . . ."

"I knew you had something on your mind. Well, now that I've spilled my beans, it's your turn."

It was as if they were two girlfriends sharing their lives as they always had, but this wasn't so. She could rarely confide her life to her mother without the woman judging and giving her opinion. It was an old pattern, and Jessica wasn't ready to let her guard down just because her mother had found a companion. She had to test the waters.

"Companionship is important. It's been lonely without Caleb."

Her mother's raised eyebrow told her she thought Jessica had found someone also. And in fact, she had, but it was a re-finding of sorts, for she'd never truly let him out of her sight. Hell, she had to come out and say it or choke it down for another time. She wasn't going to wait any longer.

"Mother, Jacob and I have been in love for . . . forever. We knew it wouldn't work, so we went on with our lives, but—"

Her mother's raised hand stopped her.

"I know. I've known for many years."

Jessica took in a sharp breath. "How?"

Her mother sat back in her chair. "Do you think your mother is blind and deaf? I knew there was something there. I hated to admit it to myself and wished I were as blind to it as June and Burt were. They always let that boy go wild."

"I don't think wildness had anything—"

"However, I saw it crystal clear and said nothing. That time he dropped you home from the gallery, you know, the first job you had after high school? What was the name of the man who owned it?"

"Yes, Mr. Cromwell, go on."

"Well, it was a snowy March day, and Jacob said he'd found you walking home, though I'm sure he planned it. You both hurried in, giddy with red cheeks, and headed for the parlor fireplace to warm yourselves. At first, I found nothing unusual about it, but when the chatter stopped for so long, I peeked in to see if you were both still there. And when I did, I saw you were holding hands."

Jessica gulped the saliva that had formed in her mouth. She'd been sure her mother was going to say she'd seen them kissing, which she vividly recalled they had done just before he grasped her hand in his. She let the memory play around in her mind. So sweet were those days and yet so imbued with danger. Little had she known what other dangers lay ahead of her.

"He's my companion now, Mother. I may even marry him one day, if he asks."

"Is that legal?"

"Um . . . I haven't thought about it."

"Of course you haven't."

Now this was more like the woman she knew. "We will certainly take it into consideration. We're still in love after all these years."

"I know he loves you. I read his letters."

Jessica leaned forward. "What?"

Her mother pursed her lips, as if she'd just accidentally revealed a misdeed. "After I moved here, I asked Caleb if I could come to the house and have something of yours as a . . . I don't know what. I was grieving the loss of my husband, my daughter was gone, and we hadn't heard from Will in ages. Caleb left me alone in your art room. I couldn't take a thing—nothing was you. I looked around and spotted the little wood box sitting on the shelf."

"So it was you. I feared Caleb might have—"

"Oh, he did, I'm sure. How could one not? You were gone, and we thought we might never see you again. We all needed something to hold on to. I thought the box held treasures you'd found over the years. I quickly realized it was filled with the treasures of you and Jacob."

Jessica was the one to turn pink now. "I'm sorry."

"No, I was the nosy one. I *wanted* to find something."

"Was I that bad a daughter?"

Her mother's head rose to meet her stare. "You weren't. And Will wasn't a bad son. Your father and I had our standards as parents in a community that had standards one had to meet to stay a part of. It was necessary. A different time."

"Your children had other ideas," Jessica said. "I tried, Mother. Frederick was not my standard but yours and father's."

"I never would have let you get involved with a man like that had I known."

"Aunt June told you?"

"Yes. Had we known of his abuse, your father would have run across country with a rifle as long as his arm and a pocketful of bullets!"

"A pocketful?"

"Well, wherever they go before you use them."

Jessica laughed out loud, then came down with a sigh. "It's all behind us now. New chapters lie ahead. Let's make them loving and kind."

Her mother nodded, and tears welled in her wrinkled eyes.

When it was time to leave, they embraced, and the violet floral perfume her mother always wore tickled her nose. For a brief moment, she was a child in her mother's arms. Coming away, she had to ask, "Will you give us your blessing?"

Her mother answered with a resounding yes. Jessica's heart lifted, and tears streamed down her face.

"Thank you." It was all she could say after years of fear that one day she and Jacob would be found out. She would leave Henry's birth a secret. There was no more need for the telling of that story.

ON HER WAY TO THE house, Jessica stopped in the meadow and picked a handful of wildflowers. Tying the bundle with a blade of grass, she walked to Caleb's grave. She placed the flowers under the headstone that had recently been carved with his name and dates of his being on Earth. She knelt down, and as she had since his passing, she talked to him.

"I have my mother's blessing to marry Jacob. I hope I have your blessing, too, but I can see your blue eyes filled with jealousy. I can't say I'm sorry enough. I loved you and still do. I hope wherever you are, you know that."

She would not get a sign from him. She had not expected to, yet when a junco flitted around his tombstone and then landed on it, she took it as a sign. It was Caleb's favorite bird, and he had created safe places for them to nest each year. She whispered to the bird, "Thank you."

CHAPTER FIFTY-ONE

August 1923

*L*ET ME TAKE YOU AWAY, JESSICA." SHE AND JACOB WERE dining on the veranda of her home.

"Take me where?"

"New York City. Just the two of us. This damn influenza is finally over. We'll be fine. Besides, I did some finagling, and I got you space in a gallery."

"In New York? What? Jacob! How?"

"Now, it's not a prominent gallery, but it is well-known and chic enough to accept a Jessica Cantrell Collection."

"That dream left my thoughts years ago!" She placed a finger to her chin as her mind worked. Jilly had rebuilt the gallery in San Francisco, and a part of the gallery had become a permanent home for her work. "Which ones should I send to them? I'll have to talk to Jilly. The gallery has one of my best pieces hanging in it right now."

Jacob smiled. "It will be in October, so you have some time to work out all the details. I wired the gallery owner that you accept. I hope that's all right."

"No, I mean, it's amazing!" Flustered, she rose and went to him. He held her, and their sensual kiss warmed the air.

Looking up at him, she saw those beautiful brown eyes with that fleck of gold in one, beaming down at her. He gently brought her away. "There's one other thing," he said.

"Whatever you want."

He looked down at his shoes, then directly into her eyes. "I want to go to New York as man and wife. Will you marry me, Jessica? I would have asked sooner—"

"Yes, I will marry you, Jacob." Jessica felt the world right itself in that moment.

They giggled. She was swimming in Mary's pond with him again, riding through the field back home, chasing behind him. Stealing moments of love in secret rendezvous. They would be together for the rest of their lives.

She had never felt more like herself. The young woman who'd wanted to become an artist and love the handsome, intelligent, and often daring and frustrating young man she had fallen for at a tender age had finally come around to where she'd begun. Time had no hold on them now. The waiting was over.

That night, they made love with abandon. It wasn't the first time in the past year, but it took them to new heights. Freedom to love him was so sweet, she could almost taste it. Tomorrow, she would make him breakfast, and later, bathe with him at their leisure.

New York City, 1923

LIKE MOST GALLERIES, THIS ONE was filled with hushed voices and slow-moving patrons. Mrs. Stanford stood to the side with her husband and watched the sign indicating the art was sold go on the last one of her paintings. The New York crowd loved her work!

Jacob slid his arm through hers. "My wife is very popular tonight."

Jessica smiled. "It's a dream come true," she whispered. First her and Jacob's simple and lovely wedding on Rail River Acres with her family in attendance showing their support, now this wonderful event.

He put his arm around her waist. "Next stop—Paris."

She leaned into him, laughing. Another life awaited her. A few patrons turned their way. Caring not what anyone thought of their public display of affection, they locked eyes, and their lips met in a sweet kiss.

The End

TRAVELED HEARTS
BOOK ONE IN THE TRILOGY

The Traveled Hearts saga begins in 1885 New England, where Jessica Messing, a spirited twenty-year-old yearns to break free from the confines of her rigid, upper-middle-class life in Hartford, Connecticut, to become a well-known and respected artist. However, her family and society have different plans.

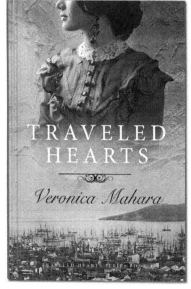

Falling in love with Jacob Stanford only complicates her life–a love affair she must keep secret.

Forced to bend to her father's wishes, she marries the charming yet deceitful English attorney, Frederick Moore, to help save the family's law firm. An arduous journey across America leads Jessica to her new life in San Francisco, California, where she finds herself trapped in life as a dutiful housewife. Compelled by curiosity, she secretly ventures into the heart of the city, where her artistic passion is fueled and her view of life is altered.

When her marriage is faced with jealousy and infidelity, Jessica is determined to carve out a truer life for herself, including her love for Jacob. Can she fulfill her dreams without destroying her reputation and her family's future?

SACRED TERRAIN
BOOK TWO IN THE TRILOGY

In book two of the Traveled Hearts trilogy, Jessica Messing finds contentment in her new life, yet Jacob is still out of reach. Promising to quit his roguish ways before leaving her after their last rendezvous, she remains hopeful of him settling down near Clermont City. As the months pass with no word of him, she is left in doubt of his love.

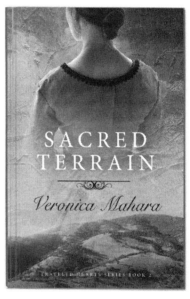

When the handsome and confident Caleb Cantrell steps into her life, Jessica finds it difficult to hold true to the man she has loved for so long. Caleb's intellect and manners deny his rough exterior. As Jessica's affection for Caleb grows, she must choose between waiting for Jacob or living in the present, where a homestead on breathtaking lands offers security and the love of a man who knows what he wants.

Falling in love with two men was not her plan, yet her heart cannot be reasoned with. Innocently, she becomes a pawn in Caleb's and Jacob's outlaw past. When she finally meets with Jacob again, she has been through a harrowing experience that forever changes her.

They come together, having been separated from society. The temptation is great, and the consequences are greater.

Secrets come to light while others remain to be seen. Above all, having been away from her home and art, she returns with a renewed purpose as she navigates the perils of love ... and loyalty.

COMING IN 2024

BEYOND DIAMONDS
A STANDALONE NOVEL

Cincinnati 1879

Thanks to her father's success in the jewelry business and the diamond trade, Jane Wallingford enjoys a privileged lifestyle as part of Cincinnati's upper class.

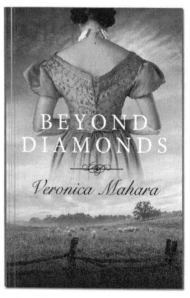

At nearly twenty-five years old, she's more interested in horticulture than marriage and children. When she finally falls in love, her new husband, Martin, sweeps her away to a Northern California town, where a rundown homestead and sheep farm await her. In the small town of Clermont City, Jane meets Martin's cousin, Harry, and is drawn to the handsome, down-to-earth sheep farmer who doesn't take her as seriously as she takes herself.

Using her substantial dowry, Jane sets out to turn the farm into her dream garden estate, while Martin becomes engrossed in the raising of sheep. However, even with Harry's help, Martin struggles to make a living at it.

Unexpected news from back home changes Jane's life. The family fortune is gone, and now she and Martin must make the farm work or lose everything.

Secrets come to light that will shake Jane's faith in Martin, drawing her deeper into a scandalous relationship while her roles on the farm and in society are forever transformed.

A heartfelt story of fortunes lost and gained and a woman's journey to find love and success on paths unknown.

ACKNOWLEDGMENTS

My team, as always, were so great at their jobs. Developmental editor, Julie Christine Johnson, cover designer, Jane Dixon Smith, and Natalia Leigh, Greg Rupel, and Lisa Gilliam of Enchanted Ink Publishing. They were there for me in the spring and summer of 2020 during the pandemic by scheduling their time and getting me in gear to meet my deadlines when I felt my creativity slipping away. Thank you all so much for making my writing better and publishable! Thank you everyone at Enchanted Ink Publishing for helping with all the revisions in 2023.

I want to thank my readers. You make my storytelling worthwhile. Thank you for your support.

Last, but always in my mind and heart, I want to thank my family and my husband, Jeff, for being so supportive of me throughout this process of bringing the Traveled Hearts series to life. Your love and encouragement helped me get to the finish line, and I love you all so much.

Veronica Mahara

Veronica Mahara is the maiden name of Veronica Stoneman who lives with her husband and their cat Toby surrounded by her family and the beauty of the Pacific Northwest. To find out more about the author and future publications, visit:

WWW.VERONICASUNMAHARA.COM

Made in the USA
Columbia, SC
25 January 2025